BANE OF WORLDS

SURVIVAL WARS BOOK 2

ANTHONY JAMES

Cover Design by Dan Van Oss www.covermint.design

Follow Anthony James on Facebook at facebook.com/anthonyjamesauthor.

LIMBO

The light from the long New Earth mid-summer day had started to fade as the yellow sun crept lower towards the horizon. There were distant clouds, already turning to a vivid red. The clouds seemed frozen in place, making unusual patterns of almost-familiar shapes. It was still hot, though the heat would rapidly escape into the night sky when it became dark.

Captain John Nathan Duggan looked down the barren slope and into the inconceivable space within the New Earth Capital Shipyard. From his position atop one of the surrounding hills, he could see most of the hundred-square-kilometre complex – it was a drab collection of concrete and metal-walled buildings, foundries and an ever-moving sea of vehicles and people. There were three deep V-shaped channels which ran from east to west, each one flanked by structures built from massive beams, with heavy cranes visible everywhere.

The nearest – and longest – of these channels contained the hull of the Space Corps' newest Hadron class supercruiser. It was almost six kilometres in length and destined to be the first of the new generation of battleships, meant to outrun and outgun the Ghast Oblivions.

"It's doomed already," said Commander Lucy McGlashan. Her face looked haunted and her eyes were darker than usual.

"Why do you say it's doomed?" asked Duggan. He already knew the answer.

"It's the same as the others. Bigger, a little more efficient. The Ghasts will blow it into pieces. We don't have anything that can target and destroy their Shatterer missiles. Even a Cadaveron will give it a run for its money."

"It's just a hull so far, Commander. The core goes in near last and the weapons are the final thing they fit. That's another two or three years for the tech labs to come up with something new. I've heard about a few lines we're testing in prototype. There's real promise, I'm told."

"I've heard plenty of promises, sir. We've spent the whole of the last year hiding from the Ghasts, trying to buy ourselves enough time to build the fleet. What's the point? It's just target practise for those bastards."

"You're not usually so bitter," he said.

She sighed in response. "Maybe it's getting to me. Being kept off duty for so long."

"These things take time to resolve, you know that. We're facing serious charges. I'd rather they got it right than rushed through a verdict."

"Will Admiral Slender be able to sway them?"

"Perhaps. He'll have to be careful he doesn't try too hard. It'll rub people the wrong way and make it look like he's got a vendetta."

"He does have a vendetta, sir."

"Against me. Not against you, Lieutenant Chainer or Breeze. The investigators won't want to be drawn into his mission to bring me down. He's a powerful man, but he has no say over their decision. Friends on the Confederation Council might get him the result he's after."

"He has those friends, doesn't he?"

"Fleet Admiral Slender doesn't have friends, Commander. He's always been respected for his abilities, rather than his personal qualities. The death of his son beat out any interest he might have had in friendship. So, the most he can expect is some nominal support. He has no one who'll risk their careers for him. No one who's willing to become embroiled in what could end up a messy business."

McGlashan looked at him curiously. "How do you know all this?"

"I have to keep my ear to the ground, in order to ensure we get treated fairly." Duggan gave a half-smile.

"Any idea when we'll hear?"

"Soon. The sooner the better."

"What'll happen if we're cleared?"

"We'll be given another ship. A Gunner. Then, we'll be sent out to do whatever it is we'll be asked to do. And I'll have to spend the rest of my time in the Corps looking over my shoulder for whatever comes next."

"I'm glad to see the *Crimson*'s still in one piece," she said, changing the subject. "I don't envy them trying to study the Dreamer tech from the inside."

Duggan looked into the shipyard's middle trench. At over two kilometres long, they could have built an Anderlecht light cruiser in it. For the moment, it held the eleven hundred metre length of the *ESS Crimson*. It looked menacing, even at such a distance, hardly reflecting the sun's warm light at all. Duggan couldn't decide if the threatening quality was because of the vessel's sleek lines or because he knew what weaponry it carried.

"They've taken some of the plating off the underside and stripped out several of the Lambda clusters and Bulwarks to give themselves more room inside. I guess they didn't want to risk breaking anything by trying to disassemble a working model."

"I hope it doesn't slow them down too much. As much as I love the ship, I'd have it torn to pieces if it meant we could copy the hardware a few months sooner. Hell, even a few weeks or days."

"They've taken a gamble," said Duggan. "A surprisingly risky gamble. It gives the Confederation an ace up their sleeve. Not one they can play every round, but if it's played right, it could change the whole outlook for the war."

"By blowing up one of the Ghast planets?"

"If that's what it comes down to," he said quietly. "The Ghasts seem to value strength, or at least the appearance of strength. We might not have to blow up one of their planets. If we destroyed something nearby, it might be enough to make them think twice about taking us on."

"We've got to find one of their planets first. There's no sign of that happening anytime soon. They already know we have the capability to destroy worlds."

"We *don't* know that, Commander. When we destroyed the tenth planet, the only Ghast ship in the vicinity was the Oblivion. One of the labs did some modelling and they figured out the battleship would have almost certainly been destroyed. The trouble with modelling the unknown is that you can never be sure."

"Two seconds to us is hardly any time, sir. To an Oblivion's AI, it's plenty of time to package and send a signal to say what happened."

"Who knows?" was all he could say in response.

"If we found one of their worlds and you had the opportunity to fire the weapon, would you do it?" She'd asked him before and he'd never given a straight answer. He could see the question and the answer were important to her.

"I can't tell you, Commander. Some questions are best answered only when you have to answer them. I would do my duty."

"Yeah." It was a noncommittal response. Duggan didn't know what she expected to hear from him.

"I've seen enough for today," he said. "Let's get back to base."

Duggan turned his gaze away from the New Earth Capital Shipyard and walked across the parched earth towards the car he had parked up on the verge. It was ancient and decrepit, running on rubber tyres, and modelled along the same lines as an early diesel-engined jeep. He climbed into the front seat and fired it up, still half-expecting to hear the clatter of cylinders. The vehicle's power plant was much more modern and it hummed in near-silence. Duggan pressed the accelerator and the car surged away along the rough-paved road, the rubber tyres skittering for grip.

The Space Corps base was sprawled across a large area adjacent to the shipyard. The military owned vast swathes of land in this area – it was out of the way, yet easy to supply from the nearby megacity of Frontsberg. By the time Duggan and McGlashan got back to base, the sky was almost completely black, speckled here and there with pinpoints of starlight. Duggan parked up in one of the communal bays and stepped onto the tarmac. He looked around – there was nothing about the base that looked remotely advanced; squat, ugly buildings of steel-reinforced concrete, thrown up quickly and without thought for the final appearance.

"They could have built this place five hundred years ago," said McGlashan, reflecting his thoughts. "If an alien race saw this place before anything else, they'd wonder if we've even learned to fly."

Duggan grunted in response, his mind already elsewhere. He bade McGlashan goodnight and went back to his quarters. Duggan was housed in one of the larger buildings on the base, where he had a room and an office. He might be on enforced ground duty, but he was still a captain in the Space Corps until he was told otherwise. Stepping into the confines of his room, he realised how difficult it was becoming for him to stay cooped in this place. When he was in the close-quarters of a spacecraft's bridge, the lack of space was somehow liberating. Here, it only served to remind him how much his future was in the balance and how little control he had over what was to come.

The lights came on automatically when he stepped over the threshold. He had a desk in one corner, made from some type of lightweight mass-produced plastic. There was a screen on the desk, along with a keyboard and mouse. The technology had been around forever and here it was in his quarters. Duggan sat in front of the screen, without any great enthusiasm. The display flashed up at once, showing a list of several new messages. When he saw the subject of one, he sat up straight and opened it. There wasn't much to read and he skimmed over it quickly, before reading it for a second time. At last, he sighed and slumped back into his seat. He called up McGlashan's number on his desk communicator.

"What is it?" she asked.

"We've been cleared of any wrongdoing," said Duggan. "In fact, the investigation found strong evidence that we went above and beyond expectations, whilst pointing out that our positive actions in no way excuse a number of minor failings. They've stopped short of suggesting we get a medal," he finished wryly.

"That's great, sir! What happens now?" She sounded stunned at the news. Duggan knew how badly it had affected her, having the charges hanging.

"We go back to our normal duty, that's what happens."

"As if nothing happened?"

"Exactly, Commander. As if nothing happened."

As he watched his display, a new message appeared. Duggan opened it and read the contents.

"Sir? Are you still there?" asked McGlashan.

"You'd best pack your things, Commander. We're shipping out tomorrow."

"Sir," she said, in that one word conveying a mixture of untold relief and excitement.

Duggan ended the call and sat in quiet contemplation for a few minutes, before he contacted Lieutenants Breeze and Chainer in turn, to let them in on the news.

CHAPTER ONE

"CAPTAIN DUGGAN!" said Admiral Teron, as if he were greeting a long-lost friend. "How have you been keeping yourself?"

Duggan gave a mental shake of his head at the greeting. Teron knew exactly what had happened since the last time they'd met. "I'm fine, sir," he said, taking a seat. The Admiral's office on the *Juniper* hadn't changed a bit since the last time Duggan had visited it. In fact, he couldn't remember it changing at all in the last ten years.

"Good of you to get here so quickly," said Teron.

"I had little choice in the matter, sir," said Duggan. The trip from New Earth to the *Juniper* had taken almost a week on the Anderlecht *ES Greeter*. They wouldn't usually employ a warship to shuttle personnel from one place to another, but the *Greeter* was to be permanently stationed near to the *Juniper*, assisting the Hadron *ES Maximilian* and almost a dozen Vincents. It didn't look as if the Space Corps was going to take any further risks with the orbital. Last time Duggan had been here, two Cadaverons had almost come within launch range of their missiles, drawn to the location by an automatic emergency signal from the *Crimson*'s alien core.

Teron wasn't fond of small talk and to Duggan's relief, the Admiral got on with business. "We're at total war, as you know, Captain. That ensures unlimited funding to our efforts, but it does not ensure we have unlimited trained personnel to fill every role. We're making ships faster than we can fill them, at least as far as the Vincent class is concerned."

"Does that mean I'm to be assigned to another Gunner, sir?" Duggan didn't know whether to be happy or angry.

"You've been cleared, Captain Duggan. Unfortunately, for you, that doesn't mean you'll be given command of a bigger ship. The Space Corps is required to keep you in your earned position, but that doesn't entitle you to preferential treatment."

"I didn't ask for preferential treatment, sir," said Duggan. "Just *fair* treatment."

"If I were you, I'd keep your head down for the foreseeable future, Captain. Your exoneration doesn't have any conditions attached, nor does it offer you any protection going forward." Teron stared intently across the table.

"A warning, sir?"

"Take it as you will, Captain Duggan. I'm sure you realise how it has to be."

"Stuck on a Gunner until I retire or get blown to pieces."

"I didn't bring you here to argue. I won't discuss it further. I brought you here to talk about your newest assignment."

Duggan didn't press the matter. He'd been around long enough to know when it was pointless. Fleet Admiral Slender wasn't a man to forget and he'd not be happy about Duggan's latest escape. The Space Corps' top man couldn't ignore the verdict of innocence, but that wouldn't stop him doing his best to make Duggan's life difficult.

"What am I to do, sir?"

"I'll get to that shortly," said Teron. "You're aware we're building warships at a tremendous rate. We've got dozens of new hulls laid down, and that's not including the one hundred and fifty Vincent class that are nearing completion. In fact, the first ten have just entered service."

"It's hardly been a year," said Duggan, making no effort to hide that he was impressed.

"Fourteen months, as it happens. Competition – it's a wonderful thing. Each shipyard has been encouraged to do its best to beat the others. You may remember the times when the Confederation constructed a lot more spacecraft. Rivalry was rife. All we've done is reminded the shipyard workers how it was in the past and I'm pleased to say they've responded as we hoped they would."

"I'm glad we're getting up to speed, sir," said Duggan. "Where are you heading with this?"

"A lot of ships need a lot of metal. The engines in particular require certain rare elements in enormous quantities."

"We're running out of raw materials?"

"Not exactly. There are numerous planets in Confederation space, many of the suitable ones given over to the mining operations needed to feed our industries. However, these mines are not able to meet the demand for metals that we're placing on them. Even if the metals are there for the taking, we lack the capabilities to mine them and transport them to our foundries. The Space Corps hasn't stood still on this matter, and we have focused many of our efforts on increasing production at these facilities."

Duggan wondered where Teron was going and began to wish the Admiral would speak clearly. "Mining operations aren't usually a concern for the Space Corps' warships, sir. Am I to be given command of a military transport?"

"In a manner of speaking, yes you are." Before Duggan could open his mouth to protest, Teron waved a hand to silence him.

"You're to escort a transport vessel to one of the mining planets in the Larax Sphere. A place called Everlong. They've recently discovered a considerable quantity of ore which they lack the equipment and personnel to exploit. We need those metals, so we're sending what they need to treble their output."

"When did we begin escorting transport vessels within the Larax Sphere?" asked Duggan. "Have there been Ghast sightings?"

Teron steepled his fingers in front of his face – an unconscious gesture which Duggan identified as meaning the Admiral was choosing his words carefully.

"No direct sightings," he said at last. "You'll be aware the Larax Sphere is only a comparatively short jump from the Axion Sector. Charistos and Angax had a lot of commerce with the Larax planets. We have concerns the Ghasts might have attempted to track some of our low-light transport vessels as they fled the destruction. It's possible the Ghasts' AIs were able to narrow down the escaping ships' destinations as they entered lightspeed. We're certain our enemy still lacks the ability to track our fast military ships, but we're not nearly so certain they can't do it to slower craft."

Duggan fixed Teron with a gaze. "We have three populated planets in the Larax Sphere. Are you telling me the Ghasts are close to finding them?"

Teron shifted in his seat. "Three of our transport vessels have gone missing in the last month. They've vanished without sending a distress signal."

"Nothing at all?" asked Duggan.

"That's what I said. If the Ghasts found and destroyed one of these smaller spaceships out in the depths of space, we'd never find out beyond guessing. We aren't certain it's the Ghasts."

"What do the sim guys tell you about the cause?"

"Fifty-fifty between a Ghast interception and accidental destruction."

Duggan wasn't buying it for a minute. Accidents did happen on modern spaceships – he knew that only too well. However, they were exceptionally rare and blaming the loss of three ships to accidents in a month was stretching the bounds of credulity. "What do you believe?" he asked.

"I'm required to give the simulation team the respect they're due, Captain Duggan. However, I know that odds of fifty-fifty aren't good odds unless you're a determined gambler. And I'm *not* a gambling man."

"Escorts for every transport, then?"

"Until we learn for definite what happened to our missing ships. On the positive side, it gives us the opportunity to introduce our new spacecraft and crew to the dangerous side of the Corps without throwing them straight in at the deep end. You'll be pleased to learn you are to be a part of this introductory process by mentoring a fellow captain on his first voyage."

"What?" asked Duggan, sitting upright.

"You're being given command of a brand-new Vincent class fighter in order to escort a heavy-lift mining transport and its personnel to Everlong. Accompanying you on this journey will be Captain Mason Graham on his maiden flight. He'll have his own spaceship, of course. I'm certain he'll become an excellent officer, given time and the right guidance. You will, of course, be the senior officer and in charge of the mission."

"I don't need this crap, sir."

"You have the experience, Captain Duggan. You cannot shirk your responsibilities by refusing to share it with others."

Duggan knew he'd spoken out of place, but couldn't bring himself to apologise. He wasn't in the mood for saying sorry. Instead, he nodded to show he accepted Teron's words, his expression making it clear he didn't like what was asked of him.

"On the bright side, it shouldn't be as dangerous as your trip to locate the *ESS Crimson* turned out to be. As soon as the heavy-lift transport has delivered its cargo, it'll return to its base. You'll stay with it until it returns to the space port on Pioneer and then you'll be given new duties."

"Are we meeting the transport at Pioneer? That'll add several days to the journey."

"No – you'll rendezvous with the *MHL Goliath* at the mid-point of its journey. The lifter has already left the space port, along with Captain Graham's *ES Ribald*."

"That means there's no time to pick up the new Gunner anywhere other than here on the *Juniper*," said Duggan.

"Correct. The *ES Pugilist* is in Hangar Bay Two. It's like your old ship *Detriment*, except everything's newer and mostly better. There are one or two additions, which you'll begin to see on some of the new spacecraft and which will eventually be retrofitted to older vessels, assuming they prove their worth."

"What sort of additions?" asked Duggan.

"Don't get yourself too excited. New high-impact Lambdas, with one or two changes to the guidance systems. In addition, there are two high-yield nuclear missiles, with their own dedicated launch tubes. After the success you had with those on the *Crimson*, we've had them added to the arsenal of a few of our warships. Ideally, we'd have liked to mount them on a modified Lambda propulsion section, but there's not been time. I'll leave you to read through the technical specifications when you're in flight to your rendezvous point."

"That's fine," said Duggan. From what Teron had told him, he wasn't anticipating any great surprises. "How is the *Archimedes* doing, sir?" he asked. The damage the Space Corps' flagship had suffered from the Ghast Shatterer missiles was a closely-guarded secret and Duggan had struggled to find out anything concrete.

"She was badly damaged. The Ghost missiles breached her armour in two places and ripped big holes in the engines and disabled almost half of the port-side weapons and counter-measures."

Duggan gave out a low whistle. "The Shatterers must have some payload."

Teron's face twisted and he pursed his lips. "They do, Captain Duggan. Though not enough to have caused as much damage as they did to the *Archimedes*. They got lucky and struck in a place where two sections were originally fitted together. They found a design flaw, if you will. We should almost be grateful."

"How long until it can fly at full capability?"

"Another eighteen months," said Teron. "In reality, we're stripping out some of the redundant systems in order to make room for the new technology we're hoping will come onstream in the interim. If needed, she could fly at almost full speed tomorrow if we released her from dry dock. She'd be lacking a huge portion of her weaponry, of course."

Duggan was left with the impression that Teron wasn't telling him the whole story. There'd be time to think about that later. "Permission to bring my own crew onto the *Pugilist*, sir?"

"I told you to bring them with you, didn't I? Permission granted."

"What about the infantry I had with me before? They were good men and good women."

"I'm afraid they've been dispersed amongst other ships. You've had fifteen picked at random from those who happened to be on the *Juniper*. I'm damned if I can remember their names and truth be told I've got better things to do with my time than spend it looking at troop lists. I've got the roster here." Teron picked up a piece of paper and handed it over. "Here we are, centuries after we were promised a paperless society and my desk is covered in the stuff."

Duggan took the paper and looked at the names. He struggled to suppress a smile as he rose from his seat. "With your leave, I'll go and take a look at the *Pugilist*, sir."

"Of course. I'll have the *Juniper* feed through the specifics of your flight. Goodbye, Captain Duggan and good luck, though I'm sure you won't need it."

CHAPTER TWO

THE *ES PUGILIST* was one of two Gunners in Hangar Bay
Two. Duggan didn't need to ask which one was which. The
closest of the two was a dull grey, with a blackened nose and signs
of extensive heat blistering. The second had a peculiarly glossy
sheen from the lacquer they applied at the factory. Duggan didn't
know why they bothered, since the coating was always burned
away as soon as the spacecraft entered a planet's atmosphere at
anything above ten percent of its maximum speed. The *Pugilist*
also had its name emblazoned along the side, in five-metre-high
letters. The painted letters wouldn't last any longer than the
lacquer. Other than that, the two spacecraft looked identical. The
hull design was a proven shape which they'd never seen fit to
alter in decades.

Hangar Bay Two was vast, with hundreds of people flowing
around. It took Duggan almost five minutes to reach the *Pugilist's*
boarding ramp, since he had to make his way around people, vehicles and maintenance equipment. The ramp was down, with two
soldiers at the bottom of it. They looked alert, with their gauss
rifles held in readiness, though Duggan couldn't for the life of

him think why they'd be agitated. Perhaps it was the presence of all the people in the area. As he came close, they recognized him, presumably from having seen his face on their assignment notices. They both saluted.

"Sir, welcome to the ES *Pugilist*, sir!" said the closest, a woman with blonde hair and sharp eyes.

"Who's aboard?" asked Duggan.

"All fifteen of our squad are ready to go, sir. And Commander McGlashan is on the bridge."

"Excellent. Lieutenants Chainer and Breeze should be here shortly. They know where they're going."

"Sir," said the woman.

Duggan was about to walk past when he stopped. "What're your names?" he asked.

"Infantrymen Powell and Casper, sir," replied the woman, her voice crisp, yet polite.

"You look on edge," said Duggan.

"Sir?" she stuttered.

"What's bothering you?"

"Nothing, sir. Sergeant Ortiz told us to be alert, that's all."

Duggan nodded to himself and made his way up the ramp. The interior was exactly the same as every other Vincent class – cramped and with pockets of stifling heat, interspersed with areas of bone-biting chill. He knew before he reached the bridge that it would be far too hot and he knew exactly what it would smell like. He wasn't disappointed.

"We could be back on the *Detriment* again, sir," said McGlashan with a broad smile.

"Feels like I never left it," Duggan admitted. "A bit shiny for my liking."

"And there're no rips in the seat coverings," agreed McGlashan, sitting in her chair. It squeaked and crackled like the cheap leather it was.

"We're on escort duty," said Duggan. "Double escort duty."

McGlashan stopped what she was doing and looked at him. "From the look on your face, I take it that's not good?"

"We're taking a heavy lifter to Everlong – a mining planet. We've got company. A second Gunner is coming with us. It's got a fresh captain. Fresh crew as well, I imagine."

"Backup is always good."

"Not when I have to hold hands."

McGlashan looked over her shoulder to make sure no one was approaching the bridge. "Sir, the new bloods are what we need to keep fighting the war."

"They are."

"You don't sound convinced."

"I feel as if I'm getting to old to teach. Too many bad habits."

"I learned more in the first two months I spent on a ship than I did in the four years I spent training to come on a ship. You have an opportunity to pass on what you've learned, sir. To beat the Ghasts."

Duggan sighed. "I'll give the man a chance, Commander."

"I'm sure you'll treat him fairly, sir," she said. It almost sounded like an order. "When are we leaving?"

"As soon as we're all aboard."

"That won't be long. The ship's life support has detected the arrival of Lieutenants Chainer and Breeze. We've got Sergeant Ortiz with us."

"So I hear. I think she'll be disappointed when she learns about our destination."

"No chance of a scrap this time?"

"I wouldn't go so far as to say that. We shouldn't need to put down on the planet's surface, at least."

While they waited for Breeze and Chainer to arrive, Duggan ran through a series of check routines on the *Pugilist*'s weapons, guidance and engines. He was suspicious of new spacecraft, ever since an accident on an Anderlecht cruiser he'd captained in the past.

"It looks good to go," he said. "They put this ship together in record time, but they don't seem to have cut any corners."

"I'll be holding tight on the first lightspeed jump," said McGlashan.

"It came to the *Juniper* at Light-F. A gentle cruise to run in the engines. We'll need to go a lot faster than that to reach the rendezvous in time."

Lieutenant Bill Breeze arrived first, with Lieutenant Frank Chainer right behind. Chainer was carrying a six-pack of hi-stim cans.

"So new you can small the paint drying, sir," he said. Then, he held the cans aloft, like a supplicant at the temple steps. "I brought supplies."

"He also wanted to stop off for a coffee on the way," said Breeze with a wink.

Duggan pointed at their seats. They took the hint and sat. McGlashan powered up their consoles. "The *Juniper* has already fed our destination coordinates into our mainframe, sir," she said.

"Start the engines up," said Duggan.

There was a high-pitched whine, followed by the familiar coarse vibration. It rapidly settled down to a smooth, underlying thrumming. The engines on a warship didn't take much warming up.

"Gravity drive at full power and ready to go," said Breeze.

"Request clearance to leave."

"The *Juniper*'s given clearance, sir. Hangar Bay Two should be empty of personnel in ten minutes." Chainer cleared his throat. "The AI has requested you engage the autopilot."

"Requested?" asked Duggan.

"It won't open the doors until you do so."

"Very well." Duggan activated the *Pugilist's* automatic control systems and sat back in his chair.

Ten minutes later, the heavy external doors that separated the *Juniper* from the vacuum outside slid open. The *Pugilist* lifted smoothly from the hangar floor, its silver alloy hull bathed in the strobing deep red of the internal warning lights. Under the guidance of its mainframe, the spacecraft exited at precisely the correct speed, and maintained an exact distance from the walls of the aperture. McGlashan looked at Duggan and raised an eyebrow. He shrugged in response.

"I can't act like a hooligan every time, Commander."

The bulkhead screen showed an image of the *Juniper* as it receded into the distance behind the *Pugilist*. None of the crew spoke for a while – there was something soothing about watching the enormity of space. Minutes passed, until the incredible bulk of the orbital was nothing more than a silvery dot, mankind's largest space-borne structure reduced to insignificance by the infinity of its surroundings. Glesta-2 was visible to one side – a large, grey sphere of rock and common metals. Soon the *Juniper* would be lost from sight as it proceeded on its wide circuit about the planet.

"Power up the deep fission drive."

"On it now. Seventy-eight seconds till they're ready. That's a bit quicker than normal – they must have been doing some optimisation."

"Could be they've already learned something from the *Crimson's* Dreamer core," said Chainer.

"Or given the Vincent mainframes a bit more oomph," said McGlashan.

"Our technology's moving forwards," Breeze replied. "That's all that matters."

"Go to full speed as soon as you're able, Lieutenant."

"Will do, sir."

Duggan kept an eye on the fission drive readouts, prepared to cut them off if he saw anything anomalous. There was nothing untoward and a series of gauges climbed steadily, until the mainframe completed its calculations and decided the engines were ready to fire. There was a rumbling thump to signify their shift to lightspeed.

"We're a fraction above Light-H," said Breeze. "Slightly faster than the *Detriment.*"

"It's a relief we're not waking up from unconsciousness," said Chainer. Lightspeed jumps on the *Crimson* had been brutally harsh on the human occupants of the ship. The *Pugilist* was much slower, and the life support systems had an easier time keeping things stable.

Duggan was also relieved. It would have only been a matter of time before one of the *Crimson*'s crew or the ship's infantry had been seriously hurt. Still, he knew which of the two vessels he'd prefer to be in command of.

"Give me the *Crimson* any day," said McGlashan, as if she'd read his thoughts.

"Yeah," said Chainer. "I never did mind a few minor lacerations in the line of duty."

"How long till we rendezvous?" asked Duggan.

"Six days until we stop, give or take. After that, it looks like we've got another ten days until we get to our final destination. A place called Everlong. Why the mid-flight break?" said Breeze.

"It's a mining planet. The Space Corps is running low on dense metals. They've recently found a whole load of what we need, waiting to be dug up. All we have to do is escort a heavy lifter to the planet. We're meeting it somewhere in the middle of the journey."

"I'm checking the specs on the ship we're meeting, sir. It's big and slow. I'm not even sure if it'll scrape past Light-E. Why are we escorting it anyway? Everlong is in a safe area of Confederation space."

"It might not be safe now, Lieutenant. That's why we're coming along with it."

"The Ghasts aren't letting up, are they?" asked Chainer. "We might be hiding from them, but they're not going to stop looking."

"Did you think they would?" asked McGlashan.

"No, Commander. I've seen the same things you've seen. I didn't for one minute think they'd let up."

Duggan pushed himself upright. The chair's leather covering squeaked and made him wonder why they'd tried to save coppers on the seats, given how much the warship cost to build. "Call the squad to the mess room and we'll go down and meet them. I'll let them know where we're off to."

CHAPTER THREE

·THE MEETING DIDN'T TAKE LONG. There wasn't much to tell the squad about where they were going or why. Duggan sized up the men and women he'd been provided with – there were a couple who looked like they'd not seen much action, but the rest had the calm, self-assurance that suggested they'd seen their fair share of combat. Sergeant Ortiz hadn't changed at all in the year since she'd last served on one of Duggan's ships. She was hard and competent, with lines at the corners of her eyes to betray how long she'd been in the Corps.

"Good to see you, Sergeant," said Duggan, when the rest of the squad had been dismissed.

"And you, sir."

"What've we got here?"

"There's some good experience amongst them. A couple of young bloods, full of themselves. I'll soon fix that."

"I'm sure you will, Sergeant. I can't see there being any fighting this time around."

"I'll take it as it comes, sir. Word is, there've been a few sightings around the Larax Sphere."

Duggan hid his surprise. He knew he shouldn't have been shocked to learn that Ortiz had heard some things. Soldiers had a knack for finding out what was meant to be a secret. "You've had Monsey hack the *Juniper* to find that out?"

"Monsey is dead, sir." She saw his face. "I'm sorry, sir. Didn't you know? She got chewed up by a Ghast repeater out in some forsaken part of the Axion sector. I didn't even know we sent ships there anymore."

"Thank you, Sergeant. I hope she gave as good as she got."

"I'll bet she did, sir."

Duggan returned to the bridge, in a foul mood. He should have heard about Monsey's death sooner. He'd been kept at his desk for the last year, but that was no excuse for him to remain ignorant of what was happening to the people who'd been with him on the *Crimson*. Duggan had lost men and women before – it never got easier. He sat in his seat and kept himself busy monitoring the *Pugilist*'s onboard systems for any fluctuations in output that might indicate a fault somewhere. The others saw his face and didn't speak. After an hour had passed, Duggan shook away the cloud, determined that he wouldn't be weighed down by it.

"Have you been through our weapons systems?" he asked. "Admiral Teron said they've made some changes."

"Nothing too revolutionary," said McGlashan. "We've got two banks of eight Lambdas each. At first, I thought it was a downgrade, since the *Detriment* had two clusters of ten. However, these are a newer model of missile. One hundred and forty thousand klicks targeting range and a higher plasma yield. They fly faster too."

"Should let us get the jump on the Ghast conventional missiles," said Chainer hopefully.

"Assuming they haven't made changes of their own," said Breeze. He wasn't usually so cynical.

"The Lambda guidance systems are different as well. I've not had a chance to look into it," said McGlashan.

"Admiral Teron said something about that," said Duggan. He frowned as he read through the top-level technical specifications of the missiles they carried. "We can manually disable the homing element of the weapon."

"Eh? Why would we want to do that?" asked Chainer.

Duggan realised why. "The Lambdas can fly a lot further than their maximum launch range. The limitation is in the targeting – they can't detect an object that's too far away. If we disable the guidance, we can fire them in a straight line from much greater distances."

"Like the *Crimson* did against that Dreamer ship?" said Breeze.

"Must be," said Chainer. "Except the *Crimson* had eighteen missile clusters and a core that's far faster than what we've got on this ship. We wouldn't have a hope of getting a straight-line hit on something that's more than twenty thousand klicks out. Even then it would be down to luck."

"It's something, Lieutenant," said Duggan. "An option we didn't have before. At least the Corps is trying to learn new ways of doing things."

"Yeah. It's got to be better than nothing."

"What about the nuclear warheads?" asked Duggan, turning towards McGlashan.

"I don't see any nukes in our arsenal, sir," she said.

"They must be locked to the captain's console. Even after all these centuries, they're still scared of an accidental launch. I've given you access to them, Commander. I'm sure you won't get up to any mischief."

"I don't like them," she conceded. "These ones are just shy of a gigaton each. Seems like they'll boost for half a million klicks. They're not exactly nimble and they won't outrun anything."

"Mankind's answer to the Shatterer missiles," said Chainer. "Can you foresee any situation where we'll need them, sir?"

"No, Lieutenant, I can't. Except that as we've learned, it's occasionally good to have an option for the unforeseen. I'd rather have them with us than not."

The remainder of the six days went by in relative quiet. The mood onboard was relaxed and Duggan reflected that they'd all had the threat of punishment and dismissal to deal with for far longer than was good for their health. The war against the Ghasts wasn't going well, but it didn't appear to be weighing down on the crew. Things had been comparatively quiet for a while – or at least the Space Corps hadn't lost any major ships for the last few months. Several Anderlechts and a few dozen Gunners had been destroyed in battle that Duggan knew about. In a way, the losses were almost acceptably low, given how many new ships the Confederation was building. In his heart, Duggan knew that something was going to change. The Ghasts hadn't given up on the war. He worried that next time there was a major confrontation, mankind was going to be in for a shock.

Two hours into the sixth day, the *Pugilist*'s deep fission engines cut out and, without fuss, the spaceship entered normal space.

"Any sign of the *Goliath* or the *Ribald*?" asked Duggan.

"Scanning the locality," said Chainer, the faraway tone to his voice indicative of his concentration.

"We're early," said Breeze. "The mainframe calculated it almost ninety minutes out."

"They're here, sir. I'm getting two pings a little over an hour's sub-light travel away. There's nothing else out here, so they're easy to spot."

Duggan took manual control of the *Pugilist* and directed the ship towards the coordinates Chainer fed through to him. "Hail both vessels."

As he waited for Chainer to get a response, Duggan zoomed in the main display to show the *MHL Goliath*. The back three-quarters of the ship was cuboid, while the nose was much smaller and looked as if it had been welded on as an afterthought. The cargo bay doors were huge and ran in pairs along the underside of the otherwise featureless superstructure. It was functional and nothing more. The *Pugilist's* mainframe listed the dimensions and overlaid the image of a Gunner onto the screen. The *Goliath* was a big ship – over five kilometres in length, but bulky and massive where a warship would be sleek and streamlined. Unlike a warship, the heavy lifter had plenty of internal space and its fission engines were comparatively small. Its gravity drive was oversized and allowed the *Goliath* to drag an inconceivable weight of cargo away into space.

"I'm getting responses from both vessels," said Chainer. "Captain Erika Jonas asks what took us so long."

Duggan gave a half-smile. "Tell her we stopped off for a bite to eat."

"Captain Mason Graham from the *ES Ribald* wants to speak to you directly, sir."

"Very well. Bring him through."

"He wants a private channel, sir."

"What the hell does he want a private channel for?" asked Duggan. He shook his head. "Fine, connect him."

Moments later, there was an almost undiscernible fizz in Duggan's earpiece as it became active. A man's voice spoke. It was of indeterminate age, but Duggan had already looked at the files and knew the speaker was twenty-six years old.

"Captain Duggan?"

"Speaking. Captain Graham, what do you need a private channel for?"

There was a short pause. "Protocol, Captain Duggan. The communication between two captains of the Space Corps must remain confidential at all times when it pertains to matters relating to their assignment or mission."

Duggan thought he could just about remember reading something about that. "What matters do you wish to discuss?"

"Formations and tactics, Captain Duggan. I have a few suggestions."

"There are only two warships and one MHL, Captain Graham. We'll be at lightspeed for ten days and in orbit around Everlong for no more than a single day. I can't imagine we'll have much need of a formation. As for tactics, if we see anything larger than a Kraven light cruiser, our tactics will be to get away as quickly as we can."

"Captain Duggan, we might encounter Ghast warships at sub-light near to Everlong."

"Indeed we might. In that case, I will tell you what to do and you will do it at once. Are those tactics clear enough for you?"

"I'm not sure that's the best approach, Captain Duggan," said Captain Graham. His voice sounded strained.

"While I'm in command, that's the approach we're taking. Am I clear?"

"Yes, Captain Duggan. Very clear."

"Good. The *Pugilist* will come to within five thousand klicks of the *Goliath*. My comms man will feed the exact flightpath to both the *Ribald* and the *Goliath*, to ensure we all exit lightspeed at close to the same place. The *Pugilist* and *Ribald* will depart ten minutes prior to the *Goliath*, to ensure we arrive first - we'll be going at Light-E, so there shouldn't be too much variation."

"Understood."

"Excellent. And Captain Graham? I trust my crew almost as much as I trust myself. There'll be no more private channels for discussions like this one."

Duggan ended the connection and stared ahead, his face like thunder. When he'd gathered himself, he noticed McGlashan grinning at him. He glowered at her and she quickly looked back at her console.

"I'm going to bring us in close," he said. "Lieutenant Breeze, get an advance calculation of our course and transmit it to the *Goliath* and the *Ribald*. Lieutenant Chainer, let Captain Jonas know that we'll be on our way as soon as we're within five thousand klicks."

"The *Goliath* needs an hour before it can break into light-speed, sir," said Breeze. "They're not built for speed or urgency."

"We're an hour away. The timing is close to perfect," said Duggan.

"I've let them know, sir," said Chainer. "Captain Jonas tells me they're putting coal in the boilers as we speak."

One hour later, the *ES Pugilist* came to within five thousand klicks of the *MHL Goliath*. The *Ribald* had taken up a position on the far side of the heavy lifter, also five thousand klicks away. At precisely the same time, the two Gunners accelerated away from local space, vanishing into the controlled uncertainty of lightspeed. Ten minutes later, the *Goliath* followed.

The *Pugilist*'s mainframe calculated the journey would take just under ten days to complete. Duggan got himself comfortable, feeling a sense of relief that the comms systems wouldn't function at the speed they were travelling. He didn't want Captain Graham bothering him with any more suggestions on the way.

"What's the *Goliath* carrying, sir?" asked Breeze. "That's a Class One MHL. We've only got a handful of those in service."

"Machinery. Drills, grinders, smelters. When it drops off all that cargo, it's going to fill up with as much semi-refined metal as it can fit in the hold."

"It can do all that in a day?" asked McGlashan.

"Probably not, Commander. I know I told Captain Graham we'd be in orbit for a day. I'd guess we're looking at closer to five days or a week."

"Is the *Goliath* leaving many personnel on Everlong?" asked Breeze.

"A few. Operations are mostly automated, since the planet isn't able to support life."

"It must be tough for the miners," said McGlashan.

"Tough and dangerous. I don't envy them," said Duggan. He got up from his seat. "The gravity on Everlong is higher than we're used to. I don't plan to set us down, but I'd suggest you get in some gym time in case that changes." With that, he set off to the *Pugilist*'s tiny gym room, intending to follow his own advice.

CHAPTER FOUR

TEN DAYS and one hour later, the *ES Pugilist* emerged from lightspeed, two hundred thousand kilometres away from its destination. Everlong was the fifth planet out of twelve, orbiting a much larger than average sun. Everlong itself was nothing extraordinary, with a diameter of fifty thousand kilometres and an arid surface of sand, rock and little else. What made it unusual was the quantity of valuable metals to be found within its crust.

"Lieutenant Chainer, scan the area."

"On it. Standard checks show the area's clear."

"Run a detailed check."

"Yes, sir. Are you expecting something?"

"Not quite *expecting*, Lieutenant. It's always best to be certain."

"We've come in more or less exactly where we wanted," said Chainer. "The mining operations are visible to our sensors from here. They're right on the cusp, though and the planet's rotation will take them out of sight within the hour."

"Any sign of anything unusual?"

"There's not a peep, sir. Everything's quiet."

"Is that good or bad?"

Chainer frowned. "I don't know, sir. I would expect there to be some traffic. They probably don't send much long-distance, but the surface operations would usually be messy with broadcasts."

Duggan crossed over to look over Chainer's shoulder. "What's your opinion, Lieutenant? Could they be in the middle of a shut-down?"

"I'd expect there to be *more* broadcasts if they were having a maintenance break, sir."

"Technical difficulties?"

"Possible. It wouldn't affect every piece of equipment on the surface. The sensors on the *Pugilist* aren't the most sensitive models available, but this is still a warship. We could detect a single hand-held communicator from here."

"How visible was our arrival?"

"Pretty visible," said Breeze. "Anything military would know we've arrived."

"If they were looking."

"They'd have to be stupid to miss us."

"Keep our comms silent for the time being, Lieutenant Chainer. I'd like to say there's nothing to worry about."

"You're not going to?"

"It's not a phrase I believe in."

"There's a fission signature nearby, sir. It's the ES *Ribald*," said Breeze.

"*Ribald*, this is *Pugilist*. Maintain silence," said Chainer.

"Roger that," came the response from the *Ribald*'s comms man. "Any reason for concern?"

"Just precautions at the moment. We're not detecting any surface activity."

"This is Captain Graham. The files report this to be a sub-surface mining operation in metal-saturated rock. I would expect any activity to be hidden from our sensors, particularly at our current angle to the planet. I recommend we approach as normal, as per Space Corps procedures."

"We'll proceed with caution, Captain Graham," said Duggan. "Keep your crew on alert and arm your counter-measures."

"The *Goliath*'s appeared in near space, sir," said Breeze. "Fifteen thousand klicks closer to the planet."

"Captain Jonas, this is the *Pugilist*. We're going to approach the planet with caution. Keep your distance behind us – recommend fifty thousand klicks."

Captain Jonas' voice filled the bridge, rich and sultry. "Fifty thousand klicks it is. We've got enough machinery in the hold to mine this planet dry in five years. I wouldn't like to have it spilled before we can put it to use."

Duggan gave a signal for the channel to be closed. "I'm bringing us closer for a look," he said to his crew. "Lieutenant Chainer, keep your eyes glued to those readouts."

"Captain Graham might be correct, sir," said McGlashan. "We keep our mining operations as quiet as we can. Ever since the early days of the war. No miner wants to see a Ghost ship arriving in orbit – it means almost certain death for the people below."

"I know this, Commander. There's nothing to lose by remaining suspicious. Remember we're effectively in contested space now."

"I thought there was no proof the Ghasts destroyed our vessels?" said Breeze.

"There isn't, Lieutenant. However, I don't like surprises."

Duggan kept the *Pugilist* at a steady speed, without pushing the vessel's sub-light engines to anything like their full capacity. He noted the *Ribald* kept a precise distance to his left and slightly behind, while the *Goliath* gathered speed early to ensure it was able to keep pace with the much nimbler warships.

At one hundred thousand klicks, he looked at Chainer for an update. The lieutenant had been quiet for the last few minutes, his brow furrowed in concentration.

"Lieutenant Chainer?"

"Sir, I'm looking. I'm getting a clearer view of the operations at this range. The mine is a big, open pit, which leaves them with an extremely low profile from here. I'd be able to see better if we were directly above."

"Any noise?"

"Nothing. When we get closer I should be able to detect the vibrations of their surface equipment. They don't keep everything below ground. Some of the processing goes on up top."

"*Ribald*, this is *Pugilist*. Something isn't right. Keep alert."

"Roger."

Duggan checked the time logs since their arrival. "We've been here almost ten minutes. If there was a Ghast ship in orbit, we'd have seen it by now, wouldn't we?"

"Almost certainly. Past data suggests they maintain a speed that would have had them visible to us by now. Even if they'd gone behind the planet the moment we'd arrived," said Breeze. "And they'd have seen our fission signature."

"I'm still not happy," said Duggan. With little choice but to proceed, he increased the power to *Pugilist*'s engines. At forty thousand klicks, the planet filled the bulkhead viewscreen completely. It was a dull shade, somewhere between a yellow and a grey - as drab a place as any other mining planet in Confederation space.

"What a shit hole," muttered Chainer to himself.

"I'll bring us higher, so we can see down into the hole," said Duggan. "I don't want us to be right on top of them by the time we get a proper look."

"This was a big mine already, from the looks of things," said Chainer. "The surface works alone are eight kilometres across. I still can't see the bottom from this angle. I'm starting to pick up vibrations – they're consistent with heavy machinery."

"You're certain?" asked Duggan sharply.

"It's definitely mechanical, sir." Chainer didn't say anything for another few seconds. "Other than that, there's nothing. I don't like it. I should be able to tap into their comms from here. They only have civilian kit at places like this. It leaks out for thousands of klicks if you know what you're listening for."

"Could the Ghasts have been here, sir?" asked McGlashan. "They might have killed everyone and left."

"There's no sign of plasma spill on the rim of the pit," said Chainer. "I guess they could have dropped some missiles dead centre and I'd still not have the angle to see it."

Duggan didn't like it at all. This was meant to have been a straightforward escort mission. Now it was beginning to seem like something had happened to the Everlong mining operations. The one reassurance was the lack of any Ghast ships in the vicinity.

"We'll be directly above them in a few seconds," he said. "I'm keeping to thirty thousand klicks. We'll get a perfect view from there."

"I can see it now, sir. Everything looks normal. They've got two big grinders on the go. No sign of any operatives. I don't know how automated the grinders are. Wait on, there's no power to their comms mast, though I can't see any outward signs of damage."

"Damnit, we're going to have to land and check it out," said Duggan. "Try hailing them."

"There's no point, sir. I've got nothing to patch into without that mast. They'll have a wired link to other comms units underground, but without the main one, I can't reach anyone or anything."

"*Ribald*, this is *Pugilist*," said Duggan. There was no response. He looked at his tactical display – the other Gunner had drifted slightly off course. "Force open a channel," he said to Chainer.

"My request isn't reaching them – something's wrong." His voice climbed in pitch. "Sir, I'm picking up an anomaly just below the surface. Ghast military alloys."

"There are no positrons coming from the *Ribald*'s hull, sir," said Breeze.

"A disruptor!" said Duggan, pulling the nose of the ship away from the mine pit. He increased the gravity drive to full and pointed them towards the surface, hoping to cut off the angle and prevent any further attacks.

"There's a missile launch from the surface, sir. A Shatterer," said McGlashan, her voice eerily calm. "We're its target. Seven seconds to impact."

Duggan wanted to hit something in frustration. They'd been drawn into a trap and there was little he could do about it. He had the *Pugilist* at full power and aimed at the distant surface. The heat readings from the hull rocketed upwards as the particles in the planet's atmosphere battered against it. He knew it wasn't going to be enough – it wasn't going to be *nearly* enough. The Ghast Shatterer missile curved in flight, adjusting its trajectory to pursue the fleeing warship. Travelling at a little under four thousand klicks per second, it struck the rear of the *ES Pugilist*. The missile's warhead buried itself into the metres-thick armour, before it detonated in a blinding flash of white plasma. The warship's armour was ripped apart, sending a cascade of burning metal in a wide arc behind.

The bridge shook violently and a deafening rumble thundered through the bulkhead walls. Chainer and McGlashan were knocked from their chairs and onto the floor. Duggan clung on grimly to his control sticks. The vessel's emergency alarms chimed and the room was bathed in red light. Duggan scanned his status screens – one of them had gone out completely, whilst the other four poured an endless list of text and three-dimensional images of the damage for him to try and make sense of. Far from subsiding, the rumbling increased in intensity, booming against his ears.

"We're screwed, sir," said Breeze. "Fission drives almost completely shredded. Gravity drives offline."

"Get them back," Duggan said through gritted teeth.

"I don't think there's anything to get back, sir."

"I don't care. Give me something."

Chainer dragged himself onto his chair, cursing loudly. McGlashan regained her feet. She looked dazed.

"Commander, is there any else incoming?"

McGlashan visibly shook herself and her expression was angry that she'd been unable to stop herself being thrown from her post. "Negative, sir. One was enough."

"Engines, Lieutenant. Where are they?"

"Still offline," said Breeze. He was too busy to say more.

"We are going to crash into the surface at almost one thousand klicks per second if you don't do something. There'll be a big new crater next to the mine."

"I'm on it, sir," snapped Breeze.

Without its gravity drive, the spacecraft was nothing more than a lump of metal. It couldn't glide and it couldn't change direction without its engines. It hurtled downwards, the bulkhead viewscreen showing a jumpy image of the planet, disrupted by noise from the ship's damaged sensor arrays.

"We'll burn up in twenty seconds," said Duggan.

"There's no power – nothing," said Breeze. "The mainframe's not quick enough to re-route in time."

Duggan acted instinctively. He shut off the weapons and also the mainframe's access to what little remained of the fission drive.

Without access to those sub-systems, the core diverted its processing to the gravity drive.

"I'm getting a utilization spike on the engines," said Breeze. "Come on, come on!"

"Now, Lieutenant."

Breeze sent the command to restart the gravity drive. Something howled for a second, before fading away until it was lost in the rumbling. "What the hell?" he asked, then, "They're online, sir! Four percent of maximum output."

"Get me more," said Duggan, struggling to keep the *Pugilist* from entering an uncontrolled spin. He detected a response from the control sticks and fought hard to correct the spiral.

"We're not gonna burn, we're not gonna burn," Chainer repeated under his breath. "Come on, sir."

At five thousand klicks above the surface, Duggan wasn't sure if he could get the ship under control. It was responding sluggishly and the nose wouldn't come up. The hull temperature was at one hundred and thirty percent and climbing. The speed of descent slowed, but it didn't look like it would be enough.

"It's going to be close," said McGlashan. "The hull is beginning to melt."

"Gravity engines are dropping off, sir," said Breeze. "Back down to three percent."

"Not now!" shouted Duggan. "It can't happen now!"

As the atmosphere thickened, Duggan found he was able to direct the plummeting warship through the resistance of the colliding atoms. It wasn't much – hardly anything – but it let him alter the *Pugilist*'s trajectory just enough to approach the surface at an angle. The gravity drives were slowing them, yet with only a fraction of their output available it wasn't going to allow a controlled landing.

"Sergeant Ortiz, I hope you're buckled up," said Chainer through the comms. "Shit, the internal voice is down."

"We're going to hit," said Duggan. "Hold on."

Seconds later, the *ES Pugilist* crashed at an oblique into the surface of the planet Everlong, at almost two thousand kilometres per hour. It skipped up once, before it began rolling, tearing vast chunks out of the stone. Where the hull crashed through an area of sand dunes, the heat from its entry fused the grains into a coarse glass. Eventually, the ruined craft came to a stop and lay motionless, while the retained heat of its alloys slowly dwindled into the thin air.

CHAPTER FIVE

DUGGAN COUGHED AND GROANED. His head felt like someone had struck it with a hammer and he was sore all over. He cracked an eye open and red light seeped in. The persistent background rasp of the ship's alarm grated through his ears and into his brain. It was so hot that he felt like he was on fire. A face appeared over him, concern etched into its features.

"How long?" he asked, the words coming out as little more than a harsh croak.

"Fifteen minutes, sir," said McGlashan. "I've sent Lieutenant Chainer to fetch Corporal Bryant."

"I'll be fine."

"Too late to say that now – there's no way to let Lieutenant Chainer know. Pretty much everything's out of action, or damaged."

"Except the life support."

"It kept us alive, sir. We'd be nothing more than bloody smears across the walls without it. I don't know how much longer it'll work. It's failing. The whole ship is failing – what's left of it."

Duggan coughed again and unclipped himself from his seat.

"What you're saying, Commander, is that I can't sit around in this chair doing nothing."

She smiled, the sight of it giving Duggan some cheer. "That's exactly what I'm saying, sir."

"Where's Lieutenant Breeze?"

"I'm over here, sir."

Duggan craned his head to look, feeling a sense of relief that Breeze was alive. With a monumental effort, he pushed himself upright. Nausea threatened to swamp him for a time, until he suppressed it with an effort of will.

"What's our situation?"

"We've come down less than fifty klicks from the mine. A good effort in the circumstances." She flashed the smile again. "The rear two hundred metres of the *Pugilist* is gone, or at least there's nothing usable there."

"Any losses?"

McGlashan's face changed. "I don't know, sir, the internal comms aren't going to work again any time soon. Lieutenant Chainer will get details on our casualties and he's going to tell Sergeant Ortiz to find out what's left in the hold. We'll need suits to get out of here. There's no air and we're spilling antimatter in a ninety-kilometre arc."

The sound of hurried footsteps at the bridge entrance alerted Duggan to the arrival of Chainer and the squad medic, Corporal Bryant. Bryant was short, slim and as no-nonsense as they came.

"Sit!" she insisted. Duggan sat. Bryant immediately linked him up to her portable diagnostic and treatment box. She watched the readouts for a full thirty seconds. "You'll live," she said, without any more explanation.

"How are the men?" Duggan asked.

"Two dead, sir. Howell and Schneider."

"Damnit. What happened?"

"You'd need to check the life-support logs. They were on the bottom bunk in the same room. If I had to guess, I'd say the life support wasn't functioning at floor level. There isn't much of them left to bury or launch into space."

Duggan dismissed her. There'd be time to mourn later. "What happened to the *Ribald* and the *Goliath*?"

"I don't know, sir," said Chainer. "The missile took out our aft sensor arrays. I've checked the logs and confirmed that we received no data after the impact."

"Do we have anything left at the front to scan for them?"

"No, sir. We're buried nose-down. The long-range comms are gone as well. We're little more than a metal husk."

"We need to get outside," said Duggan. "And get clear of the area."

"Sergeant Ortiz is heading to the hold. She's going to gather what we need. If it's still there."

"The hold is right near the bottom of the ship. It's going to be hot in there for a good while yet."

"The squad keep a couple of suits in their quarters," said Chainer. "Better safe than sorry, I guess."

"I'm glad they're prepared," said Duggan. He had a worrying thought. "If we're nose-down, can we get out?"

"I think so," said McGlashan. "The secondary boarding ramp still has power. I don't know if we'll be able to open the primary ramp. Or the hold doors."

"We'll need the tanks," said Duggan. "Assuming they've not been smashed to pieces."

"I've checked," said Chainer. "There are no status updates from any of the four vehicles. They could be damaged beyond repair or it could be down to the malfunction of the internal comms."

"Follow me," said Duggan. "We're abandoning ship. Another Gunner under my command shot down." He was still angry at being caught unawares by the Ghasts.

He ducked through the bridge entrance and into the corridor outside. Usually he'd have been struck by waves of colder air only a few metres from the heat of the control room. Now it was so hot he could feel the air searing his lungs if he breathed in too deeply. The hull of a warship was designed to dissipate heat quickly throughout the structure. The problems came if there was too much heat – at that point, the whole of the interior could heat beyond the capabilities of the HVAC to control. The *Pugilist* was dangerously close to becoming a death trap.

Duggan took the crew to the mess room – it was filled with the same red light as the bridge, but the alarm was mercifully quiet. Sergeant Ortiz would have to come through here in order to reach the bridge. They didn't have to wait long. A figure entered, wearing one of the Space Corps' flexible polymer space suits. The figure was Sergeant Ortiz, dripping with sweat and dragging a couple of suits behind her. Corporal Simmons was also there, similarly encumbered. Neither of them wore their helmets – it was too cramped in the ship to make easy progress wearing one.

"Sir, we've found suits and rifles in the hold." She dropped the pile to the ground, taking care that the oversized helmets didn't clatter off the floor. "The tanks are beat up – all four broke their moorings. There's been an explosion as well – I think a plasma grenade blew up in its locker."

"The lockers are fully insulated," said Breeze.

Ortiz shrugged. "It was too hot to stick around, even in the suits. It's getting hotter as well, sir."

"That's not good," said Breeze.

"Will the tanks work?" asked Duggan. He picked up a suit and began to struggle his way into it.

"If we can flip them over, I'm sure we'd get at least one of them going, sir," said Ortiz. "Three are on their roofs, one is on its side."

Duggan needed a direct answer. "Sergeant Ortiz, is it your opinion that we should abandon the tanks?"

"Yes, sir. I believe we should evacuate the ship as soon as possible. If we manage to get one of the tanks the right way up, there's no way to be sure we'll be able to get it out through the launch chute. The mainframe's locked everything down. I'm sure you could override, but there's no guarantee there'll be anything other than sand or dirt at the bottom of the chute. We've got a portable beacon with us – we'll be able to let the Corps know we're out here."

"We'll not be using that beacon yet, Sergeant."

"Sir?"

"The Ghasts must think we're all dead. We need to use that to our advantage and see if we can take out their disruptor and Shatterer emplacements. We're here to escort the *Goliath* and until I know what's happened to it, that's what we're going to do."

Ortiz saluted. "Yes sir!"

"Gather the squad and get them suited. We're leaving by the secondary ramp. Make sure you save a couple of rifles for us."

Ortiz nodded and left. Five minutes later, Duggan and the rest of the crew were in their suits. The feeling of being ensconced in the material was an unusual one. Duggan could feel his skin temperature dropping immediately to a more acceptable level, while his face and head remained covered in sweat. He picked up his helmet and resisted the temptation to put it on.

They left the mess room in a line. Breathing became harder and Duggan wondered how the soldiers had managed, since they were quartered closer to the outer hull than the bridge was. It wasn't long until he had to put his helmet on. The servos hissed as they made a perfect seal around his neck collar. At once, the onboard computer spilled information onto the mini-HUD, informing him of the temperature, his assumed state of physical wellbeing and who on the ship was sharing his open comms channel. He inhaled the cold air inside - it was redolent with the scent of rubber and sweat, but the relief it brought was immense.

It was crowded at the top of the secondary ramp hatch. There was a small room here which was much too small to fit a combined seventeen infantry and crew, so the men and women had been forced to line up against the wall of the two exit corridors. They all wore helmets – this close to the outer skin of the hull, it was far too hot for any of them to survive without one. Someone handed Duggan a rifle without being asked and he took it gratefully.

"Please confirm through the open channel when you're ready," said Duggan. "There's not enough air to breathe outside and you don't want to know how many positrons there are." He checked his temperature reading and saw it was over two hundred and fifty degrees – already a couple of degrees higher than it had been five minutes ago.

Duggan elbowed his way to the release panel for the secondary boarding ramp. The mainframe was slow to respond to his commands and he wondered if it was dying, or if it was occupied elsewhere. Impatient to be on, he repeated the instruction. With a scrape of warped metal, the ramp unlocked from its mounting and juddered as it descended. His helmet gave a quiet chime to alert him to the dangerous levels of antimatter.

"Seems like we're partially on our side," said Duggan, peering along the length of the boarding ramp. It was early morning on Everlong according to his helmet. Outside, he could see swirling grey sand, blowing in waves across more grey sand. The light from Everlong's sun was poor, or obscured by clouds of dust - it was hard to tell from where he was standing. The far end of the ramp was suspended in the air and Duggan made his way carefully along it. "Three metres to the ground," he said, looking down. "It could have been a lot worse."

Without giving the matter anymore thought, Duggan slung

his rifle over his back, crouched at the edge of the ramp and dropped off it. He used his hands to grab the edge and arrest his fall. From there, he dropped the remaining three feet to the ground. Above him, a figure loomed – his suit told him it was Sergeant Ortiz. Seconds later, she was on the soft, sandy ground with him. It wasn't long until the rest of the ship's occupants were outside. From this close, it was impossible to see what state the *Pugilist* was in, but the alloy hull creaked and pinged loudly as it cooled. The mine was to the north-east of their position and Duggan led them that way at once.

"Lieutenant Breeze, I was told by Commander McGlashan that our engines are throwing out positrons in a ninety-kilometre arc."

Breeze responded on the private channel. "At least ninety kilometres. It won't die down for a thousand years either, unless the mainframe's able to do some major rerouting. Even that might take months." He glanced over his shoulder to the stricken warship. The damage was much easier to see now they'd made it a hundred metres away. "Years," said Breeze, when he saw the vast rip through the metal. "How the hell did we live through that?"

Duggan didn't know. He stopped for a few seconds to study the spacecraft. When the wind died down and the sand stopped swirling, he could see how the front of the ship had melted until it was almost unrecognizable from what it had once been. It had cooled and hardened already, leaving the once sleek craft looking lumpen and ugly. The rear of the ship – or at least the part which Duggan could see – was splayed outwards, with the alloys burned and grotesquely twisted. Given the opportunity, the Corps might one day attempt a recovery in order to re-use the precious metals it contained. Certainly, it would never fly again as the ES *Pugilist*.

"I'm glad the hole is pointing away from us," said Duggan at last. "I wouldn't have felt comfortable walking for fifty klicks with an open fission drive pointing straight at us. I'm not sure how long the suits would hold up against that."

The going was rough – underfoot it was a mixture of ankle-dragging sand and strewn rocks. The soldiers and crew were fit, but even so they had to watch the ground carefully to be sure they didn't suffer an unwanted fall. On the plus side, the ground was relatively level. Duggan was keen to make quick progress, since he didn't know if any of the miners were alive, or what had happened to the *Goliath* and the *Ribald*.

"I hate going blind," he growled to McGlashan.

"Only forty-seven klicks to go, sir," she said, realising at once why he was so frustrated. "The days here are twenty-two hours long. We should get there late tomorrow."

A voice broke into the conversation as one of the soldiers swore loudly into the open channel – it was Santos. "Shit man, what's that?"

Duggan spun around, trying to see what had caught the man's attention. It didn't take much to find – something had exploded behind them. The visibility was poor and it looked like a grey-blue light had surrounded the *Pugilist's* crash site.

"Is that the engines?" asked Friedman. "Hell, I'm glad we got away in time."

Duggan felt cold, even in the cocoon of his suit. "That's not the engines, soldier," he said. "Something's just hit it from orbit."

No one spoke as they digested this information. Duggan didn't need to spell out exactly what he meant – a Ghast ship had arrived and it had decided to finish the job started by the ground-launched Shatterer missile. What Duggan hoped to achieve was about to become a whole lot harder.

CHAPTER SIX

THEY PICKED UP THE PACE, risking their safety in order to increase their distance from the *ES Pugilist*. Duggan watched his pounding feet as they left a trail of shifting imprints, which were quickly swept away by the buffeting winds.

"Lieutenant Chainer, what are the chances of the Ghast ship spotting us?"

"That really depends, sir. If they're specifically looking for us in this area, they're definitely going to see us. If they're doing a random, high-level sweep, they'll probably miss us. On top of that, you have to consider what sort of ship it is. If it's a light cruiser, it'll take them more effort as they'll have fewer sensors. If it's something like a Cadaveron, their AI could well spot us even if their comms man doesn't. Assuming they even have a comms man."

"And assuming you can call whatever it is a *man*," said Duggan wryly.

"You've gotta call them something, sir. *Man* is as good a word as any. *Woman* just wouldn't seem right for some reason, given what warmongering bastards the Ghasts are. The only real warmongering bastard I know who's a woman is Sergeant Ortiz. No offense meant, of course."

Duggan smiled to himself. "That's fine, Lieutenant, I know what you mean." He considered his next words carefully. "We're likely to see some fighting. How are you with a rifle?"

"I'm a good shot, sir. I came third in my year. Just because I've not fired one in anger for a while doesn't mean I've forgotten how to aim. We've faced death many times before on the bridge. In my eyes that's no different to facing it when you're carrying a rifle."

"Thank you, Lieutenant, that's what I needed to hear."

"One last thing, sir. We should keep comms talk to a minimum. Our channels are well-shielded and the signal doesn't have far to travel between us, but it's better to be safe than sorry."

"Agreed. I'll let the squad know."

They pushed on for the remainder of the planet's day. It made no difference to a warship's sensors if it was light or dark, so Duggan felt it best they press on rather than waiting for night. On board a spaceship, night and day lost a lot of its meaning, but Duggan knew most of the people who served on one tried to keep to a routine.

"Any of the squad going to fall asleep on us, Sergeant?" he asked at one point.

"I don't think so, sir. A few of the guys have their own sleeping patterns. If I catch them flagging, I'll make sure it's the last thing they do."

She said it so calmly that Duggan half believed her words. "Don't shoot anyone until you've spoken to me first, Sergeant."

"I'll keep it to flesh wounds only, sir," she said.

Mindful of Chainer's words about keeping comms noise down, Duggan didn't say anything further. Night came and the temperature fell far below freezing. It was nothing too extreme and Duggan hardly registered the fact. His suit kept his body at a comfortable temperature, as well as recycling his waste. On top of that, it kept him in tip-top physical shape by injecting him with a tiny quantity of a complex stimulant every three hours to ensure he was able to keep going. The drugs could keep the suit's occupant functioning for a month – longer in some cases. At the end of it you'd feel like crap, but it was mostly better than dying. Some of the men and women who saw a lot of surface action developed a craving for what they called *suit time* – their fix of the stimulants. It was an addiction that Duggan had no wish to acquire.

They stopped for a time – it could hardly be called a camp. It was nothing more than a cluster of seventeen men and women in a loose circle, clutching their gauss rifles as they tried to catch some sleep. One or two lay on their sides, hoping the coarse sand would act as a cushion against the discomfort. Duggan had been out in places like this before and he didn't even try to lie down – he knew it wouldn't help him sleep. He looked around, willing his eyes to pierce the gloom. There was nothing to look at – the *Pugilist* had come down on a bleak, open area of the planet where the wind never seemed to stop blowing and the sand didn't end. The utter darkness above was dotted with an unfamiliar pattern of stars. The speed at which a modern warship could travel meant you never got the chance to become familiar with the skies. In truth, Duggan didn't especially care. He was fascinated by space, yet he'd never developed any romantic notions about what lay there.

One or two voices carried across the open channel and Sergeant Ortiz cut them off with a sharp command. Soldiers needed the camaraderie of hearing each other's voices and Duggan felt bad for them. It could be lonely when you had to travel in silence. It was easier if your team mates were able to push you onwards.

After six hours of discomfort in impenetrable darkness,

Duggan gave the command for them to break camp. The suits could enhance the landscape sufficiently to enable travel even in the blackest of nights, but the squad still needed a break and night had been as good a time as any. Duggan hadn't slept well and he was sure he wasn't alone. The temptation was already there to instruct the suit to inject a booster stimulant into his bloodstream. He resisted for the moment, certain that many of the people around him wouldn't be so stubborn.

He picked up his rifle. "Let's go," he said.

The day progressed in the same manner as the last one. The wreckage of the ES *Pugilist* was far behind now and Duggan was sure they'd remain ignorant even if the Ghasts fired another dozen missiles at the shell. The tedium of silence gave him a chance to think. He wondered why the Ghasts would go to the effort of installing a disruptor and a Shatterer launcher on such a forsaken planet as this. He was forced to concede that whatever the reasons, it had allowed them to take three Corps spaceships completely by surprise.

He permitted himself a modest gamble by speaking to Lieutenant Chainer. "You detected the presence of Ghast alloys on the surface just before they launched the missile at us."

"I did, sir."

"How big?"

"It was big. I can't think of a more technical term for it and I didn't get time to obtain an estimate of the measurements. The missile launcher was a lot bigger than a Lambda cluster – even bigger than the ones we had on the *Crimson*."

"Maybe that's why we've not seen such a weapon on anything smaller than a Cadaveron," mused Duggan. "It might need to be mounted on a large platform."

"When the Ghasts attacked the *Archimedes*, their newest Oblivion only launched six Shatterers at a time. In the circumstances, we have to assume they weren't holding back. There was a long delay between launches."

"It must have been a reasonable investment in time and effort to bring their hardware all the way here and then install it."

"It implies a certain inclination towards permanency, sir."

"Up till now they've shown no sign they want to do anything other than destroy our resource-gathering operations. Yet here they are, putting in enough defences to knock out a couple of Gunners. Perhaps even an Anderlecht cruiser if one happened by."

"With something else in orbit as well, sir."

"They're pushing outwards and holding onto their gains, Lieutenant. If they're increasing their presence in the Larax Sphere, it doesn't bode well for the occupied Confederation planets."

"I thought it was only a matter of time anyway?"

"It is, Lieutenant. I had hopes that maybe they'd be looking in some other direction for a while. Instead, they're getting ever closer and we're definitely not ready for them."

"The topographical scans I made before we were shot down detected the presence of Gallenium, sir. Fragments on the surface and borne in the sand. The place must be rife with it for it to be just blowing around."

"If they've found big deposits of Gallenium, I'm not surprised the Corps sent a heavy lifter here," said Duggan. "I think there are only five or six known planets with significant quantities of the ore in Confederation space."

"Are we running out of it, sir?"

"As far as I'm aware, we've got sufficient proven reserves to put engines in hundreds of new Hadrons. Perhaps the Ghasts are running out. I can't think of any other reason they'd want to establish a base here."

"Why isn't the surface overrun with their soldiers?"

"You don't need a significant force on the ground to run a mine, Lieutenant. All you need are enough people to keep the machines ticking over and to say hello when the supply ship comes by. The strength comes from what you keep in orbit above."

"It's not likely to be a Kraven, then, is it?"

"I'd guess at something a little bit bigger," said Duggan.

"Damn. It's not looking good for us down here."

"We'll see, Lieutenant. We might get a chance to throw a spanner in their works."

They trudged on through midday. The temperature remained cold and the sun had a peculiar blue halo as it shone through the billowing sand. The land began to climb steadily upwards and Duggan remembered the open area of the mine had been hollowed out from a series of hills. Mining operations tended to grind up a huge quantity of surface rock and filter out the metal-bearing ores they were looking for. By the time the open cast part of the mine had gone deep enough, the operators would have identified the richest seams and would be able to focus their efforts on following these under the ground. Duggan had only seen one or two such places and his mind retained an image of ragged, dirty pits, with enormous tunnels snaking away into the earth as the miners pursued the veins of metal.

As they climbed, the surface covering of gritty sand gave way to rough stone. Visibility improved as they rose above the swirling sands and Duggan realised how oppressive it had been walking in silence and with reduced sight. On the other hand, he now felt exposed with the obscuring veil of sand gone. His suit outlined Sergeant Ortiz in red and Duggan tapped her on the shoulder. She turned and he made the signal to indicate it was time for additional caution. Ortiz gave a strange bobbing motion – it was the only way to nod in a spacesuit.

Duggan checked his helmet's positional display and found

they were less than three kilometres from the south-west lip of the mine workings. The *Pugilist* had managed to keep the space-suits fed with data until a point only a few nanoseconds before the Shatterer had hit them. The suits couldn't store a huge amount of information, but the onboard computer and databanks had enough space to hold specifics on distances, heights and terrain type. It was hard to get lost when wearing one, though not completely unheard of.

"Sir?" It was Breeze.

Duggan knew the man wouldn't have broken comms silence without good reason. "What is it?"

"The suits aren't particularly good at detecting positrons – they don't need to be. However, I'm getting some fluctuations in the atmosphere away to our left. I'd say two or three klicks, not far off our path." Breeze raised a suited arm and pointed.

Duggan looked in the direction indicated. The land continued to climb all about them – they were more than halfway up a long, gentle rocky slope that stretched off to the left and right. Rocks and boulders provided some cover and also blocked Duggan's ability to see as clearly as he'd have liked. He changed course slightly and waved the squad to follow. They wended their way upwards, taking greater care to stay in cover. There was no indication of a Ghast presence, but there was no sense in taking unnecessary risks. Duggan's movement and heat sensors remained untriggered, though the cluttered rocks meant he couldn't be fully sure there were no surprises ahead.

After ten minutes, Breeze spoke again. "The rocks are shielding the source of the positrons. There must be some real dense metal in this hillside. It means the emissions are all going upwards into the atmosphere."

"Missile emplacement?"

"I don't think so, sir."

The squad emerged from a cluster of large boulders. Duggan

couldn't help but glance into the sky, as if his eyes could somehow see a Cadaveron circling forty thousand kilometres above him. Nevertheless, he felt a menace that he couldn't shake off.

The place which Breeze had directed them turned out to be the beginning of the mine pit, just a few hundred yards from where they'd been originally going. It was almost impossible to keep hidden from eyes above, so Duggan had to trust to luck that they'd not be struck by a Ghast missile as they came closer. The squad lay flat on the edge of the pit and looked over – the amount of rock which had been chewed to make the hole was hard to believe. Duggan remembered it to be eight kilometres across and it looked as big as it sounded – a roughly circular pit with sloped sides of hewn stone that dropped at least a kilometre down, with narrow tiers every hundred metres or so. The bottom was just about flat and covered with a layer of grey gravel, the pieces crushed by heavy machinery and scattered about because there was nowhere else to put them. That same machinery was in evidence, dotted around the pit floor. That wasn't what caught Duggan's eye. There was something else in the pit – something which had crashed into the side wall with such velocity that it had left a kilometre-wide crater off to the north. Fissures spread away from the crater, upwards and across the pit floor.

Now they had a clearer view of the source, Duggan finally realised what it was. The positrons were coming from something ultra-dense - a mixture of elements bonded together in such a way that they could produce sufficient power to propel a ship many times faster than the speed of light.

"It can't be the *Goliath*?" Duggan asked Breeze.

"No sir. Too dense for an MHL's engines."

"How much to make that hole?"

"Twenty square metres if it was travelling fast enough. If

they'd slowed their fall like we did, a whole lot more. It's definitely not the entire ship."

Duggan swore to himself. This was what had happened to the *Ribald* – blown into chunks somewhere in the sky above the planet and left to rain down in pieces across the surface. Whatever tiny hope he'd retained that the young captain Mason Graham and his crew might have survived and escaped to safety, were dashed by the sight of the wreckage in the mining pit below.

CHAPTER SEVEN

DUGGAN DID his best to put the *Ribald*'s destruction from his mind. What he planned next was going to be difficult enough without being able to use the comms systems freely and the anti-matter spilling from the *Ribald*'s engines meant they couldn't take a methodical approach. He didn't know how long the suits would protect them and he didn't want to take any more chances with the lives of his squad than he had to.

"It's going to be far too dangerous as it is," he muttered to himself.

Duggan studied the lay of the land in the fading light of day. The machinery he'd noted came in several different shapes, all of it oversized. There was something which looked like an earth dredger, with towers, gantries and conveyor chutes mounted on a gravity drive. Duggan had no idea what it was called, but it was several hundred metres long and at least two hundred tall and wide. There were a few dozen diggers and dumper lorries, and other cubes of dirty metal that housed the grinders. Duggan used his suit's zoom function to look more closely - none of the mining equipment gave any impression it was operational. On the far side of the pit, three gargantuan tunnels disappeared into the earth, the distance too great for his suit to pierce the darkness within. There were ore storage containers as well, some of them up to five hundred metres long and two hundred tall. These massive, reinforced units were close to the tunnel entrances – the captain of the *Goliath* would have expected to be loading them into the cargo bay by now.

The figure next to him elbowed him to get his attention - Sergeant Ortiz was the culprit. She pointed towards the bottom of the slope, where there was a metal-walled hut. Compared to everything else, the hut was comically small. At first, Duggan wasn't sure what he was meant to be looking for, then he noticed two shapes against one of the walls. They looked like sacks of goods which had been thrown carelessly into place and forgotten about. When he zoomed in, he could see they were bodies - men or women he wasn't sure which. They were clad in the survival suits which enabled humans to operate in moderately hostile environments such as that on Everlong. It was too far to see if there were any injuries to the bodies – the Ghasts used a heavier gauss-type rifle than those used by the Space Corps and they tended to leave extensive exit wounds. Whatever had killed these people was unclear.

"Lieutenant Chainer, where did you detect the Ghast emplacement?"

"Close to the middle, sir. I've lost my bearings a little but I'd say it's behind that dredger. Our sensors didn't see anything at first, so I'd guess it's been half buried."

That would make sense, Duggan thought – keep the weapons engulfed in the Gallenium-rich earth to conceal them from attackers for as long as possible. It was a long way to the bottom and a long walk to the middle of the pit. Duggan would have much preferred a precise idea of where they were going, rather than being kept in the dark until they were almost at the target.

Suppressing the urge to look upwards, Duggan spoke into the squad channel. "Listen up – we've got a Ghast disruptor and a Shatterer missile launcher somewhere in this pit. I believe they're hidden, almost certainly by earthworks. It's likely they are on the far side of that dredging equipment in the middle. We're going to spread out and make our way to the dredger. Keep low, use cover and stay alert. I wish I could tell you exactly what we'll find, but I can't. We're going to try and catch the Ghasts unawares and disable their ground facilities. If there are any miners alive, it's our duty to find them and help them. Maintain radio silence, keep movement and heat sensors on. If you see the enemy, report in quickly and succinctly. Make sure you hold your fire until you hear otherwise."

The squad members knew that Duggan didn't need a spoken acknowledgement. A few of them performed a clumsy nod and one or two raised their rifles. Duggan crawled to the edge of the pit and looked down. The walls sloped sharply and were covered in loose earth and gravel. The uppermost tier was over one hundred metres beneath him. If he lost his footing, there'd be a lot of dust which would be visible to anyone looking. He slung his rifle across his shoulder and climbed over the edge. The gravel shifted under his feet, but he could feel the solidity underneath. He belatedly realised the miners wouldn't have left the walls prone to landslides every time something disturbed them. Even so, the going was tough, straining the muscles of his calves and upper legs as he tried to control his descent.

To either side, stones rattled and clattered past as the others of the squad began their slithering climb. To Duggan's relief, there were no accidents and within five minutes, they had made it to the first tier from the top. He was concerned about the leaking engine from the *Ribald*, but Duggan knew it would be suicide to charge all the way to the bottom without stopping to check for enemy activity. To his relief, it was still quiet and he started down again, half-crawling and half-standing in order to maximise his grip. Something struck his helmet and he caught sight of a fist-sized rock spinning away to the tier below. He looked up to see Morgan recovering from a near-fall. The man carried the squad's portable comms beacon - a heavy silver box which made running and climbing much harder. There was no need for apologies and Morgan didn't even bother to raise an arm – he had too much on his plate as it was.

They'd been climbing for over twenty minutes when they reached the last tier before the bottom. Duggan found himself in a routine where he could execute a controlled slide over the roughest parts of the slope and crab down the parts where the going was easier. As he set off on the last section of slope, his mind was already concentrating on the next phase of the approach. Then, his suit picked up a scuffing noise off to his left. He looked over in time to see one of the squad toppling headlong past. It was Casper, one of the new recruits to the Space Corps. The soldier tumbled over on his way down, bounced twice, slid for twenty metres before an outcrop knocked him away from the slope and into the air again. As he fell, gravel was shaken loose and clouds of fine dust burst away from the surface. No one spoke as they watched the event play out in front of them. The last tier was the highest of all, and when Casper eventually reached the bottom, he lay still, his body made small by the distance.

Duggan swore into his helmet and began scrambling towards the fallen soldier. There was another person closer – it was Corporal Bryant, bent almost double in order to keep balance with a med-box on her back. Duggan almost gave a warning for her to slow down. In the end, she knew the risks and he didn't want to distract her. Bryant reached Casper first and had him plugged to her machine by the time Duggan reached the bottom. There were interfaces in several places across the space suits, and wires stretched from the med-box to the ports in the soldier's helmet. Bryant didn't wait for long. Her fingers were nimble even in the suit and she plucked the wires away from Casper's helmet. They retracted into the med-box automatically. She looked at Duggan – at least he assumed she was looking, since the helmet visors were completely opaque. She ran a finger across her throat and wriggled the straps of the med-box back over her shoulders.

Duggan crouched over Casper's body, a man he'd hardly said a word to, but who was still part of his squad. He was aware that the others of the unit had reached the bottom of the slope and had gathered around. Death was impersonal in this war – you couldn't even take solace from looking in a dead soldier's face in order to commit their features to memory. Duggan had nothing to offer this man – not even the honour of being launched into space. He stood slowly and saluted, sensing the others doing the same.

It wasn't the time for mourning. Duggan raised a hand and waved it towards the vast structure of the dredger in the distance. His suit calculated it to be over three kilometres away. The ground between was open in places, though there were a few pieces of smaller machinery, as well as collections of disposable metal huts that Duggan had seen in places like this before. The huts provided shelter, yet were cheap enough that they could be left behind when operations moved on.

There was no sign of movement anywhere close by, though a warning alert in his helmet had begun a gentle, unobtrusive chime to let Duggan know about the dangerous levels of positron emissions close by. He wanted to kick something in frustration – instead, he put his head down and began a sprint towards an abandoned dump truck a few hundred metres away. The others split off in groups of two, three and four as they chose their own destinations and ran towards them.

The dump truck was forty metres long and painted a dirty

yellow, which looked even less appealing underneath the layer of caked-on grime from the years the vehicle had worked at this place. Duggan wasn't interested in its history – there was no one in the cab and nothing to indicate its engines had been fired up recently. The vehicle was valuable, but it was just another piece of ultimately disposable equipment in the Human-Ghast war. If it was no longer needed on the site, Duggan had no doubt it would be abandoned. It would form a line on an inventory list somewhere on a Corps mainframe, yet would end up rotting here since it was easier to make a new truck than send a ship out to reclaim this one. The *MHL Goliath* could fit hundreds of these vehicles in her hold in order to carry them elsewhere, but the containers of half-processed ores were needed far more than the truck.

Corporal Simmons and Commander McGlashan joined Duggan at the truck. He indicated they should wait as he peered out around the edge. There was still no movement and nothing on the suit's heat detectors. With any luck, the Ghasts weren't expecting an attack from the ground. As far as they knew, they'd destroyed the Corps spacecraft and their own warship had hit the remains with a missile strike. If they happened to notice Duggan and his squad approaching, things would get uncomfortable very quickly. A Cadaveron could obliterate anyone on the surface in twenty seconds.

The next area of cover was a collection of the portable huts. They were stacked two or three high in places and there was almost enough of them to call it a village. The light had dropped so low that it was distinctly gloomy and Duggan's suit amplified his vision, the process giving everything a green tint and making distant outlines slightly fuzzy. With his rifle clutched across his chest, Duggan ran for the huts, covering the three hundred metres in a minute. He pressed his back to the first hut he reached, feeling his heart beat in his chest and hearing his laboured breathing in his helmet. He was fit enough, it was just that running in a suit was far harder than running without.

The huts were not pleasing to the eye, nor were they intended to be. They were double-skinned blocks of metal, fifteen metres in length. They had no windows, one airlock-controlled door and one emergency exit hatch. Duggan had been in places like this a few times – they were as grim inside as they were outside. Some of them were intended to be used as housing and he guessed there'd be bunks in most of these huts. It was a shitty place to spend any amount of time.

McGlashan and Simmons arrived. Duggan motioned for them to follow him. It looked as if there might be thirty or more huts here – easily enough to house all the personnel for the mine. They were a long way away from the mining tunnels, but there'd be plenty of transport to shuttle the miners to and fro. Some of the equipment made a lot of noise, so Duggan wasn't surprised they'd left the huts here, away from it all.

He looked along a passage between two of the cabins. The gravel appeared to be well-trodden. He saw the first sign of violence nearby – one of the metal walls had been ripped, leaving a sharp-edged tear through both skins. It wasn't clear what had done the damage – the Ghasts weren't known for subtlety and had a variety of weaponry that could have punched through the toughened wall. There was no hint of movement and Duggan was already sure this had happened some time ago. Even so, he didn't plan to leave himself open, so he indicated that McGlashan and Simmons should give him cover. They crouched low at the opposite sides of the passage and aimed their rifles along.

Duggan darted forward until he was adjacent to the hole in the cabin. With his rifle pointed ahead, he chanced a quick looked inside. The opening was large enough that he got a good enough view of what had happened – the damage had opened up the two main interior rooms to the thin atmosphere of Everlong. On one side were bunks, many of them thrown around. The other room contained tables and chairs. A viewscreen on the far wall had two big holes in it. A programme continued to play on the screen, the colours smeared and blurred.

There was a body – it was dressed in blue overalls. The man had been shot far more times than was needed to kill him. Duggan counted at least ten wounds. The Ghast weapons lacked finesse but they packed a punch. The body in the hut was a mess, like a piece of meat that had been tenderized far too long. Duggan looked away. At the end of the passage between the two huts was an open area about fifty square metres, surrounded by other huts. Duggan made the signal for McGlashan and Simmons to follow him with caution. He went on, scanning for movement and heat - the suit might just about pick up both through the walls of the cabins, though not accurately enough for him to rely on.

None of the huts close by were damaged and Duggan sprinted across the open space, keeping himself close to one of the walls. He entered another passageway, where the huts had been stacked two high. Their walls seemed to close in around him, exacerbating the darkness of night. He gave McGlashan and Simmons cover as they ran to join him, taking comfort from the weight of his rifle.

There was a hut positioned cross-ways at the end of the passage, reducing the options to a right or left turn. Duggan looked both ways – across from him to the right, the door to one of the huts was missing and the frame around it was twisted. He hurried towards it. There were more bodies inside – three of them this time. They were in the far corner, facing the door. None of the three were armed – there might be a few low-level firearms on the site, but nothing that would repel an armed assault by the Ghasts. The miners had been shredded by something with a high calibre and a fast rate of fire – probably a hand-held repeater, Duggan thought. The wall behind them was pocked with fist-sized holes. There were smears of blood, brown and dried, with sprays of it reaching to the ceiling. The violence was senseless – the people in here had almost certainly offered their surrender. The Ghasts had never seemed to care in the past and here on Everlong, Duggan saw that things hadn't changed.

McGlashan looked in. She'd not fought in the Corps infantry for years and Duggan wondered how she'd take it – he was sure she'd be angry. As he thought about it, he realised how angry he was himself. It had been building gradually within him, so slowly and subtly that it had almost caught him unawares. He clenched his teeth to get a grip on it. At that moment, the voice of Sergeant Ortiz burst into his earpiece with startling clarity.

"I've got movement. There's something up on the left-hand gantry on the dredger."

Duggan held his rifle and ran through the cabins, feeling a mixture of hope that he'd get a shot at the enemy and fear that it might lead to discovery and the death of them all.

CHAPTER EIGHT

DUGGAN LOOKED around the edge of the final hut. His helmet informed him that the dredger was still two-point-three kilometres away. There was an area of clear ground before him, with another couple of dump trucks and a mobile crane the next suitable places to find cover. The distant dredger loomed above everything, its upper gantries clearly visible over the other machinery on the pit floor. Duggan checked carefully – Sergeant Ortiz was correct. There was something moving along one of the walkways. If it was a Ghast soldier, it would have a clear view across the open areas of the pit floor. The squad would be easily detected by image amplification or movement sensors.

Duggan checked to his left – Sergeant Ortiz was more or less parallel with him and was crouched behind a nondescript lump of crumpled alloy a hundred metres away. There were three others with her. Another hundred past that, Breeze and Chainer were next to a mobile crane, along with Hill, Flores and Santos. The other soldiers weren't in line of sight and Duggan wasn't about to ask them to report in.

They watched for a time. Seconds become minutes and the

distant figure showed no sign of moving. It was tall and broad like the Ghasts, yet Duggan couldn't confirm for certain it was one of the enemy. It appeared to be seated and was partially obscured by a support beam. A decision he didn't want to make became unavoidable. There was no way they could risk sneaking any closer. If it was a Ghast and it saw them, it could either escape or communicate to the others in the launcher, who could in turn relay the information to the ship in orbit.

Duggan pulled his rifle to his shoulder and peered along the length. "If you're a miner, you're a stupid bastard for being up there." He took a deep breath. "Don't be a miner." Duggan squeezed the trigger. The rifle whined. It had hardly any kick-back, producing only a gentle thump against his suit. A moment later, the distant figure pitched over. Before Duggan could release the air he was holding in his lungs, he saw it half rise again. He tried to adjust his aim, cursing that the first shot hadn't been a straight kill. He was too slow – the figure on the gantry slumped again, falling so flat that it would be almost impossible to hit from below. Duggan looked around for the source of the second shot. McGlashan tapped him on the shoulder and pointed to where Ortiz was crouched. The Sergeant was just lowering her rifle. She raised a hand and gave a thumbs up. Duggan let out his breath and responded with one of his own.

"We need to move up and fast. That Ghast's suit may have communicated its death," he said to the squad. "Remain alert, shoot on sight."

With that, Duggan broke cover and ran towards one of the trucks. After a few seconds, he realised he was pushing himself too hard. If he was too much out of breath when he reached the Ghast emplacements, his shooting accuracy would suffer. With an effort, he slowed his charge, pacing himself to a speed he knew he could maintain for hours at a time. The ground was mostly flat and he had to give only occasional glances to his footing as he crunched through the gravel. A thin layer of sand dragged at his feet and he imagined this whole pit would be filled with it in a hundred years – the entire mineworks gone as if they had never existed.

He reached the dump truck and scrambled along behind it until he could see the dredger. There was no movement. A thought formed in his mind and he didn't like it. The Ghasts might come looking for their comrade soon. The possibility wasn't a good one and it spurred Duggan onwards. He burst away from the shelter of the truck – one-point-nine klicks away from his target, the suit told him.

He reached another hut – this one had been tipped onto its side. A dark object loomed on the other side – it was an excavator which had somehow collided with the cabin. As he waited a few seconds for McGlashan and Simmons to join him, Duggan became aware of a sound, a distant noise picked up and amplified by his helmet. He realised what it was – a crushing machine was operating in the pit. It confirmed what he'd already thought - the Ghasts were keeping the mine running. Their attack must have happened within the last week or two, otherwise the Space Corps would have known about it and sent more than two Gunners to investigate. *Or ignored it in case the Ghasts shot down a few more of our warships,* thought Duggan bitterly.

He continued running, over a wide space free from industrial clutter. The natural light had gone, leaving only a deep, rich blue on the horizon, faintly seen over the northern edge of the pit. The suit helmet continued to boost the image, projecting the outside world as greens and variable greys. He saw movement – there was something climbing a gantry ladder on the dredger. He fell to one knee, sliding along through the gravel, raising his rifle as he did so. Duggan aimed and fired a shot, steadied himself and fired two more. The distant figure fell a dozen feet before it became tangled in something, causing it to hang suspended in mid-air.

Simmons and McGlashan overtook him, while Duggan pushed himself into another run, his feet leaving gouges in the dirt as he accelerated.

The three of them reached a crane. It was a yellow-painted block with a model designation painted on the side in faded white letters. The boom towered above the thirty-metre-wide base platform, while the gravity engine thrummed quietly. The Ghosts either hadn't noticed or hadn't cared that it was still active. The cab was high above and reached by a ladder. Duggan looked for a moment, though he had no intention of climbing up to see what was inside. If there was anyone up there, they were certainly dead. The visors of McGlashan and Simmons pointed straight at Duggan – they were watching and waiting for him to take the lead.

Nine hundred and fifty metres, he thought as he sprinted away from the crane. There was almost no cover between here and the dredger. From the edge of the pit, it had looked as if there was machinery all the way to the centre. The perspective had deceived Duggan and he called on his reserves of energy. The muscles in his legs stretched and complained. There was a pile of rocks to one side. He ignored their offer of cover and kept a straight line towards the dredger. As he came towards it, the enormity of the machinery struck him. From afar it simply appeared to be big. Closer up, a kilometre of movable alloy structure was somehow just as awe-inspiring as a docked warship. The main section of the dredger looked like a solid wall, tall and imposing on its thick legs. At each end, massive arms reached outwards, with bladed wheels to rip through hard-packed dirt and stone. The support towers went ever upwards, with thick metal cables anchored in countless places.

Five hundred metres. Figures kept a rough line to his left and right. The members of his squad had converged into this open space, with little more than a hundred metres separating the furthest two. At three hundred metres, there was more movement on the dredger, a way back from the edge of the central section. The angle was too sharp for Duggan to get off a shot. Butler and Flores were a few metres back and they both crouched briefly. Duggan couldn't tell if either of them had fired. He looked to the dredger and his suit was no longer able to detect a source of movement.

Duggan reached the base of the dredger, breathing hard. His suit warned him about his elevated heart rate and oxygen consumption. He ignored it and ducked beneath the central section. The support legs were only five feet high, so he had to keep his head low to prevent his helmet colliding with the machinery. The underside was scored and pitted, with deep grooves where the gravity engines had previously lowered the dredger onto sharp rocks. The opposite edge was a good distance away – two hundred metres, Duggan guessed. He tried to make sense of what was out the other side, but all he could see was grey.

"Sir?" It was Chainer. His voice sounded strained with running. "We should be okay to communicate under here as long as we keep it brief. The Cadaveron's sensors won't be able to penetrate so much metal unless they're really focused on this spot."

Duggan didn't respond directly. Instead, he opened a channel to the whole squad and spoke while he continued towards the far side of the dredger. "We can use comms under here if we keep it quick and to the point. The Ghost emplacement can't be far and we have to get inside before they realise we're here and lock it down. We might already be too late. I saw movement up top. Powell, Walker, Hill, Friedman, you're going up there to look for it along with Corporal Simmons. Once the threat is eliminated, you'll provide cover for us below. Only break silence when you have to."

"Aye, sir," came the responses at once.

"Go now. It'll give you a chance to get in position." The five soldiers he'd instructed turned as one and crabbed their way back where they'd come from. Duggan continued to give his orders. "Morgan, you're going to sit tight under here. If it all goes to shit, you're going to use that comms beacon to send a distress signal to the Corps. Let them know we think the Ghasts have a Cadaveron in orbit and a ground-installed Shatterer and disruptor."

"Damn, sir, looks like I'm going to miss out on all the fun."

"It's vital you get it right, soldier. If you use the beacon too early, the Ghast ship will destroy us all."

"I'll do my best. With your permission, I'll haul the beacon out towards one of those dump trucks back there. I'll not be able to send anything while I stay under here. At least I'll be able to fire off a quick transmission if it all goes bad."

"Fine, do it," said Duggan. He dismissed the matter and moved onto the next one. "Flores, do you still have the shaped plasma charges? We might need them." They'd not had time to properly equip themselves while escaping the *Pugilist* – they had rifles and no grenades. Duggan was grateful that Flores had kept a couple of explosives in his footlocker and had brought them with him. It was entirely against regulations, but in the circumstances Duggan wasn't going to say anything, particularly since Flores was the squad's boom man.

"Still got them, sir. Just point me in the right direction."

"Right, let's go. I don't think we're going to find any lost miners wandering around, so if it moves, shoot it."

There was a series of enthusiastic responses to this last instruction. The Ghasts were hated by almost everyone and a command to kill them was guaranteed to be met with approval. Duggan made haste across the underside of the dredger. It was still hard to be sure what was out the other side until he came to the last few metres and got a better view. Much of the open cast pit was visible, with its machinery and tiered walls. However, there was something unusual two hundred metres or so from the dredger. At first glance, it looked like someone had dug a ragged three-hundred and fifty metre hole in the floor of the mining pit and afterwards had partially filled one half of it in, forming a loose-packed mound of brown-grey dirt in the process. The mound was only about ninety metres high, so it was no wonder they'd not been able to see it from the upper edge of the pit.

"What the hell?" asked Sergeant Ortiz.

It struck Duggan what he was looking at. "That's a missile crater," he said, finding he was speaking almost in a whisper. "The Ghasts must have been in a hurry to establish their defences – they've blown a hole in the ground and dropped their battery inside. They must have used some type of transport to bring it here."

"Some of the older Cadaverons had room for cargo, sir," said Lieutenant Breeze. "Before they started filling all the available space with weapons."

"There we have it. A missile emplacement in a hole covered with soil was enough to fool two Space Corps warships long enough to blast both of them out of the sky." Duggan wasn't happy to have been so easily beaten.

"Any sign of a way in?" asked Ortiz. "I assume they've got a crew to make the decision about what to destroy and when."

"Are we looking at two different structures?" asked McGlashan. "I'm sure the disruptors and missiles would be entirely separate units on a warship."

"We're going to have to find out, Commander. I can't see anything other than dirt, so the way in must be around the far side of this mound or in what's left of the crater."

Another voice intruded on the open channel. "Sir, it's Corporal Simmons. We've eliminated a Ghast soldier up here. He wasn't wearing his mech suit. He took cover before we got him. I'd assume he got a message away. Damn they're ugly bastards."

"Understood," said Duggan. "Get in position and provide cover." He waved the members of the squad who remained with him forward, urging them into the open. "Time is running out. We need to finish this."

CHAPTER NINE

AS SOON AS he left the comparative safety of the dredger, Duggan felt vulnerable. He had to assume the Ghast had alerted someone about the presence of Corps soldiers and if the message reached the Cadaveron, there was an excellent chance a precision-guided missile would be on its way shortly. *Unless they don't want to risk damaging their own ground structures,* Duggan thought with a flickering of hope.

He reached the edge of the crater. The piled earth made it closer to a moon shape than a circle. As soon as he arrived, his earlier words that a missile was responsible for it were confirmed. The sides of the hole had been turned into a deceptively smooth-looking reflective glass from the heat of the plasma. The remaining part of the crater was well over a hundred metres deep, with steeply-sloping sides. At the bottom of the dirt mound, he could see metal, glinting to his image-enhanced sight. There was definitely something under the soil which the Ghasts had tried to conceal. This close, it was a poor job. From forty thousand klicks away, it had been good enough.

He set off at a fast jog, following the lip of the hole and looking for a way into what was certainly a weapons battery. When he reached the part of the crater which contained the mound of earth, he noticed how rough and ready the construction was. He guessed they'd forced some of the miners to do the work. There were a couple of huge excavators not too far away which could have done the job in a day or two. Ahead, he saw what he was after. Smooth metal was visible, jutting directly out of the heaped earth.

"Sir, we've got movement." It was Corporal Simmons. "There's a vehicle coming out from one of the far tunnels. Three klicks and heading straight towards us."

"I'd suggest you get your head down," said Duggan. The squad members with him were hidden from the tunnels by the pile of earth. He hoped they'd evade detection for long enough to do what they'd come for.

There was a shrieking sound, followed by a series of harsh clangs, so numerous they almost became a continuous sound. Duggan looked up and saw streaks of green from the Ghast rounds as they raked across a section of the dredger. He knew the projectiles would have been invisible to his naked sight, but they left a fleeting echo on his helmet sensors, which the suit's tiny computer dutifully fed through.

There was another fusillade, which ripped into one of the dredger's gantries, producing momentary orange traces which rapidly faded back to grey. There was a secondary noise – a screeching from torn metal shredding through other metal. Duggan kept his head low and sprinted on, doing his best to ignore the din.

"We've lost Walker," said Simmons with absolute calm. "Returning fire. We've got a Ghast light tank with a repeater turret."

"Get under cover," said Duggan tersely. "You can't scratch it with your rifles."

The words had hardly left his mouth when the Ghast repeater unleashed another punishing volley of rounds into the structure of the dredger. The noise was unbearable and Duggan didn't like to think what it would be like for the soldiers huddled up there.

He reached the metal wall he'd seen and he slowed, the others stopping with him. From here, it was possible to make out the rough shape of what was buried. It was a huge cylinder, with a diameter of more than one hundred metres. It was as high as the dirt mound, with no indication how deep into the earth it went. Duggan remembered the *Ribald* was hit with the disruptor from thirty thousand klicks. Unless the Ghasts had made huge advances in miniaturisation, there had to be a big power source in the cylinder – something with similar mass to a Vincent class fission drive.

The earth had been packed down tightly on this side of the mound, with a steel mesh in place to stop the soil coming down. The reason was immediately apparent – there was a doorway, two metres wide and three high, visible only as a fine seam in the polished surface of the alloy. Most Ghasts were seven feet tall, made even bigger in their mech suits. This must be where they came in and out.

"Flores, come here and take a look," said Duggan.

Flores came forward and checked over the door and its surrounds. He reached out and struck it with a clenched fist. The blow produced no discernible sound. "Damn sir, this must be five feet thick. It's warship grade alloy."

"This tube was probably built for an Oblivion. Can you get it open?" As he spoke, another extended round of heavy repeater fire ripped overhead, pummelling hundreds of half-metre holes across the upper deck of the dredger. Duggan looked in the direction of the mining tunnels and his suit reported the presence of a Ghast vehicle coming into sight around the banked earth.

When Flores didn't respond immediately, Duggan shouted at him. "Speak, man! That tank could see us at any moment!"

Flores slung his rifle and held up the two shaped charges. They were fist-sized and could stick to any surface. A built-in timer could be set manually or the charges could be detonated remotely through a command from a spacesuit. "There's not a hope in hell, sir. I'd need a dozen of these babies to burn a hole in that door."

Duggan opened his mouth to speak, not knowing exactly what he was going to say. In the end, he didn't need to say anything. Without warning, the door moved of its own accord, sinking five feet into the walls of the missile battery and rotating slowly sideways with the glacial smoothness of perfectly-machined gears. The space behind the door was revealed to be a large airlock, with featureless walls, ceiling and floor. There was an indistinct shape, visible to one side and waiting patiently. It was a Ghast, hulking and angular in a mech suit. It had a hand-held repeater clutched across its chest, with the weapon's power cell visible over the alien's shoulders. There was a moment, a fraction of a second, which felt like it lasted half a lifetime while the two sides looked at each other in mutual surprise. Duggan lowered his rifle and pulled the trigger, sending a metal slug into the Ghast's chest. There was a sharp hiss of escaping air or servo fluid. Duggan shot it again, while the Ghast began to swing its repeater towards him. Then, the creature was thrown from its feet by another half-dozen rounds from Duggan's squad. It thumped against the floor with a dull clunk and didn't move.

"Inside! Now!" barked Duggan. The squad didn't hesitate and scrambled past to get into the airlock. Before they could make it, a flash of pure, exquisite white lit up the night. Duggan had to close his eyes to shield them from damage. A roaring wave of heat buffeted against him and he fell flat while the other soldiers did the same. He felt the light fading and when he opened his eyes, he saw static across his vision from the overload to the helmet's sensors. A series of warnings told him the suit's exterior had suffered permanent damage from a blast of heat significantly above its design tolerances. Duggan blinked, trying to clear the white spots from his eyes. The helmet sensor recalibrated itself in moments, just as a second detonation dispersed the night. The heat roiled over the huddled squad while they tried frantically to crawl into the shelter of the airlock. Duggan scramble-crawled the last few feet to join the others. He saw what had happened – something big had struck the dredger, followed by another of the same. The gargantuan machinery had been ripped into two pieces, each one glowing bright orange from the after effects of the missile strikes. The remains looked like a hideous wreck, melted and distorted until they were something completely different to what they had been before.

Duggan rolled to his feet and pressed his back to the airlock wall, in case another strike was incoming. "I think the orbiting ship knows we're here," he said, hoping the thick alloy shielding of the missile battery would prevent the Ghast ship detecting where they were. *More dead,* he thought. *With each one, I owe those bastards a little bit more.*

Someone moved past him, stepping over the sprawled body of the Ghast. It was Sergeant Ortiz and she was looking at something. There was a panel on the wall, on the opposite side of the doorway to where the enormously thick door waited unmoving. "Anyone know how to work this Ghast stuff?" she asked. "I think we should close the door."

"They don't teach you that at the academy," said Chainer. He laughed nervously. "I think my suit's failing."

"Mine's taken a battering," said Bryant.

"And mine," said Dorsey.

"Permission to piss around with this panel, sir?" asked Ortiz.

"Go ahead," Duggan told her.

Ortiz didn't wait. She pressed a couple of fingers on it. When it was clear nothing was going to happen, she put her palm against it, then made a sweeping motion with her hand. She stopped trying and gave the panel a two-fingered salute.

Duggan was aware there was a tank outside. He didn't know if the Ghosts realised there were still human soldiers left alive. Even if the tank crew didn't come to investigate, it wouldn't be long until the Ghosts in the missile emplacement realised the airlock door had been left open. He checked the surroundings – the airlock was about four metres square. The inner door was opposite the outer and was about the same dimensions. Duggan crossed over to it. There was another panel, which he touched, expecting the same lack of response that Ortiz had found. He wasn't disappointed.

"Flores, check this door out, will you? Maybe they didn't reinforce the internal fixtures as much as the outer ones."

"Will do, sir," said Flores, walking as he talked. He gave it a hard thump with his hand. "Two feet thick and made of something softer," he said at once. "It won't disperse the heat nearly as well as the outer door. I can open this one. It'll need both charges and we'll need to get outside while they burn."

"What about the tank?" asked Chainer. "And what if the Ghosts remote-close the external door?"

"Take your pick, Lieutenant," said Flores, already placing the charges against the seam on the inner airlock door. "I can say with one hundred percent certainty that you'll fry if you stay inside. If you go outside, there's a chance you'll live."

"Look on the bright side, Lieutenant," said Ortiz, walking towards the outer doorway. "If the Ghosts forget to lock us outside, they're going to find it pretty hard to breathe in about two minutes when all their air gets sucked out."

"Yeah, sounds good," said Chainer, putting on a show of bravado.

Ortiz was first out through the door. She dropped into a low crouch and kept her rifle pointing forwards. "Go to the right," she said. "Try and put some of this dirt between us and the tank."

"Charges set," said Flores. "Thirty seconds."

"Best not trip over the mech suit, soldier," said McGlashan as she skirted around the motionless body.

"Think the Ghasts will fire missiles at this battery?" asked Chainer as he inched warily through the outer door.

Duggan was right behind him. "Not a chance of it." As he said the words, a plan formed in his head. It came to him fully formed with such force that his heart beat hard in his chest at the possibilities. Suddenly, it was of vital importance that the enemy warship – a Cadaveron, he was sure - didn't know they still lived. "Stay low, maintain radio silence," he instructed.

The remaining ten of them got outside in plenty of time. They sat to the right of the doorway with their backs pressed against the steel mesh. There was no sign of movement and Duggan gritted his teeth with each passing second. *Where's that damn tank?*

His suit detected an angry fizzing, hissing noise. Blue light flared in the doorway – the charges were purposely designed to emit as little light and sound as possible. The man next to Duggan got up and ran into the airlock – it was Flores. Hoping the soldier had a good enough idea when it would be safe, Duggan got up to follow, keeping low and close to the wall.

"Shit, the outer door's closing," said Flores.

"Get in! Quickly!" shouted Duggan, finishing the last couple of yards at a burst sprint. He leapt over the mech suit and got himself to the far side of the airlock to give the others plenty of room to follow. He turned to face the outer door and watched as it slid easily along hidden runners. The door was moving too fast and Duggan realised with horror that it was going to trap most of them outside. Sergeant Ortiz darted through at the last moment. She was a quick thinker and jammed her rifle under the door. The gauss rifles looked flimsy, when in fact they were about the hardest material available to the Confederation weapons plants. They needed to be strong to put up with the high internal forces they were subjected to. Something screeched – and the door stopped moving. The rest of the squad came through at the double. For a few moments, it looked as if Ortiz might have permanently jammed the door. Then, with a lurch, it moved a few inches, crushing part of the rifle against the floor.

Duggan looked around and saw only one option. He reached down and took one of the mech suit arms – it was a heavy, jointed tube of a metal he didn't recognize. "Help me!" he said, dragging at the arm. Duggan was a strong man, but he could hardly move the body.

Others joined him. Hands reached beneath the suit and between them they hauled it over the smooth floor and dumped it across the doorway. The suit was massive, but the door looked as it if weighed a hundred tonnes. The square slab of metal moved again, flattening Ortiz's rifle completely. Then, it connected with the mech suit. The door didn't slow and it pressed the dead Ghast against the far edge of the doorway. The suit creaked as it was crushed between the door and the frame.

"Come on! Do it!" said Dorsey.

Just as it seemed the suit might not be strong enough, there was a grating sound and the square door stopped moving. Duggan let out a breath and went over to see the result. The mech suit was badly crushed, but it had left a narrow opening between the door and the frame. It would be a tight squeeze to get out. There was blood as well – it oozed through ruptures in the suit's metal and spilled onto the floor. *Red, just the same as ours.*

Duggan turned his attention to the rest of the squad and the inner door. "What have we got here?" he asked, pushing his way through.

CHAPTER TEN

THE INNER AIRLOCK door was still in place. However, the shaped charges had burned a metre-round hole straight through the middle. Ortiz, Breeze and Butler had their rifles trained inside. The edges of the hole smoked with heat and looked glutinous. A readout in his helmet told Duggan that air of approximately the same composition as that required for human life, was rushing out through the opening. There was another room visible through the hole, as drab and metallic as anything the Space Corp's designers could come up with and lit in a cold blue. Tall, wide doorways led off to places deeper within the battery.

"It should have cooled enough to get through, sir," said Flores. To demonstrate, the man pressed his suited hand on one of the surfaces for a half-second before removing it quickly. "Still hot if you hang around."

Duggan ducked his head and did a half-roll through the gap. Once through, he crouched to one side with his rifle trained ahead. "Come on," he said. When they were all through, Duggan split them into two groups of three and a four. "Three doors, three squads," he said. "Move quickly and kill any Ghasts you see. It's a near-vacuum on this planet, so they should be dead from ruptured lungs if they weren't suited. Any Ghasts at the bottom of the emplacement may have had time to protect themselves." He paused to let that sink in before he continued. "Make sure you don't break anything. We're looking for a control room. Find it and secure it. Sergeant, Ortiz, I'm giving you the largest squad, since you don't have a rifle."

The open channel filled with acknowledgements. Duggan didn't wait around and went left, with Dorsey and Santos behind him. Ortiz went straight on and McGlashan took the right.

The way to the left entered a wide, short corridor. The three of them stuck close to the walls and advanced, their rifles at the ready. Duggan noticed there was a slight curve on both sides and he guessed they were following the perimeter of the cylinder. There was a room at the end – four metres square, with a series of free-standing metal cabinets against one wall. The body of a Ghast lay here, on its side, with one arm outstretched as if it were reaching for something. Its broad frame was clad in what could only be described as brown trousers and a shirt, made from a tough-looking cloth.

"You wouldn't think they'd dress like us, would you?" asked Santos.

"The same, yet completely different," said Dorsey, her voice a whisper.

The grey eyes of the dead creature stared at them from the smooth grey-skinned face. Duggan stepped around it and continued across the room. There was a single exit – a series of steps led down, the curvature clearly visible. The interior lights burned from indentations in the wall where they'd been embedded. Duggan looked at one of the lights as he passed – it was a fist-sized globe that emitted a diffuse light and served to illuminate heat-scarring on the walls.

"Got bodies," said Ortiz across the channel. "Three of them

at the top of what I think is a service shaft. It's steep and looks like it goes all the way to the bottom."

"Advance with caution, Sergeant," said Duggan. He continued down the steps with the other two behind.

"These steps look like they've been welded across here," said Dorsey. "You can see through the risers and there's just.... nothing. Like we're standing in a big empty space."

"I'm certain we're standing in a modified warship Shatterer tube," Duggan said. "This area is for heat expansion when the missile launches. Damn, they must have cobbled this place together in a hurry. And it's huge. No wonder they haven't installed Shatterers on their smaller vessels yet."

"If it was meant for a warship, that might be why there was no lock-down when the airlocks failed, sir," said Santos. "This place must have been a death-trap to work in."

"Yeah. It's all good if it makes our lives a bit easier," said Dorsey.

The steps went on for some time and Duggan tried to figure out how far into the earth they'd gone. At the bottom, the steps ended at a landing, with a wide passage leading to the right. Duggan followed it for thirty or forty metres, realising it was taking him to the centre of the battery. At last, the passage opened onto a ten-metre-wide platform that curved to the left and right, until it made a complete circuit of this central part of the interior. There was a thrumming sound here, which Duggan recognized at once – it sounded exactly like the engines of a spaceship. The three of them made their way to the edge of the platform, keeping alert for any sign of movement. There was no safety rail at the edge. Rather, there was a perfectly round hole, with a diameter of ten metres or more. The hole dropped deep below and vanished into green-edged darkness above.

"This is where they launch the missiles from," said Duggan. "And these walls must contain the power source for the disruptor.

They've managed to build both weapons into a single unit." He peered carefully over the edge. Far below, there was a shape, the tip of it visible to the helmet's sensors. "There's a missile in the tube," he said. "They must have to pre-load in order to fire on demand."

"They're big bastards," said Santos grudgingly. "Shame we've not got a few of them ourselves."

"I'm sure we're working on making our own," said Duggan. He dropped into a crouch at the sight of movement opposite. It was McGlashan with her squad. She gave him a single wave, which he echoed. "Anything to report?" he asked, knowing she'd have told him already if there had been.

"Nothing, sir."

"We need to get on." He changed channel and spoke to privately to Ortiz. "Where are you, Sergeant?"

"Still coming down the service shaft, sir. There's a ladder, but it's not built for us. Makes it a bit hard to climb."

"Fine, keep going." He closed the line and made a gesture to McGlashan and her squad to tell them to look for a way ahead. It wasn't hard to find – there was an exit equidistant from both squads. The area wasn't lit and it showed as a greenish square against the solidity of the surrounding metal. Duggan advanced towards it, keeping his gaze fixed firmly ahead.

Movement nearly caught him unawares. A broad shape appeared in the opening. His suit outlined it in orange, which contrasted sharply with the intensified greens. He fired at it, hearing Dorsey and Santos doing the same. The figure went down, falling back into the doorway.

"I'm hit." It was McGlashan.

"We're taking fire," said Duggan calmly. "McGlashan's hurt."

"Need backup?" asked Ortiz.

"I'll let you know. We've got Corporal Bryant up here with us."

Another shape appeared. This Ghost was more cautious than the last and it crouched close to the wall. Something pinged next to Duggan's head, ricocheting away. He fired back, not knowing if he'd scored a hit. Santos rolled away from the wall and pressed himself flat on the floor. He raised up on his elbows and fired twice in quick succession.

"I see at least two," he said.

The distant shape ducked away behind something. Duggan kept firing into the darkness, hoping to keep the Ghosts pinned down.

"Chainer, Santos, Dorsey, advance," he said.

At once, Dorsey swarmed past on her belly, using her legs to push herself across the smooth floor. Santos was a little way ahead of her. Duggan's rifle whined as he fired it again and again, the tube becoming warm to the touch. A glimpse of movement told him at least one Ghost was still alive. Something whispered by his forearm. He didn't pay it any heed and fired another couple of rounds, until a bleeping in his helmet became too insistent to ignore. He looked at his arm, suddenly aware of the pain. There was a puncture wound in the suit, already sealed over as the material re-bonded. He felt a stabbing pain in his neck – it was the suit injecting him with a burst of battlefield adrenaline as a precautionary measure.

"Get these bastards," he growled. The adrenaline reached his heart like a violent kick to the chest and almost made him retch. His breathing deepened and his skin felt cold and tight. He kept firing as the advancing soldiers closed towards the place the Ghosts were hiding. Santos got there first.

"Hold fire," he said. "I think we got them." The soldier went towards the opening, still on his stomach. "Got three dead here." The sound of his rifle carried over the channel when he fired four or five extra rounds. "Definitely dead."

Duggan left the insignificant protection of the wall and

sprinted across to where Santos, Dorsey and Chainer had established themselves. They stayed crouched, their rifles pointing into the opening. It was dark, but there was enough light for Duggan to see what he needed to. The three Ghasts were unmoving on the floor. They wore a type of space suit that he'd not seen them in before – they were made of a flimsy-looking material, with cube-shaped metal-and-glass helmets that might have been two hundred years old. There was a thick, heavy, heat-proof door on runners to one side of the doorway.

"They were about to lock us out, sir," said Chainer. "We got here just in time."

"Hold here," said Duggan. "Shoot anything that moves." He ran around to find McGlashan. She was prone on the floor, hooked up to the med-box that Corporal Bryant brought everywhere with her. Duggan could see a re-sealed hole in McGlashan's suit over her stomach and there was blood on the floor underneath her from the exit wound.

"How is she?" he asked Bryant, wondering how he kept his voice steady.

"She's in trouble, sir," said Bryant. "We need to get her to proper medical facilities or she'll die."

"I feel great," said McGlashan, interrupting the conversation. She didn't sound quite with it.

"The box has pumped her so full of crap she'll think she can run a marathon," said Bryant. "It'll induce a coma shortly, to extend her life."

"Hand me a rifle," said McGlashan. She sounded half asleep.

"Santos, wait here with Corporal Bryant."

"Will do, sir."

"You've been hit," said Bryant, as Duggan got to his feet.

"I'll be fine," he said. Bryant didn't argue. She knew a lost cause when she saw one.

Duggan returned to Chainer and Dorsey, trying to put news

of McGlashan's injury from his mind. Together, they walked into the room from which the Ghasts had ambushed them. It was four metres square, like every other room in the missile battery. There was a hatch in the floor, a metre to each side and almost a metre thick. It was folded back from its opening and had ratcheted runners to allow a series of motors to haul it open and closed. There was a shaft, with a metal ladder running up one side. There was a room at the bottom, but it was impossible to make out any details of what was down there. He thought he could see a green light, though he couldn't be sure it wasn't a false hue created by his spacesuit sensor. There was another ladder, this one going up the side wall and into a square hole in the ceiling.

"I'm going down," said Duggan. He took hold of the top rung and stretched out a foot. The gaps between the rungs were awkwardly large and he recalled Ortiz's words from earlier. A hint of pain flared up from his wounded forearm as he forced it to bear his weight. "Cover me," he said, climbing deeper into the shaft.

He descended at least forty metres. He paused once or twice to listen out for sounds that might indicate there were more Ghasts inside. There was nothing. At the bottom, he found himself in a room that was packed with screens, consoles and two more dead Ghasts, slumped in oversized metal chairs. The chairs looked as if they'd guarantee backache after twenty minutes of sitting. Duggan began to wonder if the Ghasts celebrated discomfort, or took pride in enduring it. He did his best to ignore the frozen expressions of pain on the Ghast faces and studied some of their equipment. He recognized many of the functions immediately.

"Sergeant Ortiz, I need you and your men here, at the double. Santos will give you directions. Lieutenant Chainer, come here. I need to see what you think of this."

"Roger," said Ortiz.

"On my way," Chainer added.

Above, Chainer began his careful descent, while Duggan poked around. The equipment in the room had clearly been added after the missile tube was built. There were holes in the walls, made for optical connections, with nothing routed through them. In other places, screens had been roughly bolted to the walls. Chainer arrived and glanced about.

"Definitely their control room," he said. "They've got every-thing they need. How are we going to spoil it without grenades? Are we just going to shoot everything and hope?"

"We're not going to spoil it, Lieutenant. We're going to figure out how it works. Then, we're going to bring that Cadaveron in close and hit it with as many missiles as we can. If we don't, that heavy cruiser may well be enough of a deterrent to stop the Space Corps sending out a rescue ship when we use the comms beacon. Particularly when Admiral Slender learns I'm amongst the party to be rescued."

Chainer didn't say anything. Duggan had half-expected him to offer an alternative. Instead, Chainer kicked one of the dead Ghasts from its chair. With a grunt, he dragged the seat across the floor and positioned it in front of four banked screens which Duggan had already guessed were part of the comms unit. "We'd best get on with it, sir. I don't think Commander McGlashan has long left. My suit's not got much longer either from the looks of it – enough power for two more days I reckon."

"Damnit, why didn't you mention it earlier?"

"I did, sir. There's nothing I can do about it, so I just got on with what we were doing."

Duggan sighed. "Come on Lieutenant, let's see if we can pull a rabbit from our hat."

CHAPTER ELEVEN

LIEUTENANT BREEZE ARRIVED ten minutes later. He had a vast experience earned on numerous spacecraft. "I haven't got a clue what their writing means, but I've got a pretty good idea of what console does what," he said after a few minutes.

Duggan could only nod in response. He was in a foul mood, since Corporal Bryant had just informed him that Commander McGlashan would be dead in a matter of hours, rather than the days it would take to get a Space Corps vessel to Everlong. He had the others to look out for as well and he did his best to remain focused. His arm throbbed and he resisted the temptation to take another shot of adrenaline.

"These control the power," he said. "I can't read the gauges and I probably don't need to know what the numbers are. The screens are touch-sensitive and they seem quite happy to track where I point."

"Unlike the control panels for the airlock door," said Breeze.

Duggan continued with his efforts to understand the Ghast equipment. Their method of doing things was lacking in finesse – clumsy, almost. Then he remembered that they'd picked up a lot of their tech from the parts of a wrecked Dreamer warship. Before that, they'd been decades behind what the Confederation could build. This was a mish-mash of old and new. Duggan persevered and soon he was sure he knew how to launch the Shatterer missiles. The trouble was, there was no obvious way to target them. Similarly with the disruptor – it seemed easy to fire, except the targeting was either offline or he simply didn't know how to do it.

"I think these options control the internal doors in the missile battery," said Breeze, studying one of the panels.

The suited figure of Chainer leapt up from his chair. "Yes!" he shouted.

"What've you got, Lieutenant?" asked Duggan. He noticed Chainer had got something up on one of the monitors.

"This is the Ghasts' tracking screen," said Chainer, pointing. "Look, there's an object moving in a low orbit here. It's circling around this nearby area of the planet at a low speed."

"The Cadaveron," said Duggan.

"No, sir, I don't think so." Chainer was clearly excited by something. "Over here there's another object, almost directly above us. It's hardly moving."

"The Ghasts have two warships stationed?" Duggan furrowed his brow. He wasn't sure what Chainer was getting at.

"I can't figure out the numbers, but I've worked out how to overlay the two objects on top of each other. The first one is bigger than the second – I'd say it's close to seventy percent longer, with a far greater volume."

Duggan suddenly understood. "They didn't destroy the *Goliath*!" he said. "The bastards must have guessed what it was carrying and kept it intact. They're planning to steal the cargo and use it for their own mining operations!"

"That would make sense," said Breeze. "The equipment in the *Goliath*'s hold is worth a king's ransom."

"They'll have a top-notch medical bay on the MHL, sir. They expect accidents doing what they do."

"Can you contact the *Goliath*?" asked Duggan.

"I can, sir. Unfortunately, if the Ghasts operate anything like we do, they'll be continuously monitoring our broadcasts. It's good practise. There's another thing, if it makes a difference. Assuming that's a heavy cruiser above us, it's smaller than normal – using the *Goliath* as a comparison, I'd say the Ghast ship is less than three thousand metres long."

"Must be an old one," said Breeze. "For all the good it'll do us."

Duggan's mind was racing. He went back to the console which controlled the targeting. He was now able to see a mirror of Chainer's tracking screen, with the Cadaveron and heavy lifter far above. The Shatterer could target either of the two craft, while the disruptor wouldn't acknowledge either as a target. "I can hit the Cadaveron," he said. "Even if it's an ancient model, one missile won't bring it down. If we can get them with the disruptor, we might get two or three missiles away."

"Will that be enough?" asked Chainer doubtfully.

"It might be. Those missiles tore a Hadron to pieces and put a few big holes through the *Archimedes*."

"How do we get them with the disruptor?" asked Breeze. "I guess they'll be at a hundred thousand klicks."

"There's no reason for them to come into range. They can do everything they need to from where they are, including destroying this battery if it takes their fancy," said Chainer.

"That's it!" said Duggan. "They'll not want to destroy this emplacement. However, if they think something's wrong, they'll definitely send a dropship to investigate."

"They launch their dropships from a much lower altitude!" said Breeze. "They may come close enough for us to disable them with the disruptor."

"We need to find the distress beacon," said Duggan. "And get everyone behind the blast door in the room above."

"Why haven't the Ghasts already triggered the beacon?" asked Chainer. "At least I'm assuming they haven't, since the Cadaveron is still circling happily overhead."

"This place isn't rigged up to be secure," said Breeze. "I'll bet there are no alarms or anything to let the people in the control room know there's been a breach. These two Ghasts could have been caught unawares when the air got sucked out."

"What about those three who tried to kill us in the room above?"

"Who knows?" said Duggan. "They might have been suited up elsewhere in the silo and been on their way to check out the control room." He spoke to Sergeant Ortiz. "Get everyone into the room above. We're going to try and seal it."

"Sounds like you have a plan, sir."

"There's always a plan, Sergeant. We might need to fire that missile in the tube."

Less than a minute later, Ortiz spoke. "Everyone's in, sir."

"We're going to close the door. Stand back."

"It's closing, sir." She went silent. "Completely closed now."

"Good. Sit tight until you hear otherwise."

By the time Duggan finished speaking, Breeze had found the distress beacon. It was a grey button, on its own away from anything else.

"I wonder if grey is their equivalent of our red," said Chainer.

Duggan pressed the button. It took hardly any force and it made a click. There was no visible sign that anything had changed within the missile battery.

"Any alteration in the Cadaveron's flight path?" asked Duggan after a few moments.

"Yes, sir. They've reacted immediately," said Chainer. "I'd say they're coming in for a look."

"Keep your fingers crossed they do what we're expecting, rather than blowing us up," said Duggan.

"Expect the worst and hope for the best," muttered Chainer. "They're dropping fast. If they started at a hundred thousand klicks, I'd say they're at fifty thousand now."

"Coming closer than that?" asked Duggan.

"No, sir. I think they've levelled out at fifty thousand. There's a load of mumbo jumbo coming up on one of my screens. They're probably asking how we're doing."

"Ignore it," said Duggan.

"We're going to be in the shit if they launch a dropship from that height," said Breeze.

"They normally come in lower," said Duggan.

"Yeah," said Breeze. "Come and say hello to Billy."

"Still not moving."

"Probably takes a few minutes to load up and prepare for launch. They're just being cautious," said Chainer.

"I don't like it," said Breeze.

"They're moving again," said Chainer. His exhalation of breath carried clearly through the helmet speakers. "Forty thousand klicks."

Duggan kept his eyes glued to the disruptors. "Still can't target," he said quietly.

"Thirty-five."

The Cadaveron became highlighted on his screen. "Target locked," said Duggan. He pressed an area of the display to fire the disruptor and straight after sent the launch command to the Shatterer in the tube.

"Some of these gauges are bouncing around like crazy," said Breeze. "I'd say we're out of juice for the time being."

Any other words were drowned out by a thunderous sound. Even muffled by twenty-five metres of alloy, the noise was tremendous. The whole missile battery shook and there was a howling roar that increased in volume. Then, it was silent again, as the Shatterer missile flew from its tube and into the night sky.

"Seven seconds to impact," said Duggan, remembering how long it took a Shatterer to hit the *Pugilist* at the same altitude. A green dot raced across his screen, on an intercept course with the larger green dot of the Cadaveron. The two dots met and the smaller one winked out of existence.

"The Shatterer's scored a hit," he said.

"The Cadaveron must have been pointing downwards when the disruptor got them," said Chainer. "Its altitude is still dropping. They're in free-fall, sir!"

There was a rumbling from somewhere beneath, followed by the vibration of powerful gears shifting a thousand tonnes of missile into a position from which it could be fired.

"Automatic reload," said Chainer. The vibration continued. "Is anyone keeping a timer?"

"Not a very fast reload," said Breeze. "I'm counting."

"We'll know soon enough when our minute's up, Lieutenant. We'll see missiles coming towards us."

"These gauges are settling down. I don't need to read Ghast to know there's nothing much left in the tank," said Breeze. He spat the words out in a staccato rhythm while he maintained his internal count of the time. "I'm up to thirty seconds."

The gears continued to rumble and Duggan mentally thanked Breeze for keeping a count - it was important to him that he know how long they had left. "No third strike, then." He'd realised this already – none of the Ghast warships had been able to fire the Shatterers quickly.

"Forty."

"Maybe no second either," said Duggan.

"They're at eighteen thousand klicks now. They're going to land too close for comfort."

"Fifty seconds."

The sound of the gears stopped. Still there was no option to target the second missile.

"Sixty."

The disruptor and the Shatterers lit up simultaneously. Duggan fired both at once, gritting his teeth at how close-run it was. The sound of the second missile engulfed the control room and it was a relief when the roar of its launch faded to nothingness. The Cadaveron was much closer this time and the second missile took only three seconds to strike the Ghast heavy cruiser.

"Our power's down to zero, give or take," said Breeze.

"Sir, I really think there's a good chance of their impact killing us," said Chainer. "It would be a shame, since we've technically beaten the bastards."

Something in Chainer's words made Duggan burst into laughter. "I don't want any of us to die, Lieutenant, but if we do, we can rest easy knowing we've killed some Ghasts with their own missiles."

"They're less than five thousand klicks above the surface," said Chainer. "They're going to land four hundred klicks east. The crater's going to be huge."

Duggan spoke to the squad. "There's three thousand metres of Ghast heavy cruiser about to crash nearby in the next twenty seconds. I want you all to know that if it kills us, you did a damn good job here."

"Twenty seconds notice of impending death, huh?" asked Ortiz. "That's more than we usually get."

"Now," said Chainer.

For a few seconds, there was nothing. Then, the walls of the silo began to shake. It started gradually, before building in ferocity. Duggan struggled to keep his feet and Chainer was knocked from his chair. The rumbling didn't subside, rather it built again until it reached a new intensity. The entire missile battery canted to one side and the three of them were cast helplessly into the wall. One of the screens fell loose and it smashed against Duggan's shoulder. He shouted in pain and anger. Still the shaking went on, until it seemed as if the shockwave was going to kill them all.

After what seemed like an eternity, the quaking stopped. Duggan struggled to his feet, fighting for grip on the thirty-degree tilt of the smooth floor.

"Is anyone hurt?" he asked the squad. "How's Commander McGlashan?"

"The Commander's been well looked after, sir," said Corporal Bryant. "Other than that, I'd say we have plenty of bruises."

It was better news than Duggan could have hoped for, but there was no time for celebration. "Lieutenant Chainer, do you think you can open a channel to the *Goliath*? Ask her captain to scan the crash site and tell us what's out there."

Chainer pressed a few areas of his console. He waited and then pressed them again. "It's not working, sir. Either I'm doing it wrong or our comms are down."

Duggan swore. "Everybody, get ready to move out. We're getting out of here and we're going to see what a crash-landed Cadaveron looks like." In his head, there was another thought, which he didn't speak. *And if the Ghasts have killed Morgan and disabled the comms beacon, we're going to be right out of luck.*

CHAPTER TWELVE

IT TOOK LONGER to exit the silo than it had taken to enter. The structure had been knocked at an angle by the shock from the Ghast heavy cruiser. The floor was smooth and even the high-grip soles of the space suits struggled as the men and women clambered around the central area where the missiles had launched from. In addition, the inner walls of the silo were still blisteringly hot from the launch.

"Over two hundred degrees," said Duggan. "It wouldn't normally matter, except my suit's not functioning properly."

"It feels about eighty degrees in my suit," said Chainer. "I'm not sure there's any power going to the temperature control. Natural insulation only for me."

"It's not too cold on the surface, Lieutenant."

"Colder than I'd like."

Duggan paused for a moment on the perimeter steps. Corporal Bryant and Sergeant Ortiz were carrying McGlashan. It didn't look easy.

Ortiz caught his reflective visor looking at them. "I'd rather be carrying a rifle," she grunted.

At last, they reached the entrance airlock room. The heavy outer door was in the same place, jammed against the dead Ghast in its mech suit. Duggan instructed the others to wait. He climbed onto the twisted metal-clad body and inched sideways through the door. It was still night and his suit vision flickered and jumped disconcertingly as the damaged helmet struggled to cope. The missile battery had tipped away from the edge of the crater it had been buried in and was lying against the collapsed opposite wall of the hole. There seemed to be a lot more earth and gravel than there had been earlier. Duggan had to perform a controlled slide down the exposed outer surface of the tube and jump the last few feet. He landed in soft earth and scrambled upwards towards the edge above him.

Duggan looked over the loose dirt at the crater's edge, making the most of the cover it provided. There was no sign of the Ghast light tank which had chewed up the dredger with repeater fire. There was plenty of other damage. In fact, nothing looked the same as before. The mining equipment was scattered about, most of it tipped over, or thrown from its original position. From where he was, Duggan could see most of the dredger. The remaining pieces of it had moved a great distance, and there was a huge chunk of sharp-edged metal balanced precariously on the edge of the pit near to the missile tube. It didn't look as if it was going to fall of its own accord, but Duggan was concerned there might be aftershocks from the earlier earthquake.

"Sergeant Ortiz. Bring everyone out. And thank your lucky stars we found ourselves in what must have been the most secure structure on the entire planet."

"Coming out now, sir. I take it the world's gone to shit out there?"

"It's worse than that, Sergeant. Far worse." She didn't respond to that. Duggan climbed onto the ground above and surveyed the area as best he could. The mining tunnels he could see had all collapsed – buried and gone beneath a billion tonnes of earth and stone. The sides of the mining pit were no longer carefully tiered. Instead, they were ragged from the numerous landslides triggered by the Cadaveron's impact. The eastern wall was too far to make out clearly – it looked like a dark mass, but was now much lower than it had been before. The shocks must have punched the sides in and caused the whole lot to come down.

"Infantryman Morgan, do you copy?" he asked. There was no response. "Infantryman Morgan, do you copy?" Duggan's heart lurched in his chest at the thought of losing another squad member and their only comms beacon.

"Morgan here, sir. Are the fireworks over?"

Duggan blew out noisily. "For now, soldier. Are you hurt? How's that comms beacon?"

"I'm the luckiest man alive, sir. I took a couple of knocks is all. I've looked after that beacon like it was my own child."

"Stay put for the moment. We brought the enemy warship down, but the light tank is unaccounted for. We're coming out of the silo."

The rest of the squad began leaving the Shatterer battery. Most of them followed Duggan's idea of sliding down twenty metres or so and then jumping into the earth. It wasn't so easy to get McGlashan out and her comatose body nearly slipped to the ground in the process.

"You three, stay here with the Commander," said Duggan, pointing out the chosen squad members. "The rest of you are coming with me. Morgan's alive and he's got the beacon."

The relief was palpable. The six of them set off at a good pace, using the torn dredger for cover. Morgan was in the cab of a dump truck. It had turned onto its roof in the earthquake.

"Lucky I remembered to belt in," he said. "Else I'd have landed on my head."

No one took advantage of the opportunity to comment on the benefits of Morgan landing on his head. The time didn't feel right for joking, given what had happened so far.

"Where's the beacon?" asked Duggan.

"Right here, sir," said Morgan. He opened the glove box and slid out the comms beacon. It was a metal cube, with several extendable aerials. Duggan took it and set it up at once.

"Sir, there's movement a way over to the north," said Dorsey. She was outside the cab, peering into the distance.

Duggan looked up sharply. "Coming our way?"

"I'm not sure. I'd say it's the tank."

"Of course it's the damned tank," muttered Duggan. He powered up the beacon. "*MHL Goliath*, this is Captain John Duggan. Do you copy?"

There was a pause for a few seconds. "This is Captain Erika Jonas of the *MHL Goliath*. You are not going to believe the size of the hole you just made in this planet."

"We need a pickup – urgently. We've got an injured officer here."

"What about the missile bunker?"

"We've taken care of it. Come at once. There's a Ghast tank hunting us and we've got nothing except our rifles."

"Roger. On our way."

With the broadcast finished, the beacon powered itself off. "Where's that tank?" Duggan asked.

"About a klick away. It's sweeping the area. I'd say they're looking for something, without knowing what."

"Could they have picked up our signal?" asked Duggan.

"Not sure, sir," said Chainer. "These beacons aren't well shielded. That doesn't mean every piece of military hardware automatically knows when it's sending."

"Damnit, I think they've seen me," said Dorsey. She ducked around the edge of the truck again.

"Think?" asked Duggan.

"Sorry sir, they're coming straight towards us."

"Get down!" shouted Duggan, throwing himself onto the ground.

The others followed suit. There was a clatter of metallic impacts against the side of the truck, punching dozens of holes along its forty-metre length. The force of the blows was such that each one knocked the truck a little way along the ground. The soldiers crawled on their stomachs to keep ahead of the machinery which threatened to crush them. Another volley smashed through the truck bed. Duggan could feel the depleted uranium projectiles ripping through the thin air above him. He looked frantically around for a place to run. There was no other cover within two hundred metres and the tank would see them if they tried to escape. *And it'll get us if we don't,* came the grim realisation.

"What do we do, sir?"

"Sir, should we run?"

"There's the tank!" said Dorsey.

A menacing shape came into sight around the edge of the truck, all angular sides and plate armour. The turret on top rotated with unnerving speed as it retargeted. Another round of projectiles spilled into the ruined truck as the soldiers tried desperately to crawl around to the far side, in the hope they hadn't been seen. Duggan fired a couple of shots from his rifle, determined to show at least this amount of resistance.

The seemingly inevitable death didn't arrive for Duggan or his squad. Before the Ghast tank could focus on them, a wall of earth gouted from the ground. It stretched in a line a hundred metres long, like a high fountain of grit and stone. Duggan's suit picked up hints of movement coming from above, objects streaking to the surface at an unimaginable velocity, accompanied by a deep thumping where they struck the surface. The tank was punched and flattened, flipped over and thrown twenty metres high. The fountain stopped and then returned, breaking the tank into pieces and shredding each part into something smaller again.

The fountaining stopped and fragments of stone rained down upon the huddled soldiers, rattling against their helmets and covering them with dust. Duggan raised his head and knew that on this day, he'd relied on luck far more than he should have. He stood up and dusted himself off, the gesture both automatic and pointless. Cheering broke across the open channel as the men and women became accustomed to continued life, rather than death.

A few minutes later, a shape appeared in the sky. One of the *Goliath's* four personnel transporters hovered silently overhead while its sensors scanned the ground for underlying fractures that would jeopardise its landing. At last, it settled to the ground in an open space a short distance from the truck. Duggan sent the five soldiers with him to meet with it, while he ran to help the three he'd left with Commander McGlashan. Together, they carried her across the rough ground to the transporter. The craft was big enough for two hundred people if you crammed them in tightly. At the moment, it only carried three members of the *Goliath's* crew, plus the five from Duggan's squad. Several came to assist and they got McGlashan up the wide boarding ramp and into the airlock. Minutes later, the transporter was away, heading towards the heavy lifter.

With a feeling of relief, Duggan pulled his helmet off and went to speak to the pilot. She greeted him with a smile that was as open and genuine as they came. She was in her thirties and attractive, with a mischievous glitter to her eyes.

"Glad you could join us, Captain Duggan." She extended a suited hand. "Captain Jonas."

They shook hands. "Your timing is excellent," he said. "Another ten seconds and we'd have been finished."

"The *Goliath* isn't warship, but we still carry a few Bulwarks, in case any stray missiles come our way." She winked. "Or a Ghost light tank."

An image of something was zoomed in on one of her monitors. Duggan leaned over for a closer look.

"That's the crater," she said. "How much would you say one of those Cadaverons weigh?"

"That particular one? About nine-point-five billion tonnes. There are bigger ones in the Ghost fleet."

She zoomed the image out to show the entirety of the heavy cruiser's impact crater. There was a tiny spot off to one side, which she pointed at. That's the mine operations there. You might not have seen it from where you were on the ground, but there're cracks everywhere. One of them a whole kilometre wide. It's going to take a while before they can get that site running again."

Duggan was occupied looking at the two craters side-by-side. The Ghost ship had struck the planet at a sixty-degree angle. It must have turned over a few times after impact, which made the initial crater extend into a long, deep furrow.

"Three hundred klicks across." He shook his head, dumbfounded at the damage.

"And about five hundred long. Goes down an awful long way, too. The hull stayed in one piece - inconceivable when you think about it. Would any of them have lived?"

"Depends on what damage the missiles did before it crashed. If the life support suffered damage, their bodies will be spread a nanometre thick across the walls."

"Tough luck for them, huh?"

"I'm out of sympathy."

"Yeah, me too."

Something else loomed into view. The *MHL Goliath* lay ahead, with a hatch open high on one of its sheer sides. Captain Jonas engaged the autopilot and the two of them sat in silence while the onboard computers lined them up with the docking bay and guided them in to land.

CHAPTER THIRTEEN

THE SHIP'S medic was waiting for them in the hangar bay. He was a surly man who spoke in little more than grunts. He'd brought the *Goliath*'s mobile medical robot along with him, which was an eight-feet tall block with a human-sized tube through the middle. A couple of the soldiers wrestled McGlashan into the tube, which closed up, sealing her in completely. The med-bot reversed away on its tiny gravity engine, the ship's medic close behind.

"Will she live?" Duggan called after the medic. The man just shrugged and continued walking. It was insubordinate, but this wasn't a battle Duggan wanted to start.

"I guess you're in charge now, Captain Duggan." It was Jonas. She offered a perfect salute with just the right amount of mockery. It would have made Duggan grin on another day. "What do you command? Shall we set a course for Pioneer?" she asked.

He realised how exhausted he was. He'd not slept apart from a few restless minutes snatched on the walk from the wreck of the *ES Pugilist*. His body had been running on battlefield adrenaline for too long and the pain from his forearm was making it difficult to focus.

"We can't go to Pioneer yet, Captain Jonas," he said. "We're not finished with our duties here on Everlong."

She raised an eyebrow and there was no trace of humour when she spoke. "The miners are all dead, Captain Duggan. We were in orbit long enough to find that out, at least."

"I know," he said. "The poor bastards didn't stand a chance. We can still get something out of this."

"What do you have in mind?"

"The Shatterer emplacement on the ground. Do you have room for it?"

"How big is it?"

"One hundred and twenty metres in diameter, length unknown. I'd guess no more than three hundred metres."

"Oh, I thought you meant it was big. There's almost room for that under my bed."

This time Duggan couldn't help but smile. "We'll need to get it onboard. If we get it back to a shipyard, the Corps research labs will have something to go on. We've got nothing to combat them at the moment. The Shatterers ignore all our countermeasures."

"I know," she said. "We'll get it into the hold. Tonight. Want to come up to the bridge and see how a Class One Military Heavy Lifter works?"

"Sounds like a plan."

While a Corps warship was all engines and weapons, the *Goliath* was all gravity lifter and cargo bay. The hull was triple-skinned and access corridors ran between the walls. Duggan found himself sitting in a narrow two-seater gravity-drive car that scooted along the seemingly deserted passages.

"We're a bit more spread out than a warship," said Jonas. "So we need transport to get us around."

"How many crew do you have?"

"Twenty-two. It's not as if we could lift any of our cargo by hand, no matter how many people we brought onboard."

"What've you got in your cargo bays?"

"A couple of rock-borers at fifteen million tonnes apiece. An entire smelting plant, custom-built on Pioneer for operations here. That's got to weigh at least five hundred million tonnes. Then there're all the vehicles and supplies. Nothing we can't handle. Here's the bridge."

They left the vehicle at the bottom of a grey-metal stairwell. Everything in the Corps was grey, as if a tin of paint would push the budget too far. Duggan was used to it and hardly even noticed these days. He entered the bridge behind Jonas. To his eyes, the room was sprawled across an unnecessarily large area. There were a couple of men at banks of screens on the far side.

"Second Lieutenants Green and Haster," she said. They turned and nodded at Jonas. Discipline tended to be a bit less formal on anything that wasn't a frontline warship and Duggan didn't worry about it. Jonas pointed to a chair in front of some more screens and he sat.

"What happened to the ES Ribald?" he asked, hoping she might have some more details beyond what he'd already guessed.

"Same thing that happened to you. They got hit by a missile. At least that's what our mainframe assumes happened. See, our sensors aren't made to detect objects travelling at four thousand klicks per second. Anyway, they didn't get lucky. Broke to pieces in mid-air and ended up scattered across half the planet." She turned to face him. "Captain Graham seemed like he had a good heart. He was petrified of meeting you. I could hear it in his voice. I hope he left a good impression."

Duggan sighed. "I didn't like him. Maybe I should have given him more of a chance."

"It's too late for that now," she said, her words without judgement.

"How did you know what the Ghasts wanted of you?" Duggan asked. "After they'd destroyed your escort."

"I didn't have the faintest idea. They shot down the *Pugilist* and *Ribald* and simply didn't shoot us down. I knew I couldn't outrun them, so I just waited to see what they'd do. They did nothing and I kept waiting. Then, the Cadaveron showed up. They tried to communicate with us – sent us all sorts of messages. Our mainframe's been working on figuring out what they wanted, but it's not the quickest model in the Corps. It's funny to think we've been fighting for so long and we don't even understand each other's languages."

Duggan knew the two sides had communicated in the past, though it was something he kept to himself. Even with that knowledge, he was unaware how the dialogue had taken place or how the Space Corps had figured out enough of the Ghast language to get things moving.

"I'm going to bring us over the mine area," she said. "The gravity chains have a range of thirty klicks. Like a reverse gravity engine, except slower and with more short-range grunt. Where'd you say that missile tube was?"

"Right in the middle. In a crater."

"Another crater? You make a lot of them, do you?" It was a throwaway comment, not meant to be anything.

Duggan grimaced, remembering the planet he'd destroyed while captaining the *ESS Crimson*. "It's been known to happen."

"The sensors have located the object. Half-buried and at an angle. Shouldn't present a problem and there's plenty of room in Cargo Bay Fifteen. I see it's just shy of eighty-five million tonnes. Pretty heavy for its size - it must be right up there with the other densest metals."

"It's no problem, is it?"

"No problem at all. Here, we're hovering at nine klicks. Opening the bay door."

The nearby screens each showed a different viewpoint of what was happening. One showed a pair of cargo doors sliding away into the recesses of the spacecraft – Duggan assumed there'd be room for them between the hull skins, to ensure the doors wouldn't interfere with what was in the hold.

"Got a fix on it," said Jonas. She sounded as if she were reciting the words as much for her benefit as Duggan's. "Watch what happens."

Duggan had seen before how the lifters worked. Nevertheless, he stared in fascination as one of the screens showed the Shatterer tube being dragged smoothly and cleanly from its crater.

"The invisible hand of God, we call it," said Jonas. "Five klicks away. Rotating it perpendicular. Coming in nicely."

A couple of minutes later and it was done. The Ghast Shatterer tube was safely stowed on the *Goliath*.

"The Corps engineers will be happy to see that," said Duggan.

"And I'll be happy to see the back of this planet," said Jonas. "The deep fission drives take nearly an hour to warm up. I'll bring us to a high orbit while Lieutenant Green hits them with a spanner."

"How much can this vessel lift?" asked Duggan. "If the cargo bays were all empty and you wanted to haul the heaviest item you could?"

"We've done five billion tonnes before, though that was in separate units of a billion each. We were expecting to pick up almost that amount of metal from Everlong." She looked at him sideways. "You're up to something."

"What about nine-point-five billion tonnes in the form of a single object?"

"I knew you were up to something. If you're referring to that wrecked Cadaveron on the surface below, then there's no room for it. We're full up."

"What if you removed all of the other cargo apart from the missile battery? Would there be room?"

Captain Jonas opened and closed her mouth, still not sure if she should take Duggan seriously or not. "If we emptied the hold and dumped all our inner walls there would theoretically be enough room to fit a Cadaveron inside. It's nearly ten billion tonnes." She repeated the weight as if to remind Duggan what he was asking.

"Could the gravity chains pick it up? And if so, would you have enough power to bring it into space? Captain Jonas, we have a unique opportunity to capture one of the enemy's most powerful warships. As far as I'm aware, such a chance hasn't arisen before. We've taken wreckage of course, but nothing like this. The things we could learn, Captain. Imagine what this might do for the Confederation."

"I'm too busy imagining my precious spaceship crashing into the same impact crater as the Cadaveron you want to lift out of it. It'll take us at least two days to safely unload our cargo. What if the Ghasts come back?"

"How long to jettison the contents of the hold?"

"Less than half an hour. I can't possibly authorise that. It'll take years to pay for out of a captain's salary." Her sense of humour was still there at least.

"Could you recover the wrecked spaceship?" asked Duggan quietly.

"If you approve it, I'll give it a go."

"Very well. Captain Jonas, I want you to jettison whatever cargo you're carrying. After that, the *MHL Goliath* will bring the Cadaveron into its hold and we'll take it back to Pioneer."

"You're the boss," she said. "What if there's anyone alive on board and they decide to open fire?"

"We'll find out long before we get them into the hold."

"Stick our head around the corner and see what shoots at us, huh?"

"You have nothing to worry about, Captain Jonas. If there'd been anyone alive on that Cadaveron, they'd have blown the *Goliath* into pieces by now, rather than see us escape to Confederation-controlled space. However, if we're to bring a Ghast warship to a populated planet, we need to be sure its AI is not able to transmit its location."

"We're not a warship, Captain Duggan. We might not even be able to detect its transmissions, let alone try and block them. If we do somehow manage to get it into the cargo hold, our hull won't stop outbound comms either."

"I know. I'm going to take some of my squad onto the surface and we're going to have a look onboard. You carry explosives on the *Goliath*, don't you?"

Captain Jonas could only nod, leaving Duggan to worry about the details of his proposal. He had no idea if his plan was going to work, but was determined he wouldn't give up without trying.

CHAPTER FOURTEEN

AN HOUR LATER, Duggan was in the cockpit of the same transport craft that had recently brought his squad away from the surface. In the passenger area, a row of suited men and women sat, their bodies rocking in time to the faint buffeting the transport was subjected to. They carried their rifles, and three of them had heavy packs of explosives from the stores on the *Goliath*. The suits looked worse for wear after the blast from the Cadaveron's missile earlier. Santos had been forced to stay behind because his helmet power supply had failed. As well as that, Butler had swapped suits with Chainer, since the Lieutenant's suit was too damaged to risk wearing. Therefore, they'd left Butler as well, in order to bring Breeze and Chainer who were better-placed to figure out the equipment on the Ghast ship's bridge. There were suits on the *Goliath*, they just weren't designed for combat use.

"We'll be landing in six minutes," said Duggan. "Are you all excited to see the insides of a Ghast warship?"

"Wouldn't miss it for the world, sir," said Ortiz. Duggan knew she wasn't exaggerating.

He kept the transport low to the ground, more out of habit

than anything else. When they flew over the edge of the vast impact crater, he brought them up higher so he could focus the sensors on the crash site. The view on the closest screen changed to show a zoomed-in section of the distant centre and Duggan mirrored it through to the passenger bay. The image looked unfocused - there was a distinct shimmering from the heat, which the sensors struggled to correct. Gradually, the details became clearer, revealing the damaged hull of their target. The Cadaveron was in one piece as Jonas had said. It didn't look much like a warship any more – the nose had been flattened and the sides were deeply scarred. Nevertheless, there was something unpleasantly threatening about the remains, as if the vessel were dangerous even in its current state.

"How *did* it stay in one piece?" asked Flores. "I bet it came down at a hundred klicks per second."

"It's almost solid metal, Soldier. Denser and stronger than almost any other material – our own warship engines aren't much short of thirty tonnes per cubic metre and I'm sure the Ghasts' engine technology is on par with ours. If it had been hollow, the pieces would have burned up or scattered across a million square kilometres."

"Has there been any sign of movement or life since it went down?" asked Ortiz.

Duggan touched the screen to zoom in further. He panned across the length of the Cadaveron. There were two huge holes in its port side.

"The life support can sustain the crew on a jump to light-speed," he said. "If it was functioning when they landed, there's a good chance they'd be alive. The fact that *we're* alive and not deconstructed into atoms by a missile strike tells me for sure they're all dead."

"We can learn a whole lot from that ship, I take it?" asked Ortiz.

"We need this vessel badly, Sergeant – to learn the weak spots. If the life support is vulnerable or there are other design flaws, we might even be able to program our own missiles to target those areas of their warships."

"I'll bet the *Goliath's* captain wasn't happy when you told her what you wanted to pick up," said Breeze.

"I don't think she was expecting it," said Duggan. "I'm going to fly the length of the hull, to see if there's any obvious way to enter it. If it's shut up tight we're going to be here a long time, which is bad news when we don't know if there are any other Ghost ships incoming."

He took them close, descending carefully into the seven-kilo-metre-deep crater. The sensors of the transporter reported the surrounding rock to be dense with metal ores. Duggan wondered what the damage would have been like if the Cadaveron had crashed into soft rock. Their destination loomed ahead - the hull was a dull silver, similar in appearance to a Corps vessel. However, the Ghost ship was slightly more irregular in shape, with extra angles and curves. There were also one-hundred-metre domes at each end, which Duggan knew housed beam weapons.

"Ugly looking thing," said Chainer.

"I'll bet they say the same thing about ours," said Dorsey.

"Have you been reading a book on understanding the enemy?" asked Flores. "Love Thine Murderous Bastard Alien Neighbour?"

"Piss off, Flores - before I shoot you in the balls," she retorted.

"You'd need to be a good shot," said Morgan, producing a series of jeers across the comms.

From a distance of two hundred metres, the Shatterer missile holes looked even more devastating. Their blasts had ripped deep into the craft, tearing through several dozen metres of the outer armour. Beneath, the colour of the metal changed to a greyish blue that Duggan recognized as part of the engines. The transport had only moderate shielding, so he didn't get any closer, nor stay for longer than he needed to.

"Any idea where they get in and out?" asked Chainer.

"It's usually somewhere underneath," said Duggan. "It seems to change from ship to ship."

"If it's sealed up, you know we've got a cat's chance of getting inside, no matter how many explosives we stick to it?" That was Breeze, speaking privately.

"We won't know until we've looked, Lieutenant."

The front of the heavy cruiser was embedded deep into the rock, with the tail pointing upwards at a slight angle. Duggan flew as close as he dared, hoping there'd be a visible means of entrance. There was nothing on either port or starboard. The underside of the vessel was similarly without visible opening, though it was too low to the ground to see for certain.

"I'm going to fly us over the top," said Duggan. The transporter climbed smoothly upwards at his command and he directed it to run above the length of the Ghast ship.

"What's that I can see on the screen, sir?" asked Ortiz. "There's something sticking out."

"I see it too," said Dorsey.

Duggan brought the transporter to a halt and kept it hovering, fifty metres over the vessel below. He squinted at the pilot's viewscreen until he saw what Ortiz had mentioned – it was a nondescript metal post, a few metres in length, sticking directly upward from the hull.

"I think that's an external sensor array, sir," said Chainer. "It looks similar to one of our comms beacons, except we keep ours housed under half a metre of armour. Maybe the Ghasts' tech isn't capable of operating that way."

"What happens if we plant explosives on it?"

"You'll stop that single array from working. I'd guess a ship this size would have dozens like it protruding from all over."

"Some of them on the underside?" asked Duggan.

"I'm sure there will be, sir. They might be bent or flattened, but there's always a chance they'll still work."

The fleeting hope of destroying all the external sensors to disable the Cadaveron's ability to communicate slipped away. Duggan swore. He could feel his stress rising, which he knew was a symptom of his increasing tiredness. The wound on his forearm was hurting progressively more and he'd not been able to spare the time to have anyone look at it. He'd not removed his suit and didn't know how much of a mark the Ghast projectile had left behind on his flesh. He didn't want to dwell on it.

"I'm going to put us down, so we can get out and have a better look underneath," he said.

The floor of the crater was uneven and sloped towards the centre. The transporter was designed to land on a variety of surfaces and it settled without fuss. The side door hissed open and lowered itself to the ground. As he stepped onto the heat-scalded grey rock, Duggan felt tiny in the shadow of the crashed spacecraft. The air temperature was over eighty degrees, with heat continuing to spill into the atmosphere from the Ghast ship.

"I'm not expecting trouble, but turn on your movement sensors and keep an eye out. We're looking for a boarding ramp. You all know what one looks like – theirs aren't any different to ours."

There was less room underneath the Cadaveron than Duggan had expected. The immense weight of its alloys and the speed of its impact had pushed it into the rock. There were a few hundred metres aft where they could get beneath the hull for a look. As he put one hand on the hot metal and peered into the darkness, Duggan felt a rumbling in the rock around him. The rumbling stopped and then came again, stronger this time.

"Get away," he shouted on the comms, before turning and sprinting in the direction of the transporter.

The others didn't need to be asked twice and ran with him. The vibration ended once more, leaving behind an unspoken threat that it would return.

"The Cadaveron moved, sir," said Chainer. "I had my hand on it when the second tremor came and the hull shifted a couple of inches."

"It's probably too heavy to be stable," said Breeze. "Objects this size and density weren't really meant to be supported."

"Damnit, that's going to stop us doing a proper search," said Duggan, wondering if he should call the whole thing off and return to the *Goliath*. Then, he saw something with his suit-enhanced sight. The front-most of the missile holes was over three hundred metres away. From the ground, it was possible to see something which had been concealed when looking from the transporter – there was an area of different colour, a blue glow deep within the metal hole.

"I can see light," said Duggan. "One of the missiles must have penetrated through to a part of the vessel where the Ghast crew worked." He started jogging towards it. The missile hole was way up above him, with no obvious way to reach it. The Cadaveron had taken a lot of damage when it went down, but there was no way to climb the scratched metal sides.

"I can see it as well," said Chainer. "I think we blew open one of their inner rooms or something."

"Back to the transporter," said Duggan. "We're going to try and land in that hole."

"Sir, our suits won't protect us from the emissions for longer than a few minutes," said Breeze.

"You're right, Lieutenant. Anyone who wants to wait on the ground is welcome to do so."

"Hell no," said Breeze. "I was just letting you know the risks."

"No way I'm turning down the chance to get a look inside," said Dorsey.

Duggan began the short trip to the transporter, with the others close behind.

It was much harder to land the transporter in a three-hundred and twenty metre missile hole than it was to land it on the ground next to the stricken Ghast vessel. The transporter's autopilot refused to accept Duggan's instructions, so he had to shut the system down and use the control sticks to bring them into position. He was conscious of the passing time, so was denied the opportunity to take things as slowly and carefully as he'd have liked. The hole was uneven, and some of the outer armour had melted downwards, leaving sharp fragments over-hanging the place he wanted to land. The transporter was only eighty metres long, but it was cumbersome and not designed for precision close-in flight. Duggan spent a minute lining it up so that he could fly it in sideways, cursing the gusts of wind which seemed to have sprung up from nowhere.

He got them in, slowly and cautiously. There was no smooth place to land and he struggled to get three of the four landing feet nestled into places he was confident they wouldn't slip away from. The rear of the transporter was heavier than the front and he managed to get the back two feet in place, before rotating the nose of the craft and getting one of the front feet down. The vessel tilted slightly and there was a scraping noise when the feet slid over the canted metal. Duggan held his breath as the trans-porter's nose slipped forwards. There was the thumping sensa-tion of a low-speed collision and the movement stopped. Duggan had hardly gathered himself when he heard Sergeant Ortiz exhorting the squad to get moving.

"The exit door won't extend fully, sir," said Ortiz. The door was meant to fold outwards from the side of the transporter, to create a ramp for passengers to walk up and down. It had opened partway, but a thick spear of metal prevented it from moving further. There was a V-shaped gap to either side.

"There's plenty of room to climb out," said Duggan. He pushed through the others and poked his head outside. "Three hundred degrees. Pretty hot," he said, handing his rifle to Breeze. Then, he used both hands to grip the top of the doorway and lifted himself upwards. He swung sideways and managed to get through the gap without smashing his helmet off anything.

Ortiz came next, followed by Chainer and Breeze. The others inside passed out the rifles and packs of explosives.

"I doubt we'll need any of these guns," said Duggan. "If there's a hole into the crew's quarters, they're all dead."

"They must have internal airlocks, sir." said Chainer. "They shouldn't all have died from a single breach."

Duggan couldn't deny the logic in Chainer's words. Still, he remained certain that this vessel had become a tomb for the crew it carried. His helmet chimed a warning about temperature and positrons, letting him know it was time to move on from where he was standing. He ignored it for another few seconds, until everyone had exited the transporter. It was dark and the light from their helmets flashed over the area, casting elongated shadows onto their surroundings. The high sides of the transporter prevented them from looking outwards, not that there was anything to see. The blast crater in the Cadaveron's side sloped upwards, curving over until it formed a roof far above. Duggan searched for the source of the blue light he'd seen from below and found it quickly. There was a hole a few metres square, fifty or so metres up and to their left – it had appeared much smaller from below. There was a space through the hole, with the light giving away nothing of what lay beyond.

"We must be looking at the ceiling from this angle," said Chainer, stepping back to let Duggan go past him.

Duggan scrambled over the hot alloy surface, finding it

surprisingly easy to grip. His rifle was slung across his back and it clattered against a sharp-edged piece of misshapen metal as he squeezed by. He reached the hole, just at a point where angle of the slope would have made it hard to climb any higher. There was an open area on the other side of the gap and with a deep breath, Duggan climbed into the Ghast vessel.

CHAPTER FIFTEEN

DUGGAN FOUND himself in a room ten metres wide and stretching to a hundred in length. There were two passages leading away from opposite walls. The temperature was lower here and Duggan guessed this area was heavily insulated from the mass of engines close by. He stepped a few paces forward – the floor was metal-tiled and at a fifteen-degree angle from level. Footing would have been treacherous had the Cadaveron been at more of a tilt. As it was, he found it easy enough to manage. Sergeant Ortiz appeared next at the hole and Duggan moved deeper into the room so she and the others could enter.

"Look at all these bunks," she said. "Hundreds of them."

Chainer came next. "The poor bastards in here must have been vaporised."

"And not a damn thing they could do about it," said Flores.

"Have you been reading that book you were telling me about?" asked Dorsey.

"We're all soldiers, aren't we?" muttered Flores, not pleased to have been called out.

The bunks were little more than alcoves in the walls, eight

feet long and four deep. They were stacked three high, with the uppermost ones ten feet from the floor. There were deep, horizontal grooves in the walls next to them – ladders for the Ghast soldiers to climb up to reach their beds. Duggan headed along the room, keeping close to the wall as he went. He looked into the first bunk he reached – there was nothing within. Whatever bedding there might have been was either utterly destroyed by the heat of the Shatterer missile, or sucked out into space.

"I might hate these alien bastards, but there's no pleasure to be gained from this," said Ortiz.

"Yeah," said Flores.

"We need to move," said Duggan. "This place is too hot and we might have a lot of running to do to find the bridge."

With that, he set off with his rifle in his hands. He kept it across his chest, rather than at his shoulder. Speed was more important than anything and he was certain there'd be no resistance. The passageways he'd seen earlier went left or right from the room. Duggan went left, guessing the bridge was more likely to be at the front of the ship. In other circumstances it would have made more sense to split up, but the density of the ship would stop any suit-to suit communication and he didn't want anyone getting lost.

The corridor they entered was oversized, as was everything to do with the Ghasts. Pipes and cables ran in trays high up on the walls. Every so often, there were screens embedded into the walls, with no clue as to their function. The blue light was everywhere and seemed to exude from the walls themselves, instead of having a discernible source.

"It's a mixture of old and new," said Chainer. "I've not seen a pipe on a spacecraft since we were last on the *Crimson* – I'm half expecting to see steam coming out of a loose joint. However, the lighting is technologically superior to anything on a Corps vessel."

"This Cadaveron isn't one of their recent models, Lieutenant," said Duggan. "I can't imagine we'll see exposed cables on one of those."

"I'm sure you're right, sir. It's just this particular ship can't be *that* old. If it was older than twenty years, chances are the Space Corps would have blown it up way back when we were better than them."

It wasn't worth pursuing any further and Duggan didn't respond. The passage continued and the temperature dropped steadily. They reached a branch to the right, three hundred metres from the bunk room. There was another room, fifty metres square. This room was a mess, with piles of unrecognizable metal objects flattened against the wall closest to the front of the ship. Here and there were tables and benches, still fastened to the floor. The back wall had three lockers attached to it, each one buckled and warped.

"What's all this crap?" asked Dorsey.

Duggan took a few paces into the room. "This is what tables and chairs look like when they're ripped from their fixings and smashed into a wall at several thousand metres per second."

"Any bodies?" asked Ortiz.

"If there were, I don't think they'd be recognizable as anything," said Duggan. "There's some discoloration to the metal over here. That might be clothing I can see in the corner." He shrugged, not wanting to think about it just now. "The life support had definitely failed when they came down, else this lot would still be in place. We're too far away from where the Shatterer hit for it to have caused this damage."

"This is familiar," said Ortiz. "Everything about it."

"We could be on a bigger version of an Anderlecht," said Duggan. "They don't care much for creature comforts on those either. Anderlechts and Gunners - mobile gun platforms like this Cadaveron. Put a crew onboard and send them out to fight."

There was something about this room which disturbed him, almost as much as the bunk room. There was another exit opposite, which he ignored and returned to the corridor they'd been originally following. As he walked, Duggan noticed scrapes and scratched in the walls and floor. When the life support failed and the ship crashed, anything unsecured in this passage would have hurtled along here at an incredible speed, catching the walls as it went. He paused for a moment and pressed his palm against one of the sides, to reassure himself about a suspicion. There was a humming vibration, clearly felt through the material of his suit.

"After all this, the engines are still online," he said.

"Will it fly?" asked Ortiz.

"It might," said Duggan. "Though anyone living would have a rough time of it."

They reached another turning to the right, which ended at a series of wide steps going up. Duggan led the squad towards the steps and climbed. They continued for a few metres before reaching a wide landing. Corridors went away to the left and right, their destinations unclear. There was a door ahead, heavy-looking, featureless and closed. The light flickered on and off at irregular intervals and Duggan turned his helmet light back on to compensate.

"Flores, take a look at that door," he said.

The soldier unslung his pack of explosives and stepped forward. He repeated the process he'd gone through in the Shatterer silo earlier, by hitting the door with his hand.

"Solid," he said.

"In less technical terms please," snarled Ortiz sarcastically. "Stop pissing about, man!"

Flores apologised. "Sorry, Sergeant, I was just thinking how much it'll take to open it. My brain can't work on two things at once. I can get it open but it won't be pretty. The explosives on the *Goliath* aren't meant for this type of work."

"Will there be anything left on the other side once you're done?" asked Duggan. "If this is the bridge, it's important you don't blow it to pieces."

"I'll do my best, sir. That's the only promise I can make."

"Fine, do it," said Duggan. He wasn't happy, even if it wasn't Flores' fault.

It didn't take long. In a couple of minutes, Flores had positioned a number of red cubes around the door frame. There were no wires and the charges could be triggered simultaneously by a remote command.

"That should do it. We'll need to get away from here."

"Tell me something I don't know," said Morgan.

They hurried down the steps and positioned themselves with their backs to the walls around the corner. Ten long seconds passed and nothing happened.

"Do it," said Duggan.

"The walls are blocking the remote command, sir," said Flores. "Hang on, I'm trying something else."

The sensors on Duggan's suit picked up an angry crackling sound from nearby. The noise went on for a time and was followed by a low, muted thump. Flores was off at once, sprinting towards the steps. Duggan didn't hang around and ran after him. The door was gone, or at least it had been melted into a shape that was no longer recognizable as a door. It had folded back into the room beyond, bringing chunks of the doorway with it. The metal glowed fiercely at the edges, though its intensity was already diminishing.

"Good work," said Duggan, giving Flores a clap on the shoulder.

"No problem, sir."

"Lieutenants Breeze, Chainer, I think we've found what we're looking for. Follow me."

Duggan stepped past the ruined door and onto what could

only be the bridge. It was coldly lit in blue and filled with bank upon bank of screens and consoles. Some of the screens were illuminated in the symbols of the Ghast alphabet, whilst others were blank.

"Big," said Chainer.

"I count more than thirty seats. It takes a lot to oversee a big ship like this one," said Breeze.

At the doorway, Ortiz peered inside. Duggan waved her and the others to enter. "Don't touch anything," he warned.

"Wouldn't dream of it, sir," she replied.

Chainer and Breeze had already begun looking around. The bridge was at least fifteen metres square, with contoured metal seats still fastened firmly to the floor. There were islands of screens placed evenly around, each with three chairs positioned before them.

"The Ghasts must have built this place to withstand a bigger impact," said Breeze, pressing his finger onto some of the controls. "It's all remained in place."

"Apart from the crew," said Duggan. There was a film of something across the front bulkhead and part of the ceiling. It was clear and viscous, with large patches of grey material stuck to it. He shook his head and turned away. "Let's hope there's nothing we need to access under there. The crew broke half of the equipment when they flew into it."

"I think I've located the comms area, sir," said Chainer. "I recognize some of it from what we saw in the Shatterer battery." He was at the rear wall, sitting in one of the three seats. The size of the Ghast chair made him look faintly ridiculous – almost like a child - and the oversized suit helmet only added to the effect. Duggan and Breeze joined him, with the latter having to drag himself away from the propulsion control area of the bridge.

"Can you work any of it?" asked Duggan.

"Bits and pieces," said Chainer. "I'm amazed at how similar it is to our equipment in appearance. I guess the same needs are likely to produce a similar approach in design. I'm left with the impression their comms systems lag behind ours."

"Not enough to make a difference," said Breeze.

"No, not enough."

"Any idea how to shut the sensors down?" asked Duggan. "And will that definitely stop the comms working?"

"Well, sir, there's rarely a need to power them off, so it's not as if there's a button you can press to do it. In the Corps, we do rolling restarts of each sensor array on a monthly basis – it can highlight problems when they perform their boot-up self-checks. Or if the ship is in for a full repair job in a dry dock, they might want to turn them off then. Which would be all well and good if I had any way of understanding their damned jibber-jabber."

"Will it definitely stop the comms?" repeated Duggan.

"On one of ours it would," said Chainer. "The comms are a separate system, but they fire out through the super-fars. Turn off the sensors and the comms have nowhere to go."

"What about powering down the whole ship?" asked Breeze.

"With the number of hoops I have to jump through to do that on something as small as a Gunner, I don't hold out much hope it'll be an easy job on a heavy cruiser," said Duggan, racking his brains for anything which might help.

Chainer was busily pressing at areas of the console around him. "Nothing ventured, nothing gained," he said to himself. On the screens nearby, codes and message flashed up in a language none of them could understand. "Whoops!" he said, without elaborating further. Duggan didn't ask what had happened to produce this exclamation – Chainer knew his stuff.

Time dragged on and Duggan alternated between pacing and examining the surrounding screens for something that might help. For once, his brain failed him utterly and refused to offer anything that would move matters forward. In the end, his temper and patience snapped and he opened his mouth to order a withdrawal to the transporter.

"I think I've got it!" said Chainer, stopping Duggan's words before they were spoken. "How could I have forgotten that?"

"Tell me!" urged Duggan, leaning across to see.

"They've got a simulation mode, sir. We have them on our own warships. It allows you to test the crew's performance in a variety of improbable scenarios. I remember them hitting me with one the very first day I was promoted – they made the ship go blind, to simulate a total failure of the comms. You're supposed to fail the test miserably, yet somehow learn from the process."

"And you can do that to this ship?"

"Yes, sir. There's an option to close off all internal and external comms. There are various other options to fool the young Ghast officers as well. I can throw up a hundred pings on their fars that will look for all the world like the entire Space Corps fleet is approaching."

"That won't be necessary, Lieutenant. Shutting off the sensors will be sufficient."

"Will the scenario end automatically after a set time?" asked Breeze.

"That's the best part of it – it'll last until it's manually cancelled."

"Excellent work, Lieutenant. Please do what you need to."

"It's done, sir. The Cadaveron won't send or receive a signal until we choose to end the simulation."

Duggan felt an immense relief when it was done. He led the squad at a run back to the transporter. It was still where they'd left it – he'd half expected it to have slid away from its uncertain berth and crashed to the ground below. With his helmet chiming an increasingly urgent warning about the positrons from the heavy cruiser's engines, Duggan climbed aboard the transporter, followed by the others. He eased the craft out from the Shatterer's impact hole and up into the dark sky. When he got a moment to relax, he spoke to Chainer.

"How did you do on your scenario, Lieutenant?"

"I refused to believe that all comms could fail at once, sir. They're robust, independent systems and individually their failure rate is below a tenth of one percent over the entirety of their fifteen-year lifespan. The chances of them going wrong at the same time without the ship receiving weapons damage was so low I discounted it. When I worked that out, it was easy to guess it was a test. I located the simulation program and ended it. Afterwards, I started a new one which produced a series of inbound messages to indicate the entire Confederation was in revolt. I didn't serve under that captain for long."

Duggan laughed with genuine enjoyment as the transporter continued its journey to the *MHL Goliath*.

CHAPTER SIXTEEN

"I'M GOING to dump this stuff the first place that catches my eye. Somewhere away from the mining pit," said Jonas. She had an expression of worry. Duggan sat next to her on the bridge as they discussed how they were going to jettison the *Goliath*'s cargo of valuable machinery.

"There's no life on this planet, so get rid of it anywhere that won't interfere with the lift operation," said Duggan.

"I'm going to need a code from Lieutenant Green," she said. "There are a few fail-safes to stop one of us getting drunk and accidentally leaving our cargo in space somewhere." Jonas waved a hand and Green came over. He was an unassuming man and he blanched when he heard what was about to happen. He went even paler when Jonas told him what they intended to fill the empty space with.

"Can't we send a signal to someone in the Corps?" he asked. "To get approval?"

"We *could* send that signal, Lieutenant," said Duggan. "We're not going to. I'm approving this, so please enter your codes into the mainframe." He knew it might take hours for a request from the lifter to get through to someone with enough seniority in the Corps to give the go-ahead. If this had been a warship, he could have pushed a message through to a place higher up the chain. The lifter didn't have that authority.

Lieutenant Green swallowed hard. He looked as if he wanted to say something else, but wisely chose not to. He reached over one of the panels and entered a series of digits, which the ship's mainframe combined with his biometric data. The computer noted that the lieutenant was exhibiting an elevated heart rate, but within the expected range for the enormity of the decision.

"Thank you, Lieutenant Green. You may go back to your seat," said Jonas. The man wandered off, looking dazed.

"Done?" asked Duggan.

"Just entering my codes now, overriding this, counter-manding that. All the usual stuff needed for a once-in-a-lifetime decision. We're almost over the dump zone. It doesn't feel right to call it the *drop* zone, somehow."

"Whenever you're ready," he said.

"There needs to be a big, red button to press, doesn't there?" she asked. "Like you see in the old movies, with a big '*Do Not Touch*' sign beneath it."

"How long?" asked Duggan. He could understand Jonas' nervousness, but he wanted her to get on with it. He knew he was getting tetchy from the pain in his forearm. With everything to see to, he'd still not had it treated.

"It's done," she said. "Or at least, it's started. You'll see it on this screen over here."

One by one, the cargo bay doors beneath the *Goliath* slid away into their recesses in the hull. For a few minutes, nothing else happened. Across the room, Green and Haster watched the same images on their own screens. Duggan felt sympathy for them – they probably thought their careers were evaporating before their eyes.

"Everything's got to unlatch in the right order," explained Jonas. "Then the gravity chains will release and out it'll all go."

Another ten minutes went by. Then, something dropped away from the hold – a series of huge, metal plates. Most of them fell straight, while a few turned as they fell, as if they hadn't been released cleanly. "That's the interior walling. If we didn't drop them first, there's a chance some of the cargo would bounce away and collide with the hull. Next, the gravity chains should shut off. Yep, there they go."

A silver-hued shape fell from the cargo bay – it was angular and indistinct. Other shapes fell with it, some large, some small. They rained from the *Goliath*'s hull – a hundred billion dollars' worth of plant and machinery scattering across the rocky surface below. The crew on the bridge observed in silence until there was nothing left to fall.

"That's the lot," said Jonas. "We're as light as a feather now."

"Bring us to the crash site," said Duggan.

"We're on our way. ETA less than five minutes."

"Show me the Cadaveron, please."

It came up on the display, scarred and sullen. "It's an awful-looking thing," said Jonas, concentrating on fine-tuning their approach. "Green, Haster, get over here. We're about to pick up something heavy."

The two men got up and walked the five metres to sit at an adjacent bank of consoles. "Are you sure this is a good idea, ma'am?" asked Haster. "Lieutenant Green just told me what you're planning, I checked out the design specifications for the *Goliath*. It was never intended to lift more than five billion tonnes in one go. The highest single lift we've needed to make was just over three billion."

"We'll have to worry about specifications afterwards, Lieutenant Haster," said Jonas. "The Space Corps needs us to recover that spacecraft. We need to work together to ensure it happens quickly, before the Ghosts send another one like it to see what's happened."

"Rest assured they'll have one on its way," said Duggan. "There was plenty of time to send a distress signal."

"Fine," said Haster, seating himself. "It's my duty to ask questions, that's all."

Captain Jonas looked at the viewscreens again. "The crater is almost seven klicks deep where the enemy vessel has settled," she said. "I'd like to get to fifteen above so we've got a bit of room for manoeuvre."

Duggan had a sudden thought. "Are you shielded against positron leaks? They're pouring from those holes."

"You name it, we're shielded from it. Except outbound comms and a few other things. You could set off a nuke in our hold and we wouldn't know about it."

"That's not quite true, ma'am," said Green.

"You know what I mean, Lieutenant. The radiation wouldn't cause us any harm."

"We're stable and in place," said Haster. "The mainframe is refusing to acknowledge the object as a permittable target for the gravity chains."

"You'll have to do it manually, Lieutenant. Like they taught you in college." Jonas turned her head towards Duggan. "Lieutenant Haster is a superb winchman - that's why I have him here on the *Goliath*. The little stuff like that missile tube, I'm happy to do myself. This one, I'll leave to him."

Haster was one of those men who got on with things. "I'm calculating the best places to target the chains. Eighteen at the nose, twenty port, eighteen starboard and sixteen aft should pull it up evenly. It's easy when I tell myself it's only a billion tonnes."

"Let me know when they're fixed."

"I'd like to run a few cross-checks first, ma'am."

No one spoke while Haster ran through page upon page of

numbers on his console screen. Duggan looked around the bridge, blinking to try and reduce the stinging in his eyes. He was starting to feel light-headed and knew he'd have to get someone to look at his forearm soon. He peered at the area of his suit where the Ghast projectile had clipped him. There was an indentation in the polymer where it had closed up around the hole. It would have also sealed the wound, but that didn't stop it hurting.

"I think we're ready to go, ma'am," said Haster. "Do you want to double-check?"

"I trust you, Lieutenant and I take full responsibility for this lift," said Jonas. "Please proceed."

"Okay, here we go. There might be some noticeable vibration."

A faint whining and thrumming began, which Duggan recognized as a gravity drive spooling up. The vibration started, faint at first and rapidly building.

"Look at these gauges, Captain Duggan," said Jonas. "They show the power flowing through the chains. They've got their own source, but we'll need to divert some extra power from the main engines in order to supplement what's available to them." The first set of gauges all showed one hundred percent and they flashed red. "Lieutenant Haster is drawing from our propulsion now. These other gauges will begin to climb in a moment."

Sure enough, a separate set of gauges flashed green, before turning to amber. The vibration built, accompanied by a buzzing sound from the equipment in the room. The *Goliath* was little more than a hollow box with an engine – there was a lot more vibration than there would be on a warship.

"Seventy percent from the main engines," said Haster. "The target vessel isn't moving. I'll take it up to eighty percent. If it doesn't move at that point, it's more than we can carry."

"He means if we go above eighty percent, we won't have

enough power to keep the *Goliath* in the air," Jonas said to Duggan.

"That's eighty percent," said Haster. The gauges were all red now. Screen upon screen of red.

"Is it moving?"

"No."

"Is it close to moving?"

"Probably."

"Try eighty-two percent."

"Whatever you say, ma'am."

The floor of the *Goliath* rumbled. Duggan recognized it as a symptom of distress. In the crater below, the Cadaveron remained in place.

"It's not going to happen, ma'am," said Lieutenant Green. He looked petrified.

"Take it to eighty-four percent."

"Ma'am?" said Haster.

"Just do it."

"Eighty-four it is."

The rumbling continued, until it reminded Duggan of the earthquake they'd felt when the Cadaveron had crashed.

"I'm getting something!" said Haster, excitement in his voice. "It's coming!"

"Hold at eighty-four percent," said Jonas.

"It'll take all day to get here, but it's coming!"

Duggan watched one of the screens, which he kept focused on the damaged warship below. For the first ten minutes, there was no sign that anything had happened. Then, he noticed the Cadaveron had rotated slightly from its original position.

"It's at five hundred metres," Jonas told him. "It's hard to see from this angle. Lieutenant Haster's got it clear of the stone it was embedded in, so it should come up faster now."

"Reducing our engine leech to eighty percent," said Haster.

He puffed up his cheeks and blew out. "It's coming up under control."

It took another thirty minutes. Duggan marvelled at the damage the Cadaveron had sustained – not just from the two missile strikes, but the crash landing as well. The vessel looked like a spent bullet that had been fired at point-blank range into a wall.

The Cadaveron vanished into the *Goliath*'s hold without any more drama. The rows of cargo doors closed in unison, locking the ship within. Watching remotely, it was easy to forget just how big the enemy craft was and how much it weighed.

"Good work everyone," said Duggan. "I'm impressed."

"It's what we do, Captain Duggan," said Jonas. She didn't make an effort to hide the mixture of pleasure and relief on her face. "Can we go to back to Pioneer now? I need a drink."

"There's nothing more for us here," said Duggan. "Too much death."

"It's going to be a slow run up into space," said Jonas. "We need to maintain the same power usage to keep the cargo stable in the hold. That leaves us with exactly twenty percent of our gravity drive remaining."

"Permission to hit the fission drives with a spanner, ma'am?" asked Green. It seemed to be a joke they had running.

"Hit them as hard as you like, Lieutenant. I want them ready to go as soon as we're far enough away from the surface."

"Yes, ma'am."

"I've just received a message, Captain Duggan," said Jonas, pointing at a box of text on her screen. "You said you wanted to be informed about any change in Commander McGlashan's condition."

"Yes?"

"They've stabilized her. She'll not be fit for duty for a while. Not until they can grow her a new stomach and spleen at least.

We've got some pretty good medical kit onboard and Corporal Moseley is a good medic once you learn to put up with his bad manners."

Relief washed over Duggan and he slumped back. He knew he should stay on the bridge until they went to lightspeed. He felt giddy with fatigue and his vision started to swim. Without his suit helmet on, he had no way to give himself a shot of stimulant and it was only his body's own adrenaline that was keeping him going. Now the lift was done and he'd been told about McGlashan, tiredness roared through him, leaving him with a rushing sound in his ears.

"I need to sleep," he said. "And for someone to take me to the medical bay."

He stumbled to his feet and almost fell. Someone – Captain Jonas – steadied him and helped him from the bridge. He remembered mumbling an instruction for them to let the Space Corps know they were coming. After that, his last remaining energy was spent and he fell asleep in the shuttle car.

CHAPTER SEVENTEEN

DUGGAN WOKE up in a computer-controlled semi-darkness. He was on something soft – a bed. There was a memory of pain and he looked at his forearm, noticing a raw pinkness to it. He gingerly pressed the area where the Ghost projectile had gone through. It hurt and there was the strange feeling that the skin wasn't his own. He'd been fixed up with an artificial skin that would take a couple of days to grow into the wound and tie up with his severed nerve-endings. His space suit was gone and the room looked surprisingly clean and well-appointed, with a table, a couple of chairs and a screen. He rolled out of bed, finding that someone had dressed him in a blue uniform that signified no particular rank or position. His mind was curiously alert.

Outside the room, he walked fifty metres along a featureless corridor until he found a shuttle car. He got in and drove it towards the bridge. Captain Jonas was there, along with Green, Haster and a woman whom Duggan didn't recognize.

"Captain Duggan," said Jonas warmly. "How are you feeling? Was my bed comfortable enough for you?"

Duggan had already guessed where it was he'd woken up.

"Better," he conceded. "Much better. How long was I out for and what's our status?"

"You've been asleep for over twenty hours, I'd say. As for our status? Well the Ghasts haven't blown us up and we're at Light-E, so we should be safe until we reach Pioneer in eighteen days."

"Did you send a message to the Space Corps?"

"We did. It was received by a man with the rank of ensign who promised to treat it with the utmost urgency. Naturally, we didn't hear anything before we went to lightspeed, so we must assume our arrival will be greeted with a tremendous fanfare, as well as coffee and biscuits served by Admiral Slender himself!" She saw Duggan's face. "You don't get along with the Admiral?"

"We don't see eye-to-eye." Jonas was easy going and although Duggan hadn't known her long, he found it hard to keep things to himself when he talked to her.

"I've never met the man. Not that I would expect to, being the captain of a lowly cargo vessel."

Duggan didn't want to discuss Admiral Slender and certainly not when there were other people on the bridge to overhear his words. "Do they have a spare dock to take the Cadaveron on Pioneer?"

"It's a shipbuilding planet, so they must have somewhere. I'm not sure what they'll do to plug those holes, though. I doubt the Confederation Council will be amused if they learn an exposed warship engine has been lowered into dry dock without adequate precautions in place."

Duggan left the people on the bridge to their duties. Light-speed travel could be soul-crushingly boring at times, particularly a long trip on a slow vessel. He knew that some crewmembers were more than content to sit for hours watching screens or just filling their time by doing not much of anything. Duggan had only a limited patience with downtime, before the urge to do something gripped him again. He'd recently awoken, so hadn't reached that point yet – in fact, he felt a huge relief that he and his squad had time to recuperate. He was wise enough to predict he'd be feeling like a coiled spring in a week or two.

The medical bay was a large, starkly-lit area near to the front of the *Goliath*. There was space to spare on a heavy lifter and the facility had six narrow hospital-style beds, each attended by a top-of-the-line static med-bot. Duggan doubted whether there'd ever been more than one or two beds in use at the same time. Still, it was good that they thought about the health of the crew.

Commander McGlashan was there, in the furthest bed from the door. At first, Duggan couldn't tell if she was asleep or awake. Her face was deathly pale - nearly as pale as the white robes she'd been dressed in - and her dark eyelashes made it difficult to see if her eyes were open or not. She was connected to a med-bot by numerous wires and tubes. There was a lump beneath her robe, covering her stomach.

"Captain," she said. Her voice was weak, as faint as a rustling breeze.

"I won't ask how you feel," he said. "Has anyone told you what's happened?"

"Bill was here with Frank. They said we've picked up the Cadaveron." She gave a wheezing laugh. "They're not going to know what to do with you when we get back. I'm not sure there's anything in the procedures that covers it."

Duggan laughed. "I haven't thought that far ahead. Whatever they do, at least we'll have brought something for them to study. I want us to win this war, Commander. If we have to abandon a few million tonnes of mining equipment on a distant planet, so be it."

"When they've re-grown my insides, I'll look forward to joining you on your next ship, sir."

"Has anyone told you how long?"

She tried to shake her head. "This machine on my stomach is

what's keeping me alive. I had a look when they fitted it to me. It does all sorts of wonderful things, except it can't make me a new set of organs. The military hospital on Pioneer can do that. I've seen it happen to other men and women. I'll be out of action for a couple of months."

"You did pretty well on Everlong."

"We all did, sir." Her eyes closed. Duggan watched her for a few minutes. The med-bot didn't move or show a visible alert, so he assumed she'd fallen asleep again. He didn't want to overstay, so he got up and left the room.

The eighteen days which followed could have been a relaxing time. For Duggan, it was a slow build-up of frustration. He spent time in the gym, maintaining his strength and stamina. At other times, he spoke to his soldiers about past missions, the hardships of fighting the Ghasts, and also commiserating with them over the recent losses to the squad. Sergeant Ortiz had a seemingly endless list of stories from her past, which she told in a dry style without boasting or embellishment. These activities were diverting, but weren't enough to keep him fully occupied.

In spite of Captain Jonas' protestations that she'd need to get back to Pioneer before she could have a drink, the food replicators on the *Goliath* were permitted to vend a limited quantity of alcohol. Duggan found he had sufficient authority to command the machines to produce more alcohol than the other crew members were able to - even more than Jonas herself.

"Betrayed by my own ship," she laughed, one evening towards the end of the trip. She took another sip of the thick, sweet-smelling liquid the replicator had produced. "This isn't entirely awful."

"Only partially so," agreed Duggan.

"Why are you always so on edge?" she asked, her eyes spearing him.

Duggan shifted, feeling uncomfortable. "It's how I am," he said at last. "Inaction feels like a waste of my life."

"Would you have felt this way if there were no war to fight?"

"I've asked myself that many times. I was twelve years old when the war started. Even then I was fascinated by space, by the size of the vessels humanity had managed not only to build, but to make travel so fast you could get from one galaxy to another in days instead of centuries. I knew I wanted to join the Space Corps – to see the places for myself, instead of watching other people visit them on my television at home. At seventeen, I was filled with the bravery of youth and I signed on the dotted line as an infantryman. Looking back, there's no one who's ready at seventeen to make such an important choice for themselves.

"I served for a few years. Earned myself some respect and a couple of medals. Then, someone suggested I go back to school and become an officer. It seemed like a good idea at the time – that I might one day be a lieutenant on the bridge, instead of waiting in my quarters until it was time to get in the tank. I did well and served as a lieutenant for a couple of years until I got fast-tracked to captain."

"All you've known is the war," she said.

"That's it exactly. All I've known is the war. I can't answer your question about how I'd feel if there were no war. All I can do is guess and that's a game I've never enjoyed." He took another sip of his drink. The alcohol soothed him, washing away his worries. A part of him knew it was false, but he let himself enjoy the moment. "What about you?"

"My dad was in the Corps. A couple of my brothers as well. Joining after them seemed like the most natural thing for me to do. Fifteen years later and here I am captaining the *MHL Goliath*."

"Just like that?" asked Duggan.

"There were a few ups and downs. In the end, there were

more ups than there were downs." She sat back. "I didn't like the feeling of helplessness against the Ghost missile battery and the warship. We're not normally sent to places we might see trouble."

"There's plenty of helplessness on a warship as well," said Duggan. "Times when the Ghost missiles are coming at you in waves and all you can do is hope they collide with the shock drones, or the Bulwarks take them down. Apparently, I'm a statistical anomaly, having run so many missions on a Gunner without being killed."

"It's always good to have luck on your side."

"So I've been told. I refuse to call on luck, in case it turns against me when I need it most."

She laughed. "A man who believes fervently in luck, yet fears it as well."

"Maybe. I'm not so stupid I'll deny it exists, or that I've likely had my fair share."

"Have you ever been married, Captain Duggan?"

The question caught him off-guard. "I had a wife once. I thought I could fit a family in around my duty, like a second-class citizen. I was never there and the woman I married didn't stick around to see if I'd change. It was the best thing she could have done."

"Children?"

"None. There was talk of it at first. An absent man can't father children."

"Do you regret it?"

"It's the easiest thing in the world to tell someone not to regret what they can't change. Believing yourself when you say those words is harder than anything."

"You have your crew. Commander McGlashan."

"Yes, I have my crew and yes Commander McGlashan is very dear to me. She's an officer I respect and away from the

Corps, a woman I value as a friend. There was a cloud hanging over me when I thought she might die."

"The cloud is now gone?"

"When one cloud goes, the wind is always there to blow a new cloud into its place." He sighed. "I don't normally wallow."

Jonas looked at him sadly. "Perhaps when the war is over, we can meet and see if the sky above is blue."

"I don't know if that's a promise I can keep," he said, feeling like a coward. The conversation tailed off into a long silence. Jonas was waiting to see if he'd say anything more. Duggan found a wall in front of him, one he'd always pretended wasn't there. It was the hardest thing in the world to reach up and pull himself towards the top. "I think I'd like that very much," he said at last. Jonas smiled and Duggan felt as if a weight he'd never known existed was lifted from him.

The following day was the last before their arrival. Duggan's head was only slightly fuzzy and he did his best to ignore the alcohol-induced lethargy. He did his usual rounds, visiting Commander McGlashan, who was much improved since the first time he'd found her in the medical bay.

"We'll come out of lightspeed in four or five hours," he said. "There'll be another couple of hours till we're close enough to Pioneer to get you off on a transport ship."

"I feel fine now, sir." She smiled ruefully. "I'm sure that would change at once if I unplugged any of these wires. What'll happen to you?"

"I anticipate I'll be required to stick around while the Cadaveron is unloaded. There'll be a debriefing at some point. A *thorough* debriefing."

"Do you think he'll cause you any problems?" She meant Admiral Slender.

"I hope not. I think his hands will be tied in the circumstances."

"It's going to be interesting, at least."

"I can think of several words, of which *interesting* is only one," he replied.

He left the medical bay and tried to constructively fill the remaining few hours, without much success. Eventually, an announcement came through on the internal comms to advise everyone onboard that the *MHL Goliath* was about to enter local space. There was a minor jolt as it happened, hardly enough to cause nausea or injury. Duggan made his way to the bridge, in order to see what communications might be awaiting them as they approached Pioneer on the gravity drive.

CHAPTER EIGHTEEN

DUGGAN WAS ORDERED to leave the *Goliath* as soon as he was able. After saying his farewells, he boarded one of the transport vessels, with nobody else to keep him company on the short journey. The tiny spacecraft brought him in dubious comfort to one of the landing pads at Pioneer's largest Space Corps base. From above, the internal screens of the transport showed a dimly-lit grid-pattern of dreary brick buildings, their grimness exacerbated by the driving rain and the fading early evening light.

Duggan left the transport behind, pausing only briefly to watch it take off into the darkening sky. The base was a hive of activity – there was a huge research lab here amongst many other facilities. The work within the walls of this lab never stopped and hardly slowed down at night. Duggan scarcely noticed the people scurrying around, or the vehicles which swished silently along the smooth roads. He didn't have far to go, so he chose to walk, ignoring the rain as it soaked through his clothing.

At the largest of the administration buildings, he took the steps two at a time. Inside, he stopped one of the staff officers. It appeared he was expected – the Space Corps was highly efficient when it came to the little details.

"You've been given an office on the second floor, sir," said the staff officer. "Your lodgings are in building nine-seven-five." She smiled apologetically. "You might want to take a car to get there."

"Thanks," said Duggan. "Any messages for me?"

"Admiral Teron has asked you to contact him as soon as you arrive, sir. *Any time of day or night,* it says here," she said, studying her screen. "Must be something important."

She was just making conversation, rather than fishing for information. Duggan left her and made his way through the building to his room. There was no need to ask for directions – these places were practically identical inside, whichever planet you were on and whichever base. *There must be a hundred thousand technical drawings for each warship, yet only a single architectural design for every base,* thought Duggan. He couldn't bring himself to smile at the idea.

There were no surprises waiting for him in his room either. It was a reasonable size, square and painted light blue. There was a desk, two chairs and a couple of pieces of furniture, the types of which Duggan forgot as soon as his eyes looked away.

"Let's see what Teron wants," he muttered, powering up his main screen. It didn't take long for the Admiral to respond, his face shimmering for a few seconds as the comms relays stabilised. From what Duggan could see of the background, he guessed Teron was still on the *Juniper*. His expression was unreadable.

"Captain Duggan," Teron said, his lips a fraction of a second out of sync with the image of his face.

"Sir."

"I'm not sure where to start. Your arrival has caused some consternation. Perhaps not *your* arrival as much as what it is you've brought with you."

"Sir, I've been aboard the Cadaveron. It looks like a wreck

from the outside, but I'm confident many of its major systems are still operational. We will be able to learn from it. Copy what we don't already have. The Shatterer battery we brought still has missiles inside. I'll bet we can strip them down and have a working prototype of our own in a matter of months."

"I'm aware of the opportunities you've presented us with, Captain Duggan. In fact, I think you've done us a great service. We've never even tried to capture one of the Ghast vessels before, let alone accomplished it." Teron steepled his fingers. "But damnit man, why do you have to bring baggage with everything you do? The *Goliath*'s cargo was irreplaceable – it'll take months to remake all the bespoke equipment."

"I'm sorry I had to dispose of it, sir. There really was no other way. Besides, the Ghasts know how to find Everlong now. Given our recent policy of avoidance, I can't imagine we'll try to restart mining operations any time in the near future. For every one ship we send, they'll send two."

"I've no doubt you're correct," said Teron. He leaned forwards. "This is something new, Captain Duggan. The first sign of the Ghasts using something, rather than destroying it outright."

"They might have a shortage of Gallenium, sir. It's rare enough that we're only finding traces of it on every planet apart from a handful."

"We can hope they're running into supply problems. We don't know where the Ghasts' home planets are, but we can be sure they're a long, long way from Everlong. Once our new warships come into service, we'll have more than enough spare to intercept the enemy heavy lifters as they try to ferry the metals home."

"They deployed a Shatterer tube, sir," said Duggan, reminding Teron of the fact. "Next time there may be ten such emplacements. Or twenty. We don't even know what their maximum targeting range is – it could be that their lifters can operate in safety under the umbrella of their missile batteries."

"You've seen how the new Lambdas can have their guidance disabled. We can sit a million kilometres out of orbit and launch them in a straight line into the Ghast mining operations. Even a Vincent class has the processing grunt to land a strike in time with the planet's rotation."

"A single Cadaveron in orbit could shoot down thousands of Lambdas with their targeting and guidance disabled. We need something better than that."

"We've got people working on it, Captain," said Teron. "Anyway, we're getting off topic."

"What was the topic, sir?"

"I've been asked to give with one hand and take with the other," Teron replied. "I'm to congratulate you on your fine work under trying circumstances. Bringing back an enemy vessel is something the Space Corps appreciates. There are a number of people on the Confederation Council who are speaking about you in positive terms. However, I've also been asked to reprimand you for your reckless endangerment of the *MHL Goliath* and its original cargo. We might be at total war, but that doesn't mean our funds can be wasted. Others on the Council are asking where their money has gone to. In addition, you had the chance to escape from Everlong much earlier than you did and your delay increased the chances of the Ghasts finding and destroying a Class One Heavy Lifter."

Duggan knew it was a load of crap, but he was sure Teron was just relaying a message. "What's going to happen, sir?" he asked.

"Desk duties for the moment, Captain Duggan. While the investigation into your mission is completed." Teron glanced to one side, as if he wanted to be certain no one was listening. "Don't worry about it. The Space Corps can't be seen to lose billions of dollars at the drop of a hat. We have to fight for our reputation, particularly when there are many citizens of the Confederation who are asking why we let Charistos and Angax be annihilated."

"Could we have done more?" asked Duggan.

"We both know the superiority of the Ghast warfleet. We could have dashed our ships against theirs without stopping them. The fate of those two planets was sealed as soon as the Ghasts learned of their coordinates."

Duggan couldn't deny Teron's words made sense. Even so, it didn't sit easy with him. "It's a shame we let them get ahead of us. We could have stopped them in the early years."

"Everything we know about them suggests they respect strength," said Teron, not answering directly. He opened his mouth to say more and then closed it again.

"Admiral Slender told me about our attempts to negotiate with them, sir."

Teron snorted. "Surrender, more like, that's closer to the truth of what we offered. We've seen how they respond to weakness."

"We started out stronger than they were and they didn't back off," said Duggan.

"Maybe they like a challenge. Who knows why they're doing what they're doing? I wish we'd chased them down when we still could and destroyed each and every one of their ships!"

"Their planets too?" asked Duggan quietly.

"I don't know, Captain Duggan. If it was the only alternative, that's what I'd do. In a heartbeat."

"I tell myself that as well, sir, and then in my head I see an image of a planet disintegrating on the *Crimson*'s viewscreen."

"They've called it the Planet Breaker – that weapon on the *Crimson*," said Teron. "I don't know who chose it, but the name stuck and that's what they call it now."

A thought came to Duggan, which tightened his skin and left him feeling cold with the potential of it. "The Cadaveron must hold the information we need about their ships, their planets. Maybe even their history and their way of life."

Teron frowned. "I'm sure there's plenty of information in its data arrays. You do know their AI technology is more advanced than ours? It's not like we're going to be able to plug it into one of our data facilities and stream off what we need. We might get something, but I'm sure each and every string will be so heavily encrypted we'll take years to decode it, assuming we can manage that. We couldn't even break our own encryption methods by brute force. It's only because we have the keys that we can access our own repositories. The *Juniper*'s AI cores are about the fastest we can manage and I doubt they could get anything from that Cadaveron's arrays before this war has played out one way or another."

"I'm not suggesting we use our own technology, sir," said Duggan. "One of my squad – a soldier – was able to make the Dreamer core on the *ESS Crimson* hack itself. That core is fast and it's focused. It might be fast enough to give us access to the Cadaveron's databanks. If a self-taught hacker can do it, I'm sure the thousands of programmers available to the Space Corps could work something out between them."

Teron stared straight ahead, his eyes piercing and dark. "Captain Duggan, I think you might have just come up with an idea." He banged the table with his fist and gave a bleak smile. "If you're right and this works, it could turn the war on its head. Or at least get back some of the advantage we've squandered." His eyes became distant and he talked, more to himself than to Duggan. "We've got three available shipyards on Pioneer big enough to take a Cadaveron. It's leaking antimatter. The dock in the Atican Desert is a thousand miles from anywhere. We can unload it there. The *ESS Crimson* will fly at Light-V. That makes less than four days travel from New Earth to Pioneer. We've got teams there, good teams. Interfacing the two systems will be the hard part. We managed it before, there must be records. If not, there'll be audit logs on the *Crimson*."

Duggan watched, impressed as Teron ran through the details of making it work. He didn't always betray the qualities which had made him an Admiral, yet he seemed to possess an almost encyclopaedic knowledge of the Space Corps organisation.

"Is there anything I can do to help, sir?" asked Duggan, interrupting the flow of words.

"Not for the moment, Captain Duggan. I'm afraid nothing has changed with regards to your desk duty. I must insist you remain on Pioneer. There'll be plenty of paperwork for you to shuffle until we conclude the investigation into your unauthorized cargo drop."

"What happens then?" Duggan hadn't expected any other response from Teron. There were times when even his best wasn't good enough.

"Another Vincent class, another mission. I thought you'd know that by now." The last words weren't said unkindly. "Don't worry - I'll get you your crew. They're grounded as well, not that your commander will be going anywhere outside of a hospital anytime soon."

Duggan couldn't bring himself to offer thanks. He reached across to the screen and ended the call, his mood already turning sour.

CHAPTER NINETEEN

DAYS PASSED and the days became weeks. Duggan didn't class himself as a desk officer and he hated being confined for hours on end in the same room, which was ironic given how much he craved to be back on the bridge of a warship. His in-tray remained full, owing to the fact that he did his best to ignore the contents. His rank gave him the ability to deflect much of what was thrown his way and nobody seemed interested in speaking to him about it. This period of enforced quiet was doubly hard for him to bear, coming as it did so soon after the eighteen-day journey from Everlong to Pioneer. On one of his visits to Commander McGlashan in hospital, she spoke to him about it.

"What were you expecting to happen?"

"I'm a realist, Lucy and I genuinely thought they'd give me another ship straight away. This whole thing about having to put me on desk duty over some missing cargo stinks to high heaven."

She smiled. Her strength had returned and it wouldn't be long until she was allowed to leave the medical facility. "Admiral Slender's never going to forget. He's the head honcho, remember?"

"That he is. I'm sure I'm not foremost in his mind at every hour of every day. He can't micro-manage everything I do within the Corps."

"Are you so sure? It wouldn't take much – a word here, a mention there. I'll bet he gets a report about you put on his desk every week or every month."

The thought was depressing. "What a waste of everything!" said Duggan. "A waste of his son's potential, a waste of his father's life spent haunting mine. All because of this damned war!"

"Look on the bright side, John. If they manage to crack the Cadaveron's AI, you might be the main reason humanity comes back fighting. If we can find out where the Ghasts live, it gives us a huge opportunity."

"To kill billions more? Tens of billions?" He shook his head. "The price of winning goes up every time I hear it mentioned."

"They've pushed us to it," she said. "Don't ever forget that. Your anger should be directed at them, not at what action the Confederation may be forced to take."

"You're right. Of course you're right." He changed the subject. "Two more weeks till you're out of here?"

"That's what the doctor said. Ten days if I'm lucky. I'll be whole again in seven, after that it's a case of observation to make sure everything's working properly. There'll be lots of pills, I'm sure. I feel weak and soft already." She smiled. "I need to hit the gym, or get back to some proper action, instead of watching the news all day."

"I think I'd rip the tubes from my arm after a week on that bed."

"Don't think I haven't thought about it." Her face became serious. "Have you heard anything? About the Cadaveron or the *Crimson*?"

"They unloaded the Cadaveron hull into a dock a couple of

days after we returned. I know the *Crimson* arrived five days after that. It's hard to keep things like that secret – there's always someone from the press keeping an eye on the dockyards. If not, there are plenty of spacecraft enthusiasts watching to see what's coming and going. Other than that, it's all been locked down tightly. I've spoken to one or two people and they're as much in the dark as I am."

"They must be giving this the top-top-secret treatment."

"You can see why they'd not want anything to get out. Hope that comes to nothing can produce unpleasant results."

"Anger and revolt."

"It's not what the Confederation needs right now, nor the Space Corps."

Another ten days passed and Duggan remained pessimistic that he'd ever adapt to the enforced inactivity. He saw Chainer and Breeze in passing and nothing more. They'd been drafted in to work at the research lab. They weren't capable of contributing to anything cutting edge, but they were experienced officers and able to provide input at various stages of a project's development. Duggan envied them for having the chance to throw themselves into something. He would have volunteered to help if it wasn't for the fact he'd be automatically disqualified because of his seniority. The Space Corps wanted him at a desk, yet they also wanted him to remain available.

Late one evening, a message arrived while Duggan was still in his office. The bleeping on his receiver somehow conveyed an urgency and Duggan read it immediately. *You are ordered to the Atican Shipyard. Transporter vessel Nine-Five. Do not pack, do not delay. Teron.*

Duggan looked at the words for a moment and then deleted the message. His inbox was always empty – he hated the thought of having the old messages waiting for him every time he checked for something new. It felt like having unfinished business. He left his office, letting the door close itself silently behind him. Something told him he wouldn't be coming back.

Transporter Nine-Five was a standard model, boxy, stubby and reliable. It waited in the middle of landing pad number three, with lights on and its low-powered gravity engines humming smoothly. The side ramp was extended and more light spilled from the interior, illuminating an area of the concrete. There were three figures on the ramp, no more than animated silhouettes. Duggan hurried across, recognizing the voice of Lieutenant Breeze before his eyes could resolve the man's details. Chainer was there was well.

"Captain," said Chainer, offering a salute which Duggan returned. "Do you have any idea what we're doing here at this time of night? I was just about to turn in." He waved at the third man, whom Duggan didn't recognize. "This here's the pilot. He says he's been told to wait until the three of us are onboard, then we're off to a shipyard somewhere I've never heard of."

Duggan set his gaze on the pilot. The man was stocky and with a helpful face. "Only three passengers?" Duggan asked.

"Yes, sir. Lieutenants Chainer and Breeze, and one Captain Duggan. I take it I have all three of you present, in which case we can set off right away once you've seated yourselves."

"There's a fourth passenger," said Duggan.

The pilot looked confused. "I was only told about three, sir. Do I need to wait?"

"Yes, you do. I need access to your comms."

Only the pilot was meant to operate the transporter's comms and for a second it looked as if the man might stand his ground. He was wise enough to know which fights were worth fighting. "All yours, sir. We're already behind schedule. They're going to start giving me crap about blocking this pad soon."

"I'll handle that," said Duggan, entering the transporter.

Chainer and Breeze came after, their expressions speaking of a thousand unasked questions.

The cockpit was cramped, with a single battered chair covered in worn fabric. Duggan dropped into the seat and ordered the comms system to connect him.

"Hello?" said McGlashan.

"It's me. Are you still due for release the day after tomorrow?"

"Another thirty-six hours. Not that I'm counting."

"How do you feel?"

"Bored."

"I mean, can you walk? Can you get yourself to landing pad three? I need you here now."

Excitement, clear and unmistakable came into her voice. "A couple of needles to pull out and I'll be on my way. Assuming my legs remember how to walk."

"Take one of the cars outside," said Duggan.

"You're all heart, sir."

"See you in ten minutes."

The call was cut from the other end. Duggan climbed out of the cockpit. The pilot was standing uneasily nearby, clearly worried about letting someone unauthorized use the onboard systems. Duggan thanked him and told him they'd be waiting for a final passenger.

"What's going on, sir?" asked Chainer.

Duggan smiled in response. "I have no idea, Lieutenant. All I know is that I'm pleased to be sitting here, rather than sitting at a desk."

"There were some important tests to run on a new gravity drive modification tomorrow," said Breeze, sounding disappointed.

"I have a feeling we're going to hear about something of a greater significance in the near future."

"And you're not going to tell us what until we get there," said Breeze, not quite making it a question.

"I might be completely wrong, so you'll have to wait."

A few minutes later, a white-painted car sped across the open ground. It stopped on the pad, violating several regulations by doing so. Commander McGlashan got out, walking in a manner which suggested she'd be more comfortable with assistance. Duggan helped her onboard and she dropped gratefully onto one of the hard seats.

"That wasn't as easy as I'd hoped. I had to fight off a horde of medical staff who were insistent that I stay. In the end, I had to order them to leave me alone." She took a deep breath, though she didn't appear in any way flustered. "What's this all about?"

"You'll have to wait and see," said Chainer. "The captain likes his secrets."

"We're going to the Atican shipyard," said Duggan.

"I see," said McGlashan. She knew enough to guess the possibilities that might ensue.

"She knows. I can tell," muttered Chainer. "Maybe I should have gone for that promotion after all. Then I'd get to hear this stuff."

Duggan laughed. He shouted to the pilot that they were ready to leave. The man lifted a thumb in acknowledgement. The outer door slid shut and there was a barely-noticeable lurch as the transporter left the ground. As soon as they were in the air, Duggan felt elated. Even if the trip turned out to be something other than he was hoping, at least it had shattered the monotony of life on the ground.

The Atican shipyard was nine thousand kilometres away. The transport vessel was basic and it only had a single screen for the passengers, which showed the unending blackness of outside as they swept through the night. After an hour, the pilot came from his cabin to speak to them.

"We're almost there, folks. It's still night here so you get to see something special. I'll point the camera ahead so you can see what we're coming to. It's something of a sight, let me tell you." He returned to his cockpit and the view on the screen shifted. At first, it appeared as if there was a white glow on the horizon. They came closer and the glow expanded, until it seemed as if there was a pocket of daylight in this single area.

As they approached the shipyard, details became clearer. It was huge, covering at least one hundred square kilometres. There were five great trenches running in parallel. Four of the trenches were five kilometres in length, with the last one closer to ten. There was something in the longest trench – an incomprehensibly large hull was being constructed, which filled the whole length available.

"A new flagship," said Duggan. "I didn't know."

"They've hardly started it," said Breeze. "It'll be years."

"That one next to it's got to be a Hadron," said McGlashan. "They weren't wrong when they said this was a shipbuilding planet. The hull looks complete."

"Over there," said Chainer, pointing at the screen.

Of the remaining trenches, one was empty. The next one held the damaged hull of the Cadaveron. It looked undersized and misshapen in comparison to the other two vessels. The final trench contained a fourth spaceship, this one the smallest of them all by a considerable margin. Its sleek lines and purposeful shape spoke promises of death. In spite of its size, this was the most dangerous vessel in the Space Corps.

"The *Crimson*," whispered Duggan with longing.

CHAPTER TWENTY

THE TRANSPORTER LANDED without fuss on a pad situated in one corner of the shipyard. The artificial light was so bright, Duggan found himself shielding his eyes against the glare. It was a hive of activity – there were people and vehicles everywhere, moving continuously. There was evidently a great deal of order behind the chaos, as witnessed by the rapid progress of the construction.

The four of them crossed a few hundred metres of open ground on foot and entered one of the largest buildings in the compound. It was as busy here as it was outside and Duggan saw more than one individual with unnaturally wide eyes which suggested they'd been using stimulants to keep themselves going.

"Office Seven, Captain Duggan," said a smiling lady behind a desk. "You've been asked to attend alone."

"What about us?" asked Chainer.

"The Star Building's facilities are available for your use," said the lady. "If you wish, I can show you around, sir."

"That would be great," said Chainer. "I need a gallon of hi-stim to stop me falling asleep."

Duggan left them to it. The low number of the office was indicative of the likely importance of the occupant. He was therefore unsurprised when he found Admiral Teron within. The Admiral usually looked on top of his game. On this night, he looked haggard and close to exhaustion. The room was filled with the odour of freshly-brewed coffee and an oversized cup sat on his desk.

"Captain Duggan. I hear you've brought an additional visitor."

"I couldn't leave her behind, sir."

Teron didn't seem too interested. "Well, it might be for the best anyway. I'll trust to your judgement that Commander McGlashan is ready for duty."

Those were the words Duggan had desperately wanted to hear. *Ready for duty.* "Sir, I can vouch that she's ready."

"That's good. You'll need to be prepared for what's to come."

"What's happening, sir?"

"Events have moved on apace, Captain Duggan. There's a lot to fill you in on. It would normally be above your grade, but I've been given clearance to let you know most of it. Your ability to make the right decisions may be impaired if you're kept in the dark."

Duggan was intrigued. "I'm going somewhere?"

"Yes, you are." Teron took a deep breath and shook his head, as if to clear the fog from it. "We've found out where the Ghasts are. They live on nine worlds, the closest of them a long way distant from here. The statisticians tell me we had less than a one percent chance of finding them by accident in the next five years, if that gives you any idea of how remote the likelihood was. The Dreamer core, Captain Duggan. It smashed into the Cadaveron AI two days after we made the interfaces. We pulled out so much data we've had hundreds of our intel team working on it around the clock. And we found what we were looking for. Coordinates, flight paths, codes. We already had a faint grasp of their language, now we're working on putting together an interpreting module that we can install on every ship. Perhaps even in every spacesuit."

"What are we doing with this information?" asked Duggan.

"Coming to a decision has been...difficult. There have been a number of conflicting suggestions and much of our time has been spent in coming to a unified position." He flashed a tight smile, which told Duggan there was much the Admiral wasn't going to speak about. "Anyway, here we are and we have made progress. The ESS Crimson's sensors kept a record of your destruction of that planet. We've made the footage available to the Ghasts."

"Did they respond? Did they believe it was genuine?"

"The images could be forged, it's true. However, forensic examination would soon dispel the lie," said Teron. "We've never been able to confirm if the Oblivion battleship you were in combat with at the time survived the destruction. If it escaped, the Ghasts will have corroboration the information we provided them with is accurate."

"We simply showed them what we're capable of and nothing more? What could that achieve?"

"Give us a little more credit than that, Captain Duggan. We showed them what we could do. The threat was implicit enough. However, we have also provided them with the coordinates of one of their home worlds and threatened to use the Planet Breaker on it if they don't agree to a negotiated ending to the war. Only this time, it will be on our terms, rather than theirs."

"This is huge news, sir," said Duggan. He felt bewildered at the speed it had happened and was in grudging admiration of the Confederation Council's resolve in making the threat.

"We can't pat ourselves on the back yet. We've arranged to meet with them, where we hope to agree a truce. Afterwards, we'll look for a permanent settlement. In fact, there's a contingent

of our spacecraft on route to the meeting place already, led by the
ES *Devastator* and the ES *Lancer*."

Duggan gave a nod at that. "Two of our remaining Hadrons."

"And six Anderlechts besides. The Ghasts respond to
strength and we're determined to show them just that, yet
without risking too much of our fleet. They may still decide to
ambush us."

"Where are we meeting them?"

"That's one of the things I can't tell you."

It seemed strange that Teron had been told to withhold the
information, but Duggan had no time to ponder it. "Why am I
here? Where am I going?"

"You *are* going somewhere and your crew with you. We're
sending the *Crimson* to the rendezvous and you're going to
captain the vessel."

Duggan was speechless. Of all the things he'd expected to
happen, this was not one of them. "Sir, that's got our only Planet
Breaker in it. The engines and core are irreplaceable. What if
they blow it up?"

"If they decide to destroy the *Crimson*, they'll achieve little
apart from the deaths of you and your crew. We've removed the
Planet Breaker, Captain Duggan. It's in a laboratory elsewhere,
deep underground, where a team of our best men and women are
working to create blueprints for a new one. If we lost the engines
and core, it would be regrettable. In reality, they're unimportant
to the events which are now unfolding. We win or we lose based
on that single weapon. The *Crimson* will be a show of force and
intent, nothing more. Besides, the Ghasts are ignorant of the fact
we've only got one Planet Breaker, a state of affairs we've done
our best to encourage."

"I'll be more than happy to captain the *Crimson* again, sir. I
can't help but ask - why me?"

"You know the ship. In spite of my words, we're not eager to lose the vessel. There has been some opposition, but in the end, it was deemed that you were the most logical choice for this mission. I wouldn't expect it to be a permanent state of affairs. We've patched up the damage it suffered on your last flight, refitted the Lambdas with newer models and I believe the techs have managed to increase the cluster count to twenty, as well as fitting two new, additional Bulwarks. The *Crimson* won't be an easy target."

"It never was, sir."

"Now it'll be even less of one."

"Why didn't you send us out with the *Devastator* and *Lancer?*"

"We weren't in a position to release the *Crimson* until earlier today. The plans were already made, though we weren't able to put them into motion until a few minutes before I sent you that message. The *Crimson* is faster than everything else in the fleet. You'll have to travel at maximum speed in order to arrive in time. It's fifteen days out."

"Fifteen days? At Light-V, that means the rendezvous point must be an incredible distance from anywhere populated."

"That's precisely the reason, Captain Duggan! You can appreciate there's a lack of trust, particularly on our side. If the worst happens, we want the Ghasts to think our home worlds are in a completely different sector to where they really are."

"I take it we're leaving at once, sir?"

"Would you have it any other way?" Teron gave a genuine laugh. It made him seem younger, though the tiredness in his face returned as the laughter ended.

"I recall a series of unpleasant side effects from the *Crimson's* acceleration to lightspeed," said Duggan, remembering the injuries he and his crew had suffered. He had no desire to experience the feeling again.

"We've improved the life support modules. I'd give you the

technical details if I understood them. Suffice to say, the engineers believe they've alleviated the problem."

"Alleviated?"

"That's what they told me." Teron shrugged. "You'll have to go with what you're given."

"Has the infantry been assigned yet? I'd like to speak to the sergeant as soon as I get onboard. Beforehand if possible."

"You'll have no soldiers. It'll be you and your three crew. I had a commander assigned. I assume he won't be needed any more."

"No, sir, he won't. Why will there be no soldiers?"

"You won't be landing anywhere and we don't want to encourage you into a position where you might be tempted."

"You could simply order me not to," said Duggan quietly.

"That's been tried before, Captain. Anyway, you're dismissed. You have permission to board the *Crimson*. Your destination has been programmed in and locked down. You'll go immediately to maximum speed and, with any luck, arrive in time for the rendezvous. I expect negotiations will take several days, so I wouldn't be concerned about missing anything."

"Sir."

"And Duggan? This really is good news. For everyone in the Confederation. I hope that next time I see you, we'll be able to celebrate an end to the war. I don't like to speak too much of these things in advance in case my doing so somehow prevents them from coming to pass. All I can do is wish you good luck, in the same way I did the other captains on this mission."

"Thank you, sir."

Duggan spun on his heel and marched out of the Admiral's office. The corridor outside was near the building's reception and he could hear the sound of Chainer's voice somewhere ahead. Duggan walked smartly onwards, finding it hard not to break into a run.

When he arrived in the waiting area, all three stared at him with concern. It was Breeze who spoke first. "What's wrong?" he asked.

Duggan grinned at them. "There's nothing wrong. Quite the opposite, in fact. Come on, we've been given a mission."

He waved away their questions and took them outside. He didn't know how long he'd been in with Teron – long enough for the sky to have turned from black into the deep, pure blue of early dawn. Duggan commandeered a hovercar and the four of them climbed in. He pushed the vehicle to an unsafe speed and steered it across the shipyard.

"Why all the mystery?" asked Chainer.

"There's no mystery, Lieutenant. Or at least there won't be when we get onboard. I can't tell you about it until then."

"Where are we going? Have we got another ship?"

The rapid trip across the ground came to an abrupt end when Duggan pulled up alongside an object which was eleven hundred metres long. "We *have* got another ship, Lieutenant. This one, and we're departing as soon as we reach the bridge."

CHAPTER TWENTY-ONE

THERE HAD BEEN dozens of technicians crammed into the narrow corridors of the *ESS Crimson*. These technicians were all heading in the opposite direction to the boarding crew.

"Left it to the last minute, huh?" Chainer said to a man who hurried by. He got no response to his question.

By the time they'd reached the bridge and completed their brief pre-flight checks, they were the only four on the warship. "Internal sensors report nobody else onboard, sir," said Chainer. "We can take off whenever you want."

"Anything external?"

"No gantries or cranes overhead and nothing left anywhere on the hull. Not even a hammer or a nail."

Duggan laughed at that. There wasn't a single screw or nail anywhere on a fleet warship. "Engines?" he asked.

"Our gravity engines are warming up, sir. They were still hot from the last time they were powered. Maybe they were doing some last-minute tests."

"How are our weapons, Commander? Admiral Teron advised me we've had a few upgrades."

"He wasn't lying, sir. Twenty Lambda clusters with a dozen tubes in each. Range and payload look good. Ten Bulwarks, two of them newer than the others. They've all had updated tracking and targeting modules fitted. The originals must have been good enough that they've not needed replacing. They've been working fast to get this done so quickly."

"I don't think the technology of the base gun has changed much – only how they aim," said Duggan, relieved to hear their defences had been improved.

"We've got shock drones as well. Super-Warblers according to the tech specs."

"Super-Warblers?" asked Chainer. "Sounds like some kind of bird that can peck a whole tree down in one go."

"We should be happy the Space Corps isn't standing still, ladies and gentlemen. Anything that can give us an advantage should be celebrated," said Duggan.

"I'm celebrating, believe me," said Chainer. "I'll save my happy face for when these Super-Warblers have intercepted their first missiles."

McGlashan continued to run through their armaments. "We've still got the disruptors fitted, sir. There's no trace of the other weapon. It's not locked down like it was before – it's just plain gone."

"I know, Commander. Admiral Teron told me as much. They've taken the module away. It's called a Planet Breaker now – I don't know if that's how it'll be listed in the specification manuals."

"Planet Breaker?" said Breeze. "I can't think of anything better to call it. By the way, I'm denied access to set a course and destination. It's only the gravity drives that'll respond."

"We're not permitted to know our destination. It's been programmed in for us – we're going to sit back in comfort as we're steered to where we need to be."

"Strange," said Breeze. "Anyway, we can lift off now. The engines are good to go."

"I'm getting clearance from the shipyard flight control," added Chainer. "No other craft are permitted to land or leave until we're gone." He whistled. "This must be important."

"It is, Lieutenant. I'll tell you all about it as soon as we hit lightspeed." With those words, Duggan took hold of the *Crimson*'s control bars. He closed his eyes as the coolness of the alloy on his palms exactly matched the memory.

"The shipyard flight computer asks if we'll kindly engage our autopilot for departure," said Chainer.

"It really asked kindly?"

"Really, truly, sir."

Duggan allowed the autopilot to take over, with a pang of disappointment. "I never could refuse a polite request," he muttered.

The autopilot didn't delay. It confirmed the permission to depart and then lifted the *Crimson* directly into the air, taking care not to cause any turbulence that might affect those on the ground. The higher it climbed, the faster it accelerated.

"Two thousand klicks, three thousand," said Chainer.

"The deep fission drives are going through their build up procedures," said Breeze.

"Already?" asked Duggan with a frown. "I thought they'd wait until we were much further away."

"It sounds like this is important enough to ignore procedures," said Chainer.

"Twenty-nine seconds and we're out of here," said Breeze.

"We're at sixteen thousand klicks now, nothing on the fars. All set for a jump."

"Power at exactly one hundred percent. Twenty seconds remaining."

Chainer spoke, his voice suddenly worried. "Are we going straight to maximum speed?"

"Yes we are, Lieutenant," said Duggan. "As fast as we can go."

"Doesn't that mean we're going to wake up covered in bruises an hour from now."

"Ten seconds."

"I'd recommend you hold on to something, Lieutenant Chainer."

"Crap, I forgot about this."

"Three, two, one..."

The *Crimson* jumped. The engines whined as they unleashed their power, hurling the vessel onwards at an unimaginable velocity. It tore through space, pointing directly towards its pre-programmed destination. On the bridge, the crew felt a momentary giddiness which threatened to become outright nausea. There was a sensation of being crushed, as if by a billion cubic metres of water. The feeling passed almost before their brains could register it. Then, everything was as it had been before the jump. Duggan suppressed a smile when he saw how tightly Chainer had been gripping his chair.

"That wasn't so bad was it, Lieutenant?"

"You knew, didn't you, sir?"

"Knew what?"

"They've given us some additional life support modules."

"I think Admiral Teron may have said something about it," said Duggan, pretending to study one of his screens. Chainer huffed and puffed, but he was clearly relieved he wouldn't have to suffer unconsciousness every time they decided to do a full-power shift to lightspeed.

"We're just over Light-V and holding steady," said Breeze. "The *Crimson*'s lost none of her speed in the time she's been in

ANTHONY JAMES

dry dock. Our destination is fifteen days away. That's going to take us way out."

"Yes, it is, Lieutenant."

"Can you tell us what's going on now, sir?" asked McGlashan. In spite of her recent convalescence, there was a glow to her cheeks and her eyes were bright and inquisitive.

Duggan told them. He recounted his most recent conversation with Admiral Teron, to bring his crew up to speed with the situation. They deserved to know exactly what was at stake here, in order that it could shape their actions if they encountered any trouble ahead. Duggan knew the information was top-secret, yet he trusted his crew and preferred them to know what was going on.

When he heard the news, Chainer jumped up and cheered. Even the normally-reserved Breeze had a look of dazed happiness on his face.

"You mean this could all be over, sir? We could actually beat the Ghasts?" Breeze asked.

"Not beat, Lieutenant. Force into a position where they have no choice other than to make peace."

"Just like that?" asked Chainer, calming down. "They've killed billions of our people, sir. Do you think we'll let them get away with it?"

"What do you suggest? A punitive strike on a few of their planets, Lieutenant? Kill a billion more of theirs than they did of ours?"

Chainer looked ashamed. "That's not quite what I was saying. It just doesn't seem right somehow for them to get away with what they've done. It's not as if we asked for this war in the first place."

"Look at it this way," said McGlashan. "We were facing annihilation. Our entire species may well have been wiped out a few years from now. With this new weapon, we've been given the

166

opportunity to settle on our terms. If we negotiate properly, we could ensure the Ghasts make reparations for what they've done."

"There's not enough money for that," said Chainer.

"It doesn't have to be about money, Lieutenant. The lives of those people are lost. We can't get them back and we can't fix what's happened to them. We need to ensure there are measures to prevent this happening again. There's a chance to learn and for the Confederation move on from this war. Who is to say it won't make us harder, such that next time we find ourselves in this position, we act differently?" asked Duggan.

"I don't have any answers, sir. I can only say what I think and hope the people who make the deals exceed my expectations," said Chainer. "I want this to end as much as anyone."

"I know, Lieutenant. We should be pleased at the situation we find ourselves in. Sometimes we can try looking too far into the future and forget to enjoy what's going on in the present. We have fifteen long, boring days ahead of us in which to contemplate what might happen. And don't forget – we should be proud of what we achieved as a team, not only in returning the ESS Crimson, but in recovering the Cadaveron from Everlong."

"A shame we had to lose some people along the way," said Breeze.

"We couldn't have done it without their sacrifice," said Duggan, refusing to feel morose.

Talk of the dead brought the conversation to an inevitable end. Each of the four crew sat in quiet thought, watching the unending stream of updates and status reports which rolled from the Crimson's mainframe and onto their screens. The spaceship continued at an unchanging speed, hauling them towards a rendezvous which could define mankind's destiny.

CHAPTER TWENTY-TWO

"LOOK AT THIS!" exclaimed Chainer, delight plain in his words. "They changed over the food replicators as well! They must have been expecting to show members of the Confederation Council around the place."

"What's that you've got?" asked Breeze suspiciously.

"Steak and a hi-stim!"

"You sure know how to live," said McGlashan with a shake of her head.

"He's a true bastion of fine dining," joked Breeze.

Chainer ignored the banter and sat down with his plate and his drink. The smell of the meat swept aside the usual scent of oil and ozone. Breeze was the first to crack and he ducked outside to find the replicator, pursued by the sound of Chainer's laughter. Soon they were all eating plates of food which were acceptable facsimiles of the originals.

"Not bad," admitted McGlashan, eating a sandwich. "Better than what they served up in hospital."

Duggan had a cheeseburger that dripped clear, greasy liquid onto his metal plate. He'd promised himself long ago that he'd never have another burger, but on this occasion, he thought there were reasonable grounds for breaking his word.

"The trip may end up long and boring, but at least the food will be worth eating," said Breeze. "Even if it somehow feels wrong for me to enjoy it."

"Yeah, you sort of get used to the swill on a Gunner," said McGlashan. "I feel as if I'm cheating on all the other Vincent crews who have to put up with brown sludge."

"Some people will never learn how to enjoy themselves," said Chainer. He finished his can of hi-stim and burped with satisfaction. "Say, Captain? How come we're not allowed to know the location of this meeting with the Ghasts. Did Admiral Slender think you were going to run to the press and spill the beans about what's going on?"

Duggan put his empty plate aside. He remembered asking himself why he was being kept in the dark and hadn't had much time to think about it. "That's a good question, Lieutenant and one to which I don't have an answer. If anyone in the Space Corps was worried I'd go to the press, I think they'd be more concerned that I'd know about the Planet Breaker and about the potential for a negotiated settlement. If the newspapers learned peace was in our grasp, there'd be hell to pay if talks broke down and the fighting resumed. This makes me think there's a different reason for them keeping the location of the rendezvous a secret."

"Call me cynical if you like, but it seems really strange to hide where we're going from us," said Breeze.

"It does," mused Duggan. He crossed the tiny bridge until he was standing at Breeze's shoulder. "What information can you see about where we're going?"

"Nothing whatsoever. We're flying blind and trusting whoever programmed the mainframe to get us where we want to be in one piece."

"I don't think anybody wants us to be destroyed, Lieutenant.

There are easier ways to achieve that. Why bother telling me a load of secrets and then killing us for them? That would be completely senseless."

"There was a lot of secrecy surrounding the design of the *Crimson*, wasn't there, sir?" asked McGlashan. "Could the Space Corps want the ship to become lost, to save them having to answer difficult questions?"

"Questions from who?" asked Chainer.

"I don't know. Are there factions in the Confederation Council who have been kept in the dark about the Dreamer technology? Members of the press? Concerned citizens, wondering why an ancient hull is getting so much attention in a shipyard? It's not as if they can keep ship watchers from seeing it. There're plenty of civilians out there who know exactly which ships the Space Corps has in its fleet. I'll bet they're very interested in the *Crimson*. We might find the fission drives never switch off and we keep on going and going until we die of old age. They could make it seem like an accident."

Duggan wasn't convinced. "That's not how it works, Commander. They would have reduced our weaponry if they intended to do something as clumsy as losing us. Why upgrade the Lambdas and add extra Bulwarks?"

"I was just opening my mouth to see what came out, sir," said an unabashed McGlashan.

Duggan peered at Breeze's status screens. "We'd normally punch in a destination and the mainframe would take us there. Can you see our trajectory? We should be able to predict where we're headed if we know which direction we're going."

"That's the first thing I thought about, sir. I'm locked out of both course and destination details."

"Doesn't the *Crimson* have a greater level of authority than an Admiral?" asked McGlashan. "You could use that to override anything they programmed into software."

Duggan's interest levels were climbing, especially since he foresaw nothing else to keep him occupied in the coming two weeks. "I'll have a check of that," he said, returning to his console. A few tests left him disappointed. "I could see how they'd overlook something as unexpected as a ship having such a high authority. On this occasion, they've spotted it and disabled the facility."

"That would have taken Fleet Admiral Slender's direct approval?" asked Breeze.

"Or Fleet Admiral Gibson, though she no longer has frontline duties," said Duggan. "There are several people on the Military Oversight Committee who can override more or less anything."

"It doesn't really matter if they've hidden the direction of our travel, sir," said Chainer. "Our databanks hold records of all known stars. I can use the sensors to read which ones we pass and should be able to build up a picture from there. It'll not be as precise as simply knowing where we're going."

"It should be enough," said Duggan, rubbing his chin in thought. "How long will it take?"

"I could give you a guess ten minutes after starting. It won't be accurate, thought. The longer I have, the better an answer I can give you."

"There's plenty of time, Lieutenant. How about we give it twenty-four hours?"

"That'll be more than enough to give you something as close to perfect as we can achieve," said Chainer. "Honestly, I don't know why they even bothered trying to hide this information from us. Any good comms man could find out."

Duggan smiled to himself. "Don't belittle yourself, Lieutenant. If it was that easy, I'm sure they wouldn't have bothered taking steps to try and cover up our destination."

"Never underestimate the potential for another man's incompetence," said Chainer, a born cynic.

Duggan spent the rest of the day in the gym, which he was relieved to find they'd installed at some point recently. It was as if there'd been two separate teams working on the *Crimson* at the same time – one team to extract information about the Dreamer technology and a second to ready it for the next crew. It was better to be prepared than found wanting and the Space Corps had all the money and personnel it needed.

He spent a full seven hours in bed at his allotted time and rose feeling refreshed. The rest of the crew were on the bridge, their turn to sleep not yet due.

"What do we have, Lieutenant?" asked Duggan. "Do you have enough to tell me where we're going?"

"I'm just collating the latest batch of sensor readings, sir. We should have enough to be pretty accurate."

"Show me, please."

"Here we are," said Chainer, bring up a chart across the bulk-head. The image hung in the air, a carpet of black, speckled with near-invisible motes of white. "I've had to zoom right out, since we're travelling so far. I'll highlight the extents of Confederation Space and put a red marker at our current position and also where I expect us to be when we come out of lightspeed."

Two red dots appeared on the screen. Duggan could see them clearly enough, yet he couldn't stop himself taking a couple of steps closer. "That's way outside Confederation Space," he said. "Any idea what's there?"

"Not a clue, sir," said Chainer. "Our databanks hold nothing on the place we're going to."

"Has the information been hidden or expunged?"

"I don't think so. We've just never explored so far away from our home planets. We've got a map of one or two stars close by. Presumably the monitoring stations occasionally detect something new and add it to the catalogue. Otherwise, it's a blank canvas."

"What the hell are we going there for?" asked Duggan, his mind whirling.

"Beats me. You said we were going for somewhere neutral to negotiate with the Ghasts. Maybe this is the place."

"Something doesn't feel right," said Duggan. "And usually when something doesn't feel right, I get suspicious."

"A coverup?" asked Chainer.

"Why would they bother?" said Breeze, returning to the question they'd already found themselves unable to answer.

The questions plagued Duggan and refused to give him peace. He sat thinking for an hour, without being able to figure out why the *Crimson* had been sent fifteen days towards a place there was scant information about. He stood. "What's the standard maximum velocity of an Anderlecht cruiser?" he asked.

"Light-H?" said Breeze. "I think they've upgraded a few to go faster. It won't be many tiers higher. Why do you ask?"

"I'm trying to figure out the timelines. Admiral Teron told me they'd sent two Hadrons and a number of Anderlechts to negotiate with the Ghasts, except he didn't say how much earlier they'd left than us. They'll be forced to travel at the same speed as their slowest ships. How long would it take an Anderlecht to reach our current destination, if it travelled at Light-J?"

"Thirty-five days? Forty? Maybe a couple more," said Breeze. "There are a few variables stopping me predicting an exact duration."

"If we take the fastest-case scenario, in which an Anderlecht has been upgraded to Light-J and takes thirty-five days to get from A to B, they needed to leave approximately twenty days before us, in order for us to arrive in good time."

"Or as many as twenty-five days before us at Light-H," said Breeze.

"It was seven days from the time we brought the *Goliath* home, till they landed the *Crimson* in the dry dock next to the

Cadaveron. They'd have had to set up the interfaces, and Admiral Teron told me it took two days for the Dreamer core to unlock the Ghast AI. After that, they had to search through everything they'd extracted, make sense of it, and come to a high-level decision about how they were going to proceed. After that, they approached the Ghasts, who would have then needed to agree to negotiations and decide on the place for the negotiations to take place."

"It's starting to look a bit tight time-wise," said McGlashan.

"Very tight, Commander. So tight, I'm left wondering exactly what is going on."

"There could have been enough time, couldn't there, sir?" asked Chainer. "We were on Pioneer for over a month. If everything fell into place, it could have all worked out?" He sounded as if he were looking for confirmation.

"Yes, there could have been time, Lieutenant. In fact, there must have been, because however hard I try to guess, I can't for the life of me think why we'd be sent alone to a place that's not even on the charts. It makes so little sense, that I'm trying to convince myself everything must be fine."

"Except you're not convinced?" said McGlashan.

"I'm damned sure I'm not convinced, Commander. Now I'm left trying to decide what we're being used for. I had enough of this crap when we went looking for the *Crimson* in the first place."

None of the crew had answers and Duggan was left trying to figure out exactly what, if anything, was going on.

CHAPTER TWENTY-THREE

THE *ESS CRIMSON* came steadily closer to its destination. The crew had not been idle during this time. In fact, they'd applied themselves to the task of trying to disable the lockouts on the deep fission engines and the guidance systems. Duggan wasn't quite sure what he intended to do if they succeeded. First and foremost, he wanted to leave lightspeed so that he could use the long-range comms to speak to Admiral Teron. After that, he wasn't sure what the plan would be. If everything was above-board, he'd definitely be in for a stern lecture from Teron, but he could handle that. It was the hurtling into the unknown that he didn't like.

"They went to a lot of trouble, sir," said McGlashan. "This isn't an amateur job – they really didn't want us to play around with what they programmed in. There's all sorts of encryption and I wouldn't be surprised if they've fitted some additional hardware for extra security."

"I don't suppose there's one of those simulations you can run, is there Lieutenant? To let us take control again?"

"The *Crimson's* too old, sir. They probably didn't start adding that stuff until later. Besides, I'm not certain there'd be any sim that could do what we want."

"Particularly since you told the Space Corps how we'd disabled the Cadaveron's sensors, sir," said Breeze. "I imagine they realised we might try and pull that trick again. I don't think it matters anyway. We're coming out of lightspeed in less than five hours."

"Might as well see what they've got in store for us, eh?" asked Chainer. His tone suggested he had no genuine desire to find out and he sounded on edge. He'd been drinking hi-stim almost continuously and Duggan wondered if he should speak to him about it.

"It doesn't seem as if I'm going to be given the choice," said Duggan. "Another mystery to be solved."

"Not long to go," said McGlashan.

"I want everyone on full alert when we enter normal space. Weapons ready and a full sensor check of the area. Lieutenant Breeze, you will check to see if the fission drive lockout persists after our arrival. If any of you needs to rest, now is the time to do it."

None of them left the bridge. In truth, they'd arranged their sleep shifts around the projected arrival time. On a Gunner, the mainframe could dump you out of lightspeed many hours either side of the estimated time. The Dreamer core on the *Crimson* could pin it down to the minute, so the crew had been able to plan their rest breaks with a high degree of confidence.

As the minutes ticked down, the air on the bridge became progressively more stifling. Chainer kept blowing out his breath and running a finger around the inside of his collar. He shifted constantly, until his fidgeting started to bother Duggan.

"I need another hi-stim," said Chainer at last.

"I'd rather you held off for now, Lieutenant. It's making you jumpy."

"Sorry, sir. It happens when I'm on edge. I'm worried about where we're going to end up."

"That's fine. No more hi-stim until we've found what lies ahead," said Duggan. He didn't know if Chainer's excessive consumption was a matter for concern. It seemed better to err on the side of caution and ask him to stop drinking the stuff.

"Coming out of lightspeed in less than a minute," said Breeze.

"All weapons online," said McGlashan. "Disruptors powered up, countermeasures ready."

"I've programmed in a full scan to begin as soon as we slow down," said Chainer.

The engineers had done a good job with the life support and they experienced hardly any nausea when the *Crimson* appeared in local space. What they found was completely unexpected.

"We've been dropped twenty minutes out from the fourth planet orbiting an unknown sun," said Chainer. "It's a big old place from what I can see. A quick sweep shows nothing to be concerned about in our vicinity."

"Nothing at all?"

"Give me time, sir. There could be something behind this planet. They'd be hidden from view, though."

"Where're our warships?" asked McGlashan.

"Sir?" said Breeze. "The lock on the deep fission engines is still in place. However, I'm now locked out of the gravity drives as well."

"What do you mean, locked out?" asked Duggan sharply.

"Exactly that, sir. I have no control over our speed or direction."

"Are we moving?" Duggan checked his own console and discovered the *Crimson* was flying at one-hundred percent on the gravity drive. "What the hell is going on?" he asked.

"We're moving directly towards that planet, sir."

"Still no data on it?"

"Nothing in the *Crimson*'s arrays. Doesn't this stuff normally get fed from ship to ship as soon as they find somewhere new?"

"Not always," said McGlashan. "And only if you're within range of the ship carrying the new data."

"Uh, sir? You might want to look at this," said Chainer, fear in his voice. "I mean, *right now*."

Duggan jumped up and stood next to him. "What is it?"

"This planet is populated, sir. *Densely* populated. In fact, there's hardly a part of the surface which isn't covered in metal or other signs of building."

"A Ghost planet," said Duggan. A coldness swept into him, which dried the sweat on his skin immediately.

"I'm picking up activity in high orbit," said Chainer. "Coming towards us."

"Ours?"

"No, sir. I'd say it's two Ghost light cruisers."

"What's on the planet? Can you find our ships, Lieutenant? Could they have stopped here and been captured or destroyed?"

"That's a lot to look for," said Chainer. "I'll let you know as I find out."

"Damnit, I don't want us to fire on those Kravens and then find out our ships are on the other side of the planet, negotiating for peace."

"We could have got here first," said McGlashan.

"It'll take at least one orbit before I can give you an educated guess as to whether or not our warships are here, sir. On the other hand, I don't need a full orbit to tell you the Ghasts have at least five surface areas which could function as shipyards or landing areas. Those Kravens will be in firing range in a few minutes."

"Anything on the engines, Lieutenant Breeze?"

"I'm trying, sir. They're still pointing us straight ahead. No deviation in our course."

"Have we been programmed to crash?" asked McGlashan incredulously.

Duggan didn't think they were going to crash. He'd begun to realise exactly what they were here for and exactly why the *Crimson's* weapons systems had been upgraded. "I think we've been betrayed by our own side, Commander. Target those Kravens and launch everything we can bring to bear."

"I can see activity on three of the landing areas," said Chainer. "If I'm not much mistaken, there are at least a dozen gravity engines warming up. Big ones and small ones. They're scrambling everything they've got."

"Lieutenant Breeze, I want us to get away from here. Now."

"Not a hope, sir. Whoever's been playing with the gravity engines, they've done the same job as they did with the fission drives. It won't override from here."

"First Kraven at one-hundred and forty thousand klicks," said McGlashan. "Firing clusters one through ten."

The external missile coverings slid back to allow one-hundred and twenty Lambdas to burst away from their launch tubes. The coverings slammed back in less than a quarter of a second, leaving the *Crimson's* hull smooth and pristine once more.

At his console, Duggan tried everything he could think of to give him control of the ship again. He engaged the autopilot and disengaged it. He instructed the mainframe to begin full evasive manoeuvres, and he pulled at the manual control levers. Nothing worked. The *Crimson* followed its pre-programmed course exactly, bringing them ever closer to the Ghast planet.

"There's a power spike," said McGlashan. "And another."

"Disruptors," said Duggan. "They're trying to shut us down."

"It hasn't worked," said McGlashan. "We've got the Dreamer core. The first Kraven's launched missiles. Only thirty."

Only thirty. The number seemed pathetic in comparison to

what the *Crimson* could launch. Duggan found no satisfaction in the thought. "Shut down the second Kraven at one-hundred and sixty thousand klicks. Destroy it with Lambdas."

"The first Kraven's launching its countermeasures. Three Vule cannons and plasma flares. I don't think it'll be enough."

The Ghost light cruisers outgunned the Vincent class vessels in the Space Corps. The Kravens which had been equipped with disruptors could easily give an Anderlecht a run for its money. Against the swarm of Lambdas from the *Crimson's* arsenal, this one had little hope. The ten-metre missiles twisted and turned as they homed in on their target. The Kraven swung away, trying to hide behind its cloud of countermeasures. Some of the Lambdas were fooled and detonated against the white-hot plasma flares. A few more were shredded into pieces by a hurricane of Vule fire. The rest – almost fifty – crashed into the light cruiser at a combined speed in excess of three thousand klicks per second. Plasma warheads blazed with shocking intensity, engulfing the Ghost ship. When the light faded there was nothing remaining except a cloud of fine debris, scattering in all directions.

"Launch our own countermeasures?" asked McGlashan.

"Wait, please," said Duggan. "If we release too soon, we'll have flown past the cover of our drones when their missiles reach us."

"Ten seconds to impact."

"Launch countermeasures. Where's that second Kraven?"

"Shock drones away. Second vessel coming to one-sixty thousand klicks."

Thousands of reflective shapes spilled out from the *Crimson*, their tiny engines boosting them away on a course given to them by the ship's mainframe a nanosecond before they were launched. Each drone was slightly different in shape and each one gave off a mock-signature that was meant to confuse or fool missile guidance systems. The drone cloud was enormously expensive, but it did its job. Twenty-eight of the Kraven's missiles unleashed their payload onto a drone, rather than the *ESS Crimson*. The remaining two missiles were tracked and destroyed by depleted uranium projectiles from the four port-side Bulwarks.

"All thirty incoming missiles destroyed," said McGlashan.

"Sir, do you have any idea what's happening here?" asked Chainer. "In less than two minutes, we're going to have half of the Ghast fleet launching from the surface."

"We've been sent on a mission, Lieutenant. I'm certain it's not one of peace. If I'm correct, those Ghast ships won't reach us."

"Sir? I don't understand," said Chainer.

"Disruptors fired," said McGlashan.

"That's taken the fission drives to thirty percent," said Breeze. "Positronic output from the Kraven hull at close to zero."

"Fire," said Duggan. "Eight tubes, this time. No need to waste ammunition."

"Ninety-six missiles gone. They should impact a few seconds before the Kraven comes back online. I'm seeing activity on the weapons console, sir. I don't know what it is. There're utilisation spikes on the mainframe, like it's powering something up."

"I can access the gravity drives!" said Breeze.

Knowing it was too late, Duggan gripped the control rods and swung the *Crimson* away from the planet, still at full power. Deep within the hull of the vessel, something howled. The noise built rapidly until it was painful to hear.

"What the hell?" said Chainer, his words drowned out by the sound. Duggan saw realisation dawning on the man's face.

The floor and walls vibrated angrily, as if they fought to contain something of incredible ferocity. The howling turned to a whine, which dropped away to nothingness as quickly as it had started. On the bulkhead viewscreen the image showed the

Ghast planet breaking into pieces. It was slow at first, nearly serene. The *Crimson* was already far distant, so when the world behind them exploded, the crew were given a perfect, terrible view of it happening. The largest fragments split and split again, becoming smaller fractions of the whole as they cracked away from the centre. To Duggan's eyes, it appeared as if the pieces moved lazily, though in reality he knew they were travelling at hundreds or thousands of kilometres per second. The light cruiser they'd targeted was lost amongst the chaos, its destruction a certainty.

Ahead of it all flew the *ESS Crimson*, her gravity drives sufficient to keep the vessel ahead of the tumbling shards of a broken world.

"Planet Breaker," said Duggan, so softly he wasn't sure he'd spoken aloud.

CHAPTER TWENTY-FOUR

FOR A TIME, there was silence. No one spoke while they stared at the bulkhead screen. Eventually, Duggan switched it off. The bridge was eerily dark without the illumination it provided.

"The deep fission drives are available, sir," said Breeze. His voice was expressionless. "Want me to get them ready?"

"Where will we go?" asked Duggan. He sighed. "Hold tight for a moment, Lieutenant. I need to gather my thoughts."

"I've got Admiral Teron on the comms, sir. He wants to speak to you, privately."

"I don't give a damn what he wants. Put him through on the bridge open channel."

"Will do, sir."

Teron's voice spoke through the speakers positioned all around, giving it the appearance of floating in the air before them. "You have done what you have done, Captain Duggan?"

"Yes, sir, it's done." He felt too tired to shout his anger.

"I'd like to say well done, but I don't believe it's a time for congratulations. You should have been left in full control of the *Crimson* once the Planet Breaker discharged. I'm sending you a new set of coordinates. The meeting with the Ghasts is taking place, just not here." Teron sounded genuinely sorrowful.

"Where are we going, sir? If we're permitted to know."

"You're coming to Pioneer and bringing the *Crimson* with you."

"Why do you need us there?"

"To remove the Planet Breaker, of course. We're not even close to being able to copy it and it's far too valuable to have it flying around the universe."

"What about the negotiations? The fleet we sent to meet the Ghasts?"

"I'm sorry, Captain Duggan. We've already had our first meeting with the Ghasts. We showed them what we could do and they either didn't believe us or didn't think we'd have the determination to carry out our implied threats. We have another series of talks due soon. This time we decided it would be best if we showed our intent beforehand. To encourage them to pursue a more peaceful relationship with us."

"There must have been another way," said Duggan. "Conventional arms could have sent a message."

"This is the way we have chosen, Captain. It's finished now and we must look forwards to a brighter future for the Confederation."

"Why me? Why us?"

"I think you know the answer to that one, Captain. For what it's worth, I would not have chosen to handle matters in this way."

"Is the Space Corps planning to use the Planet Breaker again?"

"I genuinely hope not. We will see what the Helius Blackstar brings. That's where it started and that's where we should end it. Twelve days from this point and we should have news. Keep your fingers crossed that we achieve the result we want."

"What happens at Pioneer, sir?"

"No one will know about your mission and it must stay that way. We've got a dozen Vincent class fighters at the Pioneer shipyards, waiting for men and women to act as their crew. You'll be assigned to one and put onto your usual duties. Only this time, you might be able to perform them without an expectation that death will result from your endeavours."

"Yes, sir."

There was silence for a few seconds, as if Teron had gone. His voice returned. "If the war ends, there'll be no one we can thank more than you. You'll already know you won't get the recognition you deserve."

"It's not recognition I was looking for, sir."

"I know, Captain. I'll see you for a full debriefing once you return."

This time Teron didn't say anything more.

"He's gone," said Chainer.

"Sir?" It was McGlashan. She spoke hesitantly, unable to read Duggan's mood. "We should get away from here. The Ghasts will have definitely got a signal out. There'll be dozens of their warships inbound."

"You're right, Commander. There's no point in remaining. Lieutenant Breeze, get the fission engines going."

"Yes, sir. A course for Pioneer." Duggan detected the smallest suggestion of a question in the man's words.

"How far away from the Helius Blackstar are we?"

"Just shy of thirteen days, sir."

"That's where we're going."

The crew exchanged glances, though none of them said anything about this disobeying of a direct order.

"Fission drives at one hundred percent and calculating our course. Thirty seconds."

"Proceed when ready," said Duggan. "Remember what

you've seen here today. The price of peace is a harsh one to pay – on both sides."

"Never again," said Chainer.

The giddiness came, brushing up against the edges of nausea. Duggan felt his body tighten, before the sensation eased. The *ESS Crimson* flew away from the solar system in which the remains of the Ghast planet were left drifting. Some of the fragments were large enough to wreak devastating damage on the nearest planets and perhaps the sun itself. *It hardly matters,* thought Duggan. *There's nothing left to kill.*

"Light-V attained," said Breeze. "I have full control over our propulsion systems again."

"Until next time," said Chainer softly. "I'm not sure I trust this spaceship after what's happened."

"I agree with you," said McGlashan. "If I get the chance, I'm going to see if I can do something to prevent it happening again." She smiled. "I'm just not quite sure what."

"We've been properly screwed, haven't we?" said Chainer.

"Yes, Lieutenant. I'm sorry you had to be a part of it. That goes for each of you."

"I'd have rather been here than somewhere else," said McGlashan. "Not for the killing, just for being a catalyst." She looked uncertain. "I don't know what I'm trying to say."

"What happens when we get to the Helius Blackstar?" asked Breeze.

"I don't know, Lieutenant. We've been used as a tool, without our knowledge. I don't like the dishonesty. Maybe I feel we deserve to be there when they make peace. It's something we're owed."

"Won't the arrival of the *Crimson* piss the Ghasts off? They might think we're rubbing their faces in it." said Chainer.

"If they respect strength as much as the Space Corps believe they do, the Ghasts will appreciate the *Crimson*, rather than hate it. Whatever the truth, I'm damned well going to be a witness to the proceedings."

"They'll kick you out for this, Captain," said McGlashan.

"They might. Perhaps it's my time. If the war ends, they won't need people like me anymore. There's still time for this one last adventure." He grinned. "The bastards won't grind me down."

For once, the journey passed quickly, as if the speed of their travel somehow affected their perception of time itself. Duggan kept himself physically busy in the gym and tried not to brood over what had happened. Chainer estimated from his sensor records that there'd been over fifteen billion inhabitants on the Ghast world – the number was so big it felt unreal. Duggan tried to grasp it and picture the enormity of the Confederation's actions and discovered how futile it was. One phrase returned to him again and again, when he slept and when he was engaged in his daily duties. *It was us or them.* He often asked himself if there was an alternative. In the end, he gave up thinking about it. He'd been given command of the mission because of one man's hatred and spite. Duggan couldn't allow that man to be victorious.

Mid-way through the twelfth day, the four of them were on the bridge, contemplating what was to come.

"What happens when we get there, sir?" asked Chainer. "I don't think the Space Corps fleet will open their arms and welcome us."

"They'll have little choice," said Duggan. "If the Ghasts get the impression something is wrong, they may try and capitalise on it."

"By shooting us to pieces?"

"Probably nothing so overt, Lieutenant. If the Confederation doesn't look united, it may affect the Ghasts' attitude during the negotiations. They might become stubborn or hold out for an unreasonable settlement."

"The fleet will *pretend* to welcome us with open arms," said McGlashan. "It's only afterwards we'll be punished."

"There's only one person who'll be punished," promised Duggan. "And I won't go down without a fight."

"How will the talks happen, sir?" asked Breeze. "Will they meet face-to-face?"

"I doubt it," said Duggan. "There's no common language."

"So how do we speak to each other? Did you say something about us having developed an interpreter?"

"Admiral Teron said we'd figured it out. He was a bit cagey about it."

"Want me to dig around in the comms for anything new?" asked Chainer. "They've pinned a lot on the *Crimson* – it would make sense for them to have fitted the ship with all the important stuff."

"Go on, have a look," said Duggan. "I'm interested."

Chainer went quiet as the others talked about the potential outcomes.

"I hope something good comes from what's happened," said McGlashan. "It would break my heart if we had to destroy more of their worlds."

"Do I recall you saying it was a price worth paying?" asked Duggan.

"I can't settle on what I think is right. That either means everything is right or nothing is. Ultimately, I don't want to die and I don't want humanity to be wiped out for a war no one understands. If the only alternative to our extinction is theirs, I'd pay the price."

"I've got something, sir," said Chainer.

"What have you found?"

"New language modules, tucked away amongst a selection of New Earth sub-dialects."

"Hidden?" asked Duggan.

"I don't believe so. Probably just shoved in there at the last minute. I'm running a couple of the language modules up onto the bulkhead screen." The screen in question lit up with rows of characters and symbols. "This is the written version of the language – it looks just like what we saw on the Cadaveron and in the Shatterer battery."

"It's definitely the same," said Duggan.

"There's an audible version as well," continued Chainer. There was a series of harsh, barked sounds from the bridge speakers. "I think that's Ghast for *hello*."

"Doesn't sound very friendly," said Breeze. "From the tone it sounds more like *piss off* than *hello*."

"It probably needs some fine tuning," said Duggan drily. "At least we'll be able to understand any Ghast broadcasts that come our way."

"We are going to kill you," mimicked Chainer, trying his best to replicate the roughness of the Ghast speech.

"Give us all of your hi-stim," said Breeze in a similarly rasping voice.

"Enough," said Duggan without anger, waving them to silence. "Lieutenant Chainer, I want you to keep those language modules running constantly when we get there. If there's anything important happening, I'd like to hear about it."

"Aye, sir."

"How long, Lieutenant Breeze?"

"Just less than one hour, sir."

"Bring us out of lightspeed a little way out. How far from the Blackstar is the planetary system where we found the *Crimson*?"

"Too far for gravity drive travel."

"Take us to three hours away from the Blackstar, then. I don't want anyone to become alarmed by our unexpected arrival. I'd like them to have plenty of warning we're coming."

"And for us to have plenty of time to see what's ahead?" asked McGlashan.

"Exactly right, Commander."

"I've made the adjustments," said Breeze.

"Fine. Put your feet up while you can, ladies and gentlemen. I'm certain things will be interesting when we get there."

CHAPTER TWENTY-FIVE

THE FIRST IMPRESSIONS were not interesting at all. "There's nothing here, sir," said Chainer. "The fars and super-fars are showing a total blank."

"Can we see the wormhole from here?"

"We're a long way out, but I should be able to get it up on the screen. Here it comes."

"Docon't look like much," said Breeze, "Like a black dot on a sheet of black paper."

"The screens can only go so dark," said Chainer. "They're incapable of showing anything darker than zero light. If you watch, I can overlay some movement indicators to show where it is."

Their destination became visible on the bulkhead screen – it was a circle of pure darkness. A swirl of red, computer-generated specks surrounded it, gradually spiralling inwards.

"How fast at the centre?" asked Duggan. It had been a while since he'd studied the physics of a wormhole.

"It's not the speed, so much as the weight," said McGlashan.

"And the overwhelming, crushing force of gravity," said

Chainer. "We've got nothing capable of surviving a trip through one. If we managed to overcome that obstacle, the next problem is to have enough power to escape the pull at the far end. We'd then need to figure out where the other end actually is. It's conceivable a ship could emerge so far distant that even our comms would take weeks, months or years to reach home."

"Yet the Dreamers got something through," said Duggan. "One of their ships was intact."

"The *Crimson* might stand a chance," said Breeze, rubbing his chin in thought. "At least as far as the propulsion goes."

"The gravity engines couldn't pull us clear of that," said McGlashan. "Not a hope."

"No, but if we engaged the fission engines at the exact moment of arrival, I reckon she'd be able to get clear."

"You'd need to know the precise amount of time you were in the wormhole," said Chainer. "That would take an immense amount of processing power."

"We're carrying the most advanced core in the Confederation. I'm certain the Ghasts have nothing like it," said Duggan. He saw their faces. "Don't worry, we're not planning a trip through the wormhole. It's time humanity studied them in greater detail, I think. While the Space Corps has unlimited funding, it would be a good idea to learn a few things. The Dreamers came twice, which suggests they didn't give up after the first attempt."

"We don't need any more crap going on," said Chainer. "The Dreamers can stay exactly where they are, wherever that is."

"I'm taking us straight towards the wormhole," said Duggan. "I have no idea where the proposed negotiations are meant to take place. I'll assume it's close to the Blackstar, since that's the place Admiral Teron mentioned. Lieutenant Chainer, continue with an in-depth scan of the area. In particular I'd like you to focus directly ahead to where we're going."

"If they're on the other side of the wormhole, we won't see anything until we circle around it. I'm sure I don't have to remind you how these things do crazy tricks with the sensors."

"That's fine, Lieutenant. I simply need warning of whatever there is to be seen."

"I'll keep on it. At this distance, it takes longer to sweep the area."

"Is there no comms chatter?" asked McGlashan.

"Again, we're a bit far out, Commander. Military comms are tightly focused and hard to intercept if you're not the intended target. I'm not surprised there's nothing to be heard."

Duggan frowned at the thought. "Our fission signature should have been easy enough to spot when we arrived. Why haven't we been contacted?"

"There's a chance it could have been missed," said Breeze. "We're quite a distance. On the other hand, I'd be having stern words with anyone on my team who didn't notice a ship emerging from Light-V a mere ten million klicks away."

"Try hailing the *Devastator* directly," said Duggan. "Tell them we've come for the party."

"There's no response, sir. I've sent out a request on her direct channel and there's no answer. I've also tried routing through the *Juniper* and I got the same thing."

"Try the Hadron *Lancer* as well," said Duggan, trying to remember if Teron had mentioned the names of any other vessels due to be in attendance.

"Nothing from the *Lancer*."

"Are you sure the *Devastator* and *Lancer* are here, sir?" asked McGlashan. "Admiral Teron has told you a whole pack of lies up to now. They may have sent the *Archimedes* or the *Maximilian*. Hell, they might have sent a lone Gunner with Admiral Slender himself on the bridge."

"The skill with telling lies is to keep them as simple as possible," Duggan replied. "I'm convinced Teron stuck as close to the truth as he was able. I believed him when he said there was a delegation and I believe the *Devastator* and *Lancer* are with it."

"Wherever they are, they're not answering the telephone," said Chainer. "That means the only place they could be is across the wormhole from our position."

"I'm altering course to take us around the other side," said Duggan. "Keep searching until I tell you otherwise. If there's an object bigger than a speck of dust, I want to know about it."

"I'll have to pause for a moment, sir. I've got Admiral Teron here. He's asking to speak to you."

"Don't keep him waiting," said Duggan.

Teron spoke, his voice fluctuating in volume because of the distance. "Duggan, what the hell are you doing there?" He sounded angry and worried.

"Sir, I figured I should show my face at the negotiations. To let the Ghasts know we mean business."

"Damnit man, it's all gone to shit! Get out of there now and come back to Pioneer." Teron didn't usually swear. Duggan caught McGlashan's eye – something serious was wrong.

"Sir, what's happened?"

"That's not for you to know. Leave that sector and return at once. That's a direct order, Captain!"

Duggan took a deep breath. "Sir, please tell me what is wrong. We are armed and ready to assist with any conflict."

"Whatever it is, you can't deal with it. We've lost communication with our delegation fleet. Ten ships, incommunicado."

"There's nothing on our sensors. Have the Ghasts double-crossed us?"

Teron sighed. It wasn't the sigh of a man who was frustrated – it was the sigh of a man who was neck-deep in quicksand and didn't know how to get out of it before he was dragged under. Duggan was the man at the edge of the pool, offering a stick to pull him out. Teron took it with both hands. "If it's the Ghasts, they're putting on a good show of it. I've spoken to their overall fleet commander personally and he has told me they've lost track of their ships as well. They sent two Oblivions and eight Cadaverons that we're aware of."

"They were really beating their chest," said Duggan. "Is there any trust remaining?"

"I can't be certain. We are not on the best of terms, but I don't think they're desperate to have another one of their planets destroyed. They're hoping our dealings are honest."

"What happens next? Are we sending more spacecraft to this sector?"

"Not a chance, Captain Duggan. We're going to sit tight, rather than throw more of our dwindling fleet at an unknown threat."

"What about the Ghasts?"

"They can do whatever they choose. They have more ships than we have, but they lost a number of them when the *Crimson* destroyed Lioxi. Plus whatever casualties they may or may not have suffered at the Helius Blackstar."

A name to the place at last, thought Duggan. "We're going to stick around for a look, sir. The *Crimson*'s faster than anything else in the fleet and with more weapons than anything this side of the *Maximilian*. I won't let a chance at peace fail because we lack intel."

"I won't give you another direct order on the issue, Captain Duggan. I can see I'd be wasting my breath. Don't lose the *Crimson*, whatever you do. If the Ghasts aren't playing fair, it's the only hope we have left."

"No orders from you and no promises from me, except one, sir," Duggan replied grimly. "I promise I'll do my best, nothing more."

"It had better be enough, Captain. Good luck."

"He's gone," said Chainer.

Duggan blew out and realised he'd been holding so tightly onto the *Crimson*'s control bars his knuckles were white. "How did he know where we were?"

"The *Juniper* must have logged my comms request and told someone we were broadcasting from way off our expected location. I'll have to remember they can do that next time I try routing through the *Juniper* or one of our monitoring stations."

"It's no problem, Lieutenant. I'm glad I got to speak to Admiral Teron."

"Nothing is ever simple," said McGlashan.

"Life on the *Detriment* was a lot more straightforward," said Chainer. "Even if it felt like a peashooter in comparison to the *Crimson*."

"Lieutenant Chainer, resume your efforts in scanning the area. I need to know about *anything* that shouldn't be here. We may also be looking for debris."

"I will do, sir. The first sweep completed while you were speaking to Admiral Teron. I've managed to scan in a narrow cone between here and the wormhole. There's no object greater in length than four kilometres. If there was a Hadron or Oblivion anywhere in that cone, I'd know about it. I'm running a sweep for anything two kilometres long, which will tell us if there are any Anderlechts or Cadaverons. I get this feeling I'm going to come up empty-handed."

Duggan agreed with Chainer's gloomy assessment. Nevertheless, they had to keep on searching. "I'm holding course. We'll circle the Blackstar at ninety minutes distance. That should be close enough for you to detect anything."

"Anything big," said Chainer.

"We're staying for as long as it takes to get answers. I'd prefer to know sooner rather than later."

On the bulkhead screen, the Helius Blackstar was now to the

far right as Duggan's course took them around it. The gravity was immense, but it was only the final million kilometres that would cause the *Crimson* any problems with maintaining its distance. Ninety minutes out on the gravity drives was a little over ten million kilometres, which gave plenty of margin in case something went wrong. He could have taken them closer and completed the circuit a few minutes faster, but for some reason he felt reluctant to do so. A voice in his mind chimed up to suggest it was his body's in-built primal fear of something with such colossal power that it utterly dwarfed anything made by mankind or Ghast alike.

After two-thirds of a circuit, Chainer spoke up. Duggan recognized the concern in his lieutenant's voice at once.

"Sir, I've got something. Wreckage, I think."

"Ready on the weapons," said Duggan.

"As ever," McGlashan replied.

"Anything running under its own steam?"

"Definitely not. I'm analysing now."

"I can read some of it," said Breeze. "Positrons."

"Ours?"

"Some of ours. Some Ghast as well, if I were a betting man. There's something strange about it. Usually there's a pattern from a warship engine, even when it's been destroyed. It'll pulse out in a defined wave. These emissions are completely irregular."

"You're sure they're ours?"

"I can confirm what Lieutenant Breeze says, sir," said Chainer. "It's part of a Space Corps hull. Three hulls to be precise."

"Do you know which vessels?"

"Can't be sure. If you wanted me to guess, I'd say from the thickness of the plating on one of the pieces, we've lost the *Lancer* or the *Devastator*. If you wanted me to guess some more,

I'd say there are parts of an Oblivion floating a couple of hundred thousand klicks away."

"Any other details? I need something that'll tell me what's happened here. Who betrayed who? If none of our ships have reported in, that means we've lost them all. It beggars belief to think they might have been destroyed so quickly that not a single one was able to send a report or a warning."

"More wreckage, directly ahead," said Chainer. "I'd say this is predominantly Ghast – parts of a Cadaveron, drifting towards the Blackstar. There are some big pieces amongst it. There could be more than one vessel."

"Can you detect signs of damage?" asked Duggan.

"They were hit by something hot. I'm not sure if it was missile plasma."

"What do you mean you're not sure?"

"It's not clear-cut what's caused the heat damage, sir. It could be plasma."

"You think it's something else?"

"I'd need more time to analyse and from closer range."

"We'll be going past the wreckage anyway," said Duggan. "The more I see, the less I like."

"Sir, I'm detecting something else. It's a long way away – I'd guess it's twenty klicks to a side. I have no idea what it is."

"Where?" asked Duggan sharply.

"We're on course to meet it. It would have been directly behind the Blackstar from our arrival position."

"I'm convinced the Ghasts have nothing close to that in size," said Duggan. "What the hell?"

"What if they've come back, sir?" asked Chainer.

Duggan sat still for a moment as the answer to Chainer's question came to him. "The Dreamers," he said.

CHAPTER TWENTY-SIX

DUGGAN WAS CONVINCED – the mysterious species of aliens had returned. The little he knew about them suggested they were hostile and their appearance would explain the destruction of the human and Ghast fleets.

"How far away is it?" he asked.

"An hour away on the gravity drive, sir."

"I've seen enough," said Duggan. "Get the fission drives ready."

"On it. Where to, sir?"

Duggan's mind raced through the options. "We don't know if they can follow through lightspeed," he said. "Bring us out somewhere halfway between here and Pioneer. At least if they follow, we won't have led them anywhere important."

"The unknown vessel has performed a hop, sir," said Chainer. "They disappeared from where I first saw them and reappeared less than thirty minutes distant. The time which elapsed between them disappearing and reappearing is a decimal with several zeroes after the point."

"Twenty-eight seconds for the fission engines," said Breeze.

Duggan was worried by Chainer's words. With the other vessel so far away, there should have been plenty of time to escape. *My first encounter with the Dreamers and I've already underestimated them,* he thought. He hauled the *Crimson* around, pointing it in the opposite direction to the approaching ship.

"Send a signal to the *Juniper,*" he said. "Tell them we have an unknown, advanced and potentially hostile species in Confederation space."

"I'm trying," said Chainer. "We've had our comms knocked out."

"What's happened, Lieutenant? Without specifics I can't decide on what to do."

"I have no specifics to give you, sir," said Chainer, exasperated and angry. "Nothing is working on the long range comms."

"What about the emergency beacon?"

"Nothing – it's dead, all of it."

"Shit, we better hope we can get out of here before that ship does another jump," said Duggan.

"Five seconds," said Breeze. "Almost there."

Several events occurred at almost the same time. The first event was the arrival of the unknown vessel. It winked out of view and reappeared less than a hundred thousand kilometres away. A pulse of something washed over the *ESS Crimson.* Then, the *Crimson* launched itself into lightspeed.

"Made it," said Chainer," breathing hard.

"Only at Light-C," said Breeze. "Engine power falling away. Dropping to Light-A. We'll be back in normal space any moment."

"What's happening?" asked Duggan. He sprang over to stand next to Breeze.

"We're out of lightspeed," said Breeze. "Deep fission engines at less than ten percent and still falling."

"Where are we, Lieutenant Chainer? Did the enemy ship manage to follow us?"

"Calculating our position. Damn, sir, we're right back where we started. This is the system where we found the *Crimson*."

"Lieutenant Breeze, can you tell me what's happening to our engines?"

"I can tell you what sir, I can't tell you why. Our logs picked up a pulse from the Dreamer vessel right as we jumped. It's scrambling our engines quicker than the core can straighten them out – like it's reversed the mass configuration that takes weeks to set up on a new spaceship. When it's done, we'll be little more than a lump of heavy metal, waiting to start again."

"I'm going to set us in an orbit around the closest planet, until whatever happened to us finishes what it's doing. After that, we can see if we can fix it and get home."

"Prot-7, sir. Someone in the Space Corps decided to give the place a name after we brought the *Crimson* back. They've called the planet Prot-7."

Duggan aimed for the planet Prot-7 and plotted a course to take them to a high orbit. He could tell something wasn't working correctly. "Why are we going so slowly, Lieutenant Breeze? Our velocity is at eighty percent of maximum."

"We're losing the gravity drives as well. I'm trying to partition what we have left, so they're separate to the scrambled areas. It's not responding as I'd hoped."

"The Dreamer core isn't fast enough?"

"It's not a question of speed. It's like someone's shoved a big stick into our engines and stirred everything up. It'll need to settle before any attempts to fix it will work."

"You'll need to put us down, sir," said McGlashan. "While there's still time for a controlled landing. What if the life support fails next? We'll need to be prepared."

"Good thinking, Commander, except we can't spare anyone

to fetch the suits. We'll have to sit tight for the moment. I'm taking us onto Prot-7 while I still can."

The planet would have been a few minutes' distance on full gravity drives. They'd only had eighty percent of power when Duggan directed them towards it. In a vacuum, there was nothing to slow the *Crimson* down from the speed it had attained – it was controlling the velocity as well as the steering which was the biggest concern.

"Fifty percent," said Breeze. "The rate of decline is reducing."

"Will we have anything left at the end?"

"No sir, the curve is still closing in on zero."

"The sensors run off the gravity drives, don't they?" asked Duggan.

"Yes they do, sir," said Chainer. "They don't take much as a percentage of the overall output, but if we end up at zero, they won't function. It's only the life support which is fully isolated and independent of anything else."

"The mainframe has its own power source," Breeze corrected him.

"Of course."

"Make good use of the time you have," Duggan told Chainer.

"What am I looking for, sir?"

"Anything, Lieutenant. We are not in a good situation. I want to know about anything that might help or hinder us."

"Assuming the unknown vessel was the Dreamers, is there a chance they might choose to follow us through lightspeed?" asked McGlashan. "We didn't get above Light-C and they could have the technology to allow them to predict our destination at such a comparatively low speed."

"I didn't intend us to arrive here, Commander," said Duggan. "For them to follow, they'd need to predict the rate of decay in our engines and decide where that would drop us into local space. It's a stretch to imagine they're advanced enough for that." He grimaced. "What do you suggest?"

"Nothing complicated. Try and land in a cave beneath metal ore, so they have a harder job detecting us from orbit."

"You don't have lots of time," said Breeze. "Prot-7 is five minutes away at current speed. Slowing down for a landing will be tight enough as it is."

"Do we have the data from our first scans when we arrived on the *Detriment*?" asked Duggan.

"I was sending it to the Corps network as I was gathering it," said Chainer. "It's standard practise to do so, and it's standard practise to update the databanks of fleet spacecraft with anything new. We should have the records."

"I need to know how long it'll take me to reach the cave we found the *Crimson* in originally," said Duggan. "At least we know it's suitable."

"That's a lot of calculating," said Chainer.

"Work it out with Lieutenant Breeze. There's not a lot of time."

"You'll have about one minute in low orbit before we have to land," said Breeze.

"Urgent, huh?" Chainer muttered. He was lost in thought, his left-hand screen a mess of green-glowing numbers and lists.

Chainer and Breeze conferred quietly. Duggan kept an eye on their destination and course.

"I need something, gentlemen," he said calmly.

"I appreciate that, sir," said Breeze.

The planet Prot-7 filled the main screen, as grey and lifeless as Duggan remembered it. They were close enough to see the pocks and scars which littered the surface.

"Beginning my approach," said Duggan. He altered their trajectory in order to bring them into a fast, low orbit. They didn't have much time, so he planned to get them as close as possible in order to maximise the time for manoeuvring. Prot-7 had a very thin atmosphere, but it was enough to burn them up if Duggan misjudged it. He could have handed it off to the mainframe, except the built-in safety features simply wouldn't permit what he was attempting. The ship's core assumed they'd stay in orbit if the engines were failing. It had no way to take into consideration the possibility that an enemy ship could be in pursuit, making a forced landing imperative.

"We won't make it to the original cave," said Breeze. "We'll be about a minute short, unless you want to do a crash landing or risk the hull melting."

"I'm assuming you've planned the alternatives," said Duggan.

"I'm sending you some coordinates, sir. There's a place near to the planet's equator. There's plenty of dense metal ore overhead and the landing should be easy."

"It'll not be the perfect location to evade enemy sensor detection," said Chainer. "I think it's the best hope we've got, though."

"That's good enough, Lieutenant," said Duggan. "I'm taking us to the coordinates you've given me."

Duggan brought the *Crimson* in at a steep angle, waiting until the last possible moment to level them off. The hull temperature climbed immediately, pushing up to fifty percent as he tried to reach the landing site as quickly as possible.

"Gravity drives at ten percent, sir," said Breeze. "Take care – they won't be as responsive as you expect."

"Got it," Duggan replied. He had no time to lift his head and kept focused on pushing everything as close to destruction as he could, without stepping over the line.

"Just under a minute and there won't be enough power to land."

Duggan didn't respond. This was a big test of his ability. From the corner of his eye, he saw McGlashan taking her seat. She'd been standing at her console up till now and was evidently wise enough to take the additional precaution of fastening herself in.

Chainer spoke up, letting them know the situation had gone from bad to worse. "We've just flown over a Cadaveron, sir. They've flattened half a mountain range. Nothing from its engines, but the hull looks in one piece."

Duggan couldn't spare the time to think about it. The *Crimson's* hull was at ninety percent of its design temperature and still rising. They raced over the planet's surface, heading towards the equator.

"Come on," said McGlashan.

They were close enough and Duggan hauled up on the control rods. The *Crimson* shuddered and there was a peculiar grating rumble from somewhere. He knew what the sound meant – the engines were overstressed. The hull temperature was at one-hundred and ten percent and they were travelling at thirty klicks per second when Duggan saw their destination, overlaid with a red circle on his guidance screen.

"There's a fission signature just appeared, sir," said Breeze. "Not like anything I've seen before."

"I see it," said Chainer. "The type isn't in our databanks. I'm assuming it's a Dreamer vessel. We should be undetectable to their sensors for the moment."

Duggan clenched his jaw tighter, feeling his teeth grating against each other. They were approaching the landing area faster than he'd intended and it was a struggle to slow the *Crimson* down.

"There's the canyon," said Chainer.

"Twenty-eight klicks long, two wide and three deep where we're going," said Breeze.

In the watery light of the planet's morning, the orange-glowing outline of the *Crimson* stopped in mid-air, directly above and parallel to the rough, grey-stone chasm. Heat poured away from its hull, distorting the air around. Then, the spacecraft dropped vertically downwards, the speed of the motion defying its eleven-hundred metre bulk. There was something else beneath – an object which had escaped detection by taking refuge in the very same location. This object dwarfed the *ESS Crimson*. It was near four-and-a-half kilometres in length, part wedge, part cuboid. It had metal domes at the front and rear. The object was both ugly and sleek at the same time, possessed of an otherworldly menace.

Duggan saw the spacecraft too late to abort his landing. With his gravity drives at zero percent, it was all he could do to keep the *Crimson* from landing on its side, or worse. Rock cracked and splintered as it bore the two-billion tonne weight of a second spacecraft. Then, all was quiet and the crew of the *Crimson* found themselves stranded less than five hundred metres from a Ghast Oblivion.

CHAPTER TWENTY-SEVEN

"PERMISSION TO SAY *BALLS,* SIR?" asked Chainer.

Duggan slumped in his chair, feeling the leather stick to him in the heat. "Why can't anything be easy?" he asked. He wiped his forehead with one sleeve and saw the dampness on his uniform. He'd been sweating more than he realised.

"The sensors have shut down. Not enough juice for them to keep going," said Chainer.

"Engines at a flat zero," added Breeze. "You couldn't power an electric toothbrush off them."

"We're not in a good position, ladies and gentlemen," said Duggan. "Sensor blind, no comms and without power."

"The Ghasts didn't shoot us to pieces, sir," said McGlashan. "They had time and opportunity to do it."

With an effort, Duggan pulled himself together. He stood and addressed the crew. "We're in the crap, make no mistake about it. I need to know exactly what our status is and I also want your opinions. Lieutenant Breeze – you start. What about our engines?"

"Sir, it's my educated guess that the Dreamer weapon has

disrupted the links at a subatomic level. Rather than pulling in the same direction, everything is swimming around at random."

"Can we fix it?"

"I think so. It's going to take weeks for the core to reconfigure the engines. It's like when we first located the *Crimson*, except then it had already been rerouting for a long time."

"Meaning we only had to wait hours," said Duggan.

"That's right, Captain. Now we'll need to start at the very beginning and that's where the reconfiguration is slowest."

"How could a weapon do that?"

"It's strange and I don't have an answer."

"Start work on it at once, Lieutenant." Duggan turned his attention to Chainer. "What about our sensors? When will they work and when can you get the comms running?"

"Basic operation of the sensors will become available before the engines are at a fraction of one percent. Long-range stuff will take more time, because that draws more power."

"What about our comms?"

"I can run diagnostics if you want me to tap into the main-frame's cycles. Gut feeling is we've been jammed."

"Permanently? Is that possible?"

"We can't do it, sir. Neither can the Ghasts as far as we know. I'm sure it's possible – I'm one of those people who believes everything is possible."

"Do you think you can get them working again?"

"Truthfully? I have no idea. Given the time, I'm sure I could provide you with an explanation as to what's happened. Resolving it might be a different thing entirely. It may be that our comms gear has been completely ruined such that it needs a complete replacement at a shipyard. The internal stuff looks like it's working for some reason. That's a lot less sophisticated than the long-range comms. I don't think it's been affected."

"Commander McGlashan. Are our weapons online?"

"Everything apart from the disruptors, which run off the engines. I'm assuming the Planet Breaker needs an external power source as well. It's still hidden from my console, so it doesn't really matter anyway. The Lambdas have their own power systems and we can instruct them to launch using the mainframe. I'd say we have nine or ten missile clusters which are unusable owing to our proximity to the side wall and floor of this canyon."

"If our weapons are working, it would be a wise to assume the Ghasts can launch as well."

"Definitely, sir," she said.

"And if the Ghasts can launch their missiles, yet haven't done so, we must assume they have chosen to let us live."

"Or they've suffered damage we're unaware of," said Breeze.

"For some reason, I don't think that's the case," said Duggan, rubbing his chin. "Did we manage to capture any data on the Oblivion prior to the sensors going off?" he asked.

"Whatever the sensors see, they keep a record of," said Chainer. "Let's have a look."

"I'd like to know if they are showing external signs of damage."

"Nope, sir. Nothing at all. They're clean on top and on the one side we got a view of. There's something else as well – it's the same Ghast warship that we encountered on this planet when we took the *Crimson* out of the cave. The one we got away from."

"Well damn," said Breeze. "Funny old world, isn't it?"

"From what we know, the Confederation fleet met up with the Ghasts at the Helius Blackstar and several of them were destroyed, presumably by the Dreamer spaceship. We've found a Cadaveron and an Oblivion on this planet, apparently stranded. Therefore, it's likely they've been hit with the same engine scrambler as we have and they managed to escape this far. There must be other ships as well. The Oblivion hasn't fired on us, so they do not see us as the enemy," said Duggan, letting his mouth run.

"Or they see us as the lesser of two enemies," said McGlashan.

"We came here for peace and found something we hadn't bargained on," said Duggan.

"I wonder if they realise who and what we are," said Breeze.

It was a question to which Duggan dearly wanted to know the answer. "If they recognize the *Crimson* as the vessel carrying the Planet Breaker, I don't want to predict what they'll try and do," he said. "Even less do I want to predict what they might do to the people who were onboard when Lioxi was destroyed."

"Yeah, the results might not be pretty. Least of all for us," said Chainer.

"All we can do is hope they remain unaware," said Breeze. "There's a chance."

Duggan brought matters back on course. "Lieutenant Breeze, you detected the arrival of what you took to be a Dreamer vessel just prior to our landing. We can be absolutely certain *they* will be hostile. I think our primary objective should be to figure out what we're going to do about them. They can only have come for one reason, which is to finish what they started. The Ghasts are secondary."

"I'm sure you recall the logs from the *Crimson*'s last battle with the Dreamers," said McGlashan. "The Lambdas couldn't track the enemy craft and the *Crimson* fired hundreds of missiles before it scored a win. We don't have the luxury of being able to out-fly anything at the moment."

"How much cover do we have in here, Lieutenant?" asked Duggan.

"If we assume their sensor technology to be similar to ours and not too far advanced, they'd need to overfly us directly. It depends on how determined they are and how many orbits it takes before they happen to get the right angle to see where we are."

"You're saying it's down to luck," said Duggan. He shrugged to show he wasn't blaming Chainer.

"Would you have it any other way?"

Duggan wasn't even tempted to smile. "For once, it doesn't seem right to be talking about luck. We're going to need a lot more than that to get us out of here."

"There's no way the engines are going to be ready to fly us out of here in time," said Breeze. "Even if they were, who's to say they won't get scrambled again?"

Something occurred to Duggan. "The fission signature you detected just before we landed wasn't big enough to be the Dreamer ship we saw at the Blackstar, was it?"

"Not unless their engine technology is vastly, inconceivably different from ours. I'd say it was something much, much smaller."

"The mothership sent out a fighter to do the mopping up," said Chainer.

"I need some time to think," said Duggan. "If the Ghasts or the Dreamers decide to blow us up, there's not a great deal we can do about it."

He got to his feet and left the bridge. He walked along the tight, turning corridors of the *Crimson*, through areas where it was too hot and other places where it was so cold that moisture beaded on the walls and ceiling. The ship was dead – utterly silent where there would normally be a familiar, comforting humming vibration from the engines. The quiet was strangely distracting and Duggan found it a struggle to ignore the hush for long enough to allow his brain to slip into its familiar analytical mode, where it was able to view and evaluate the options dispassionately. When there wasn't much to go on, it gave him more time on each of the few choices and it was easier to discard the ones that were least likely to bring success.

After ten minutes alone, Duggan was left with one clear thought as to what they needed to do. He wasn't sure if it was viable or not, but he was determined to find out. He was a few hundred metres from the bridge and he found his feet carrying him faster and faster, suddenly impatient to get on with matters. When he arrived, his crew watched him carefully, their eyes occasionally jumping to what he was carrying.

"Lieutenant Chainer," Duggan began. "We spoke about the Ghast language modules you uncovered in the *Crimson*'s data arrays."

"Yes, sir."

"Our comms are offline, so we can't communicate with the Ghast battleship?"

"No, sir."

"During our earlier conversation, did I mention that Admiral Teron talked about one day putting the language files into spacesuits?"

"I don't think so, but it would make sense."

"I'm going to put on this space suit I'm carrying. If it doesn't have those language modules installed, will you be able to add them?"

"The files aren't enormous. They should be easy enough to pass across."

Five minutes later, Duggan was in his space suit, with the helmet in place. He searched through the options and couldn't find anything related to the Ghast language. He asked Chainer to patch the *Crimson*'s mainframe in and assist with the search. It didn't take long to realise the space suit didn't have the facility he wanted.

"Please install them," Duggan instructed.

Less than ten seconds later and it was done. There was a new option within the suit's communicator, that was meant to interpret Ghast words into human language and vice versa. He tried one or two phrases, but had no way of verifying if he was saying what he intended to say.

"Want me to come with you?" asked McGlashan, having guessed where he was going.

"I don't think we need take that risk. One person should be sufficient to see if the Ghasts are hostile and if they're willing to work with us."

"Do you have a plan beyond that?"

"No, Commander. I intend to play it by ear."

"Our inventory lists three low-powered portable beacons in cabinets at various locations on the ship," said Chainer. "They're meant for surface use only. It would be a real risk, but they should have the power to get a signal to the Space Corps. It might take a few weeks for our message to get there, but it's an option."

"Thank you, Lieutenant, I'll bear it in mind. I would prefer to speak to the Ghasts before I risk jeopardising us further. After all, we know very little about the Dreamers and what they can do."

"Yes, sir. I'll dig the beacons out while you're gone in case we need to use them. I might be able to set them to send a predefined message at some point a few days from now. That way we'll still get a message out, even if we've all been killed."

"That's a fine idea, Lieutenant. I'll leave you to it." Duggan paused before he left the bridge. "Since I'll be unable to communicate with you once I'm away from the *Crimson*, please take whatever action you deem necessary if any harm comes to me. Commander McGlashan will be in charge."

"Are you taking a rifle?" asked Breeze.

"I don't think I'll need one," said Duggan. "They'll either shoot me or listen to me. One way or another, a rifle won't help."

"What if they don't see you?" asked Chainer.

"I'll have to hope they do."

He exited the bridge, taking exaggerated care to avoid hitting his helmet against the side walls. In the corridor outside, he walked swiftly to the *Crimson*'s secondary boarding ramp. There was an airlock, which he entered and sealed behind him. A red warning light cycled as the boarding ramp released with a clunk of gears. It lowered to the ground below. The light outside was almost non-existent. When he was set on a course, Duggan rarely felt trepidation. With confidence, he strode down the boarding ramp.

CHAPTER TWENTY-EIGHT

THE CANYON WAS deep and wide, its floor covered in rocks and boulders. It jagged away in both directions and its walls loomed ever upwards, sheer in places and overhanging in others. Light reached here, though it was feeble and hardly enough to give the impression it was day. There was no river at the bottom – in fact, Duggan couldn't recall if there was any water at all on Prot-7. It made no difference. A single object dominated everything - the Oblivion towered several hundred metres high, yet it also managed to appear low-slung and intimidating. From the ground, Duggan was able to see the warship was on dozens – perhaps hundreds - of pillar-like legs, each of which must have been strong enough to support a Vincent class fighter. Fractures spread away in all directions, many of them several metres in width. It was easy to see the rock wasn't strong enough to support this burden and the heavy cruiser might soon sink into the ground.

Duggan walked purposefully across the intervening space. Here and there, he had to jump across cracks in the ground and once he needed to backtrack to find his way around a five-metre-wide fissure that vanished into emptiness beneath the surface. When his helmet sensor told him he was only one hundred metres away, he stopped. From this close, he could make out the variations in the Oblivion's surface. There were dents and scrapes here and there from where small objects had collided with it in flight. In one place, there were faint, round indentations, in a cluster of twenty, which Duggan took to be launch tubes for the Ghast missiles. There was another, much larger hatch underneath the spacecraft, which most likely housed one of the Oblivion's many Vule cannons. All-in-all, it looked like a perfectly-designed implement to destroy as much of the Space Corps fleet as possible.

Duggan had never possessed the patience necessary to wait for extended periods. It appeared the Ghasts weren't patient either. With no indication how they'd detected his presence, they lowered one of their boarding ramps. At first, Duggan didn't notice it had happened, since it was several hundred metres away and there were numerous support legs between him and the ramp. His suit picked up sound and movement and he turned his head to see six Ghasts walking towards him. He'd expected them to be in their mech suits and they were. A lone, unarmed human presented them with no threat and Duggan wondered if everything about the Ghasts necessitated an outward display of strength.

They approached, two abreast and three deep. The dull silver of their armour was an almost perfect camouflage for the terrain here. They stopped in front of him and Duggan noted they carried light repeaters. In spite of the name, nothing about these weapons was lightweight. They were powered by a cell on the mech suits and they could spray a large number of projectiles in a short amount of time.

The front two Ghasts were eight feet tall in their suits – probably not much shorter out of them. They towered over Duggan, broad and threatening in their metal armour. The visors on the suits were large and almost square, wrapping around the front of the Ghast helmets. Duggan looked into their eyes and could read no emotion in the wide, thick-boned faces of this strange species.

Duggan knew that without communication, he was open to whatever the Ghasts decided to read into the situation. If they got his intentions wrong, it would be easy to kill him. This was his only chance to get it right and Duggan activated the language module in his helmet. His suit scanned for receptors nearby and it located six channels, all of them blocked and encrypted. Duggan sent a query to one of these receptors. At first, nothing happened. Then, the receptor allowed his helmet to pair with it. Duggan cleared his throat.

"I've come to talk," he said. His helmet converted the words into the Ghast tongue and sent them off to the receptor.

The front two Ghasts continued to look at him, their gaze unflinching. Duggan had no idea if this was a threat or a test, so he stared back, meeting the grey eyes with his own. His visor was opaque, so it made his job much easier and all he needed to do was bend his neck and keep his helmet pointing towards the two aliens.

He got his answer. He wasn't sure which of the Ghasts spoke, but the response was succinct. "Come," it said. The helmet's interpretation gave no idea as to the tone or intent behind the words. It was going to be hard to reach an agreement without having a misunderstanding.

The six Ghasts turned and began walking away, as if they'd already forgotten about Duggan. He followed them, finding their pace matched his natural walking speed. His past encounters – where there'd been only fighting instead of talking – told him the Ghasts weren't especially fast in their suits. He had no idea how quickly they could run in whatever normal clothes they wore.

His escort took him into the darkness amongst the towering

support legs of the Oblivion and to the bottom of the support ramp. There were steps, which Duggan saw had been perfectly designed to match the strides of a Ghast wearing a mech suit. The aliens didn't wait and climbed upwards at once. Duggan took the time to stare into the cold blue interior of the vessel, twenty or thirty metres above. For the first time since leaving the *Crimson*, he felt the first suggestions of fear, tendrils of it working away at his confidence. It wasn't fear for himself, rather a fear that he might fail to capitalise on the opportunity which lay before him. He swept the feeling aside, replacing it with determination. The Ghasts surely wouldn't deal with a man who quailed before them.

There was an airlock at the top - a high-ceilinged room with smooth walls. Duggan was instantly reminded of the Shatterer tube on Everlong, which had a similar room. Everything was bland and featureless. *Pretty pictures distract a soldier from fighting.* The words of one of Duggan's old trainers jumped unbidden into his mind. He'd never thought them important enough to waste time thinking about, so he had no idea why his mind chose this moment to serve them up.

The outer ramp rose at speed and it thumped closed. There was the sound of a dozen metal bolts sliding into place somewhere within the warship's hull and the hiss of a seal being created. One of the Ghasts clanked across to a metal plate on the wall. It pressed the metal knuckles of its suit gauntlet onto the panel and the interior door slid aside. There was a passage beyond, blue lit, in the same hue as the airlock. Duggan followed the Ghasts through and was struck by the absence of other sounds. Aside from the metal-on-metal of the mech suits, there was no noise. The humming of the engines was missing and Duggan could tell this ship was dead, in the same way the *Crimson* was dead. It confirmed the Ghasts had suffered the same fate, not that there'd been any doubt in Duggan's mind.

Like most warships, whose vast exteriors concealed a compact interior, the Oblivion appeared to have little internal space to spare. There were some Cadaverons which had been known to carry in excess of one thousand troops and Duggan assumed the Oblivions could carry substantially more. Even so, he didn't see much evidence of places where troops could be stationed. They went along a long corridor, which branched several times. After one branch, Duggan thought he could see steps at the end, and wondered if the Oblivion contained several different levels. Certainly, he saw no one else apart from the six Ghasts who led him onwards.

Duggan was taken to a room, bare of decoration. The walls were ten metres apart and the ceiling five metres up. There was nothing on the floor and a single door led away opposite to the one he'd entered.

"Wait here," said a voice. With that, the alien soldiers passed through the far door, leaving Duggan alone. There was nothing to sit on and nothing to look at. He knew the Ghasts used seats and he was fairly sure they were civilised enough to have other furniture. It could have been a calculated insult to leave him here, he thought. For some reason it didn't seem likely – it would be far too subtle.

The Ghasts had left both doors open, since they evidently didn't think Duggan was a threat, nor that he'd try and escape. He looked through the exit door – there was another corridor beyond, which went to the left and right. To Duggan's surprise, he saw a Ghast walking towards him. This one was dressed in a stiff-looking grey cloth uniform. It wore no helmet and carried no weapons. It entered the room, watching Duggan as it did so.

The figure walked to the centre of the room and stopped, barely ten feet away. Up close, Duggan saw the age-lines across its broad forehead and at the corners of its eyes. It had hair, thick, dark and almost humanlike. The grey eyes never left him and

Duggan sensed the creature was waiting for him to do something. There was intelligence – fierce and honed, backed up by the powerful, heavy-boned frame common to all of this species. It made the average Ghast stronger than almost any man or woman.

Duggan's helmet readout informed him the air here was good enough for him to breathe. He activated the external speaker on the helmet and broke the seal around his neck. He lifted the helmet over his head and placed it on the floor next to him, feeling cold air rush across his skin. He was convinced the alien before him was in a position of seniority and there would never be any trust without eye contact. Duggan remained quiet for a few seconds and he could sense the Ghast evaluating him.

"I am John Duggan, captain of the Space Corps vessel *ESS Crimson*," he said.

The helmet speaker hummed and then spat out a series of rasping syllables. The Ghast narrowed its eyes and responded. Duggan's untrained ear immediately picked out differences in tone between the helmet's interpretation and the Ghast's speech. He hoped it wouldn't be too much of an impediment.

"I am Nil-Far. I command this Oblivion." There was a pause before the word 'Oblivion' and Duggan guessed the Ghasts used a word or phrase which wouldn't translate directly. The language modules weren't complete and probably weren't able to catch the subtleties of vocabulary as well as tone. The helmet produced more words, these ones not a part of the conversation.

"By the pattern of this specimen's voice, there is a ninety-five percent chance it is male."

Had Duggan been a trained negotiator, he would have littered his words with niceties and flowery phrases. He had no time for pleasantries. "Both our fleets have been destroyed by a third species. We have named them *Dreamers*. Humans and Ghasts alike utilise technology scavenged from an earlier Dreamer incursion through the wormhole."

"Their technology is powerful," said the Ghast. "You used it to destroy Lioxi."

There was no way to tell if there was accusation in the words, or a simple statement of fact. Duggan didn't hide behind excuses. "We used it on your planet to bring about an end to the war. The Confederation could not permit you to destroy more of our planets."

"It is understandable," said Nil-Far. When he spoke, he revealed straight, white teeth in perfect proportion to his face, though there was no hint of a smile. "We came to this sector to end the hostilities."

"Had you reached a settlement before the Dreamers arrived?" asked Duggan.

"There was progress." Nil-Far lowered his heavy brows, giving the impression he was thinking. "We will go elsewhere to speak, instead of standing here like [word not recognized]."

Duggan was relieved. It didn't seem likely they could accomplish anything worthwhile in this room. Nil-Far left the room without a backward glance. Duggan grabbed his helmet and walked quickly after. He fell into step, determined not to show potential weakness by following behind. They climbed a set of steps to a higher level and went through a series of doors. Here there were a number of much larger rooms, some open and some only glimpsed through clear panes in their doors. There were many Ghasts and Duggan wondered at the numbers onboard – from what he saw, they carried more personnel on this battleship than anything in the Space Corps fleet. Those he saw were clearly not soldiers. They sat in threes at consoles set against the walls. Many carried metal cylinders or cubes, from which wires and cables dangled. There were hatches in the walls and what he imagined to be maintenance tunnels. The Ghasts were everywhere and they were all busy with something. Nil-Far walked on without a word. Here and there, the helmet picked up a snippet from nearby Ghasts, and translated it into speech Duggan could understand. He found himself impressed – everything he over-heard was about how to get the Oblivion moving again, rather than time-wasting or joking. *Do they even have jokes?* he wondered idly.

Nil-Far stopped outside a door in a much quieter area of the vessel. He raised a broad hand and placed it palm-out on a panel. The door slid open, to reveal another ten-metre square room of the sort Duggan had seen many of. Unlike the other rooms, this one had what was unmistakeably a metal desk, with thick legs and four chairs fixed to the floor on one side, and a single chair on the other. There were screens in the walls, showing a constantly-changing list of characters and symbols. There was something about it which reinforced a feeling he'd had before – the Ghasts had a mish-mash of old and new. It was like they'd advanced too far and too fast and they struggled to control the technology they'd built. That was why they had so many maintenance crew onboard.

Nil-Far took the single seat. The Ghast didn't offer, so Duggan took one of the four seats opposite. It was as flat and cold as the walls.

"Our Admiral was killed," said Nil-Far. "After his death, I could see my primary objective was to protect my ship." It was as close to conversation as anything the Ghast had spoken so far.

"There is a Cadaveron elsewhere on this planet," said Duggan.

"We were not the only ones to escape. Why are you here, John Duggan?" Still there was nothing readable in the face of the creature.

"I have come to finish what was started," Duggan replied.

CHAPTER TWENTY-NINE

"ARE you in a position to speak for your Confederation?" asked Nil-Far.

"No, I am not," said Duggan.

"We do not need to talk if you have nothing."

"I bring an opportunity to carry the truth of what happened here to the Confederation home planets. The Dreamers jammed our communications, preventing news from reaching my superiors. We have Planet Breakers mounted on eight new prototype warships and we have the coordinates of your remaining populated worlds." He stopped to allow the translation to catch up. "It is not in your interest for a misunderstanding to exist. As it stands, nobody in the Confederation knows with absolute certainty that this is not a result of Ghast treachery."

Nil-Far's face twisted in an emotion that took no empathy to identify. He clenched a fist and banged it hard upon the metal table top. "There is no Ghast treachery! We do not break our word when it is given! We fight and we bring death to our enemies, but an oath is [words not recognized]!"

Duggan didn't flinch at the Ghast's anger. He didn't allow his expression to change at all. "There needs to be more than talk of oaths. The Confederation wishes to have peace. They would prefer to have peace without further deaths. If they can't have peace on those terms, they will destroy each of your remaining worlds in turn, until peace comes through your extinction."

"Why not destroy us anyway?" asked Nil-Far.

"Is that what the Ghasts intended for the Confederation?" asked Duggan.

"We fight to win," Nil-Far replied. "This is not a war my species wanted."

This time it was far harder for Duggan to keep his expression neutral. Nil-Far's words contradicted everything he knew about the war. *Each side has its own truths,* he thought. "You will settle with the Confederation?"

"We will settle."

"You have told me your species is honourable and I accept what you have said. We are not the people to set anything in stone, but we can provide an example to show our hostilities are no longer necessary. I wish to escape this planet and return to the Confederation with details of the Dreamer assault on our fleet. I am sure you wish to return to your own worlds."

Nil-Far didn't answer at once. His eyes became distant as he considered what Duggan had said. The Ghast looked different to a human, yet in many ways there were striking similarities. "These Dreamers destroyed four of our most recent warships in seconds," said Nil-Far. "They warped amongst us and their beam weapons ripped us to pieces. We were unable to communicate and tried to withdraw. Our engines shut down in moments, leaving us stranded here."

"We experienced the same," said Duggan. "Do you know if any vessels from the human or Ghast fleet escaped? Were there any successful strikes on the Dreamer craft?"

"I think my warship was among a handful given the time to

fire upon them. Our standard missiles refused to target, even though the enemy was so large. We launched six [technology not recognized] from our forward tubes. They were destroyed prior to impact. Our lightspeed drive took us away before we could try again."

"What destroyed them?" asked Duggan, assuming Nil-Far referred to his use of Shatterer missiles.

"We have not been able to confirm with certainty. The warheads detonated a short distance from the target."

"An energy shield?" asked Duggan. The Confederation had been experimenting with this technology. The labs had got it working in principle, except the energy draw was so huge, the shields would knock out the engines of a warship in a split second's use.

"If I understand your words correctly, an energy shield is exactly what we believe stopped our weapons."

The more he heard, the greater a feeling of dread seeped into Duggan's bones. The Dreamers were advanced and they were hostile. If they'd come here for war, which was an inescapable conclusion, both Ghasts and humanity were in deep trouble. There wasn't time to pursue each detail fully, so Duggan moved on.

"Do you know how they jammed your communications?"

"We are working on it," said Nil-Far. It wasn't clear if he was withholding something, or if he didn't have more to say.

"How long until you can fly?" asked Duggan. "Our engine re-routing could take days or weeks."

Nil-Far narrowed his eyes, another humanlike expression. "We have damage to our AI," he conceded. "We passed many of my crew on the way here. You will have noticed we are reduced to doing some repairs by hand."

There was much Duggan wished to ask and much he wished to learn. The time wasn't now and he wanted to deal with the most pressing issue for both sides. "We detected a fission signature when we entered orbit," said Duggan. The helmet struggled to translate.

"I don't understand."

"A ship emerged from lightspeed somewhere above this planet. We believe it to be a Dreamer vessel, though not the large one which destroyed our fleets. We suspect this one to be a smaller fighter. We think it wishes to find and destroy us."

"I do not wish my vessel to be destroyed."

Nil-Far appeared to accept much of what Duggan said without questioning it, as if the Ghasts hadn't learned to lie or it simply wasn't part of how they communicated.

"If it's looking, it will find us. This will happen before either of our vessels can escape."

"The enemy craft will remain until it has finished what the larger ship started," said Nil-Far. There was certainty, clear in the translation.

"I agree," said Duggan. "It may succeed against us whether or not our engines are functioning."

"Our weapons may have the power to deplete its energy shields," said Nil-Far, giving away his knowledge of the technology.

"The ESS *Crimson* destroyed one of the first Dreamer craft to come through the wormhole," said Duggan. "The logs of the combat show the enemy warship possessed a technology which prevented missiles from targeting it."

"That is what we discovered," said Nil-Far. "I can think of ways around the problem, though I will be unable to put them into action without a great deal of time."

"Your Shatterers can target."

"They can. We have six batteries as I'm sure you are aware. What you might not know is that only four of these are capable of firing upwards. The other two fire downwards."

"Four should be sufficient, assuming it has no energy shield."

Nil-Far gave a single nod of his head. "The Shatterers are the pinnacle of our weapons technology."

Duggan stood. "I need to get back to my ship and speak to my crew. There may be a way for us to defeat this common enemy. I do not wish our peace to fail."

Nil-Far's grey eyes glittered dangerously in the blue light and Duggan could see the Ghast had reached his status because he was skilful and competent. "We might soon find our ships side-by-side against a new foe, John Duggan."

"We might," said Duggan. After everything which had gone before, it felt peculiar to be talking so openly to a representative of the species he'd fought so long. He put the thoughts to one side. "I will need to communicate with you again. It is not suitable for me to put on this space suit and cross between our vessels."

"I will send my soldiers to escort you from the ship. I will have one of them wait outside until this is done. You can pair one of your helmets to his battle armour and use it as a relay to carry information. I assume your internal communications are working?"

"They are," said Duggan. "Very well, I will do as you suggest."

"My troops are already outside. Go," said Nil-Far.

Duggan climbed to his feet and picked up the helmet. He caught sight of his face, reflected in the visor. The sternness of his features shocked him and he put the helmet on again while he walked towards the door. It opened and, as Nil-Far had said, there were six Ghasts in the corridor outside, still in their mech suits and still with their repeaters. Duggan walked past them, taking the lead. He'd memorised the route they'd taken to reach Nil-Far's room. The soldiers fell in behind and made no attempt to stop him or ask him to slow down.

Standing in the airlock gave Duggan a few moments to play over the recent events in his mind. There was too much to think about and no hope of settling anything with himself. At last, the boarding ramp swung away and crashed against the ground beneath the Oblivion. Duggan walked down without a backwards glance. He took a measured pace to the *Crimson*. Some of the cracks in the ground had widened or extended and he hadn't been gone long. The Oblivion was sinking.

The *Crimson* felt like a welcome return to home when he boarded it. He stayed in his suit and fetched another suit helmet from one of the lockers. He interfaced with it and transferred the language modules across. When it was set up, Duggan walked down the boarding ramp again and placed the second helmet on the ground. He looked towards the Ghast ship and, as promised, there was a lone figure waiting, the visor of its mech suit pointed in his direction. Duggan initiated the connection between the suit helmet and the mech suit.

"This is Duggan. Acknowledge."

A voice responded, routing from the bridge on the Oblivion, through the mech suit, on to the second helmet and then into Duggan's earpiece.

"Acknowledged." The suit's translation only had one voice and there was no way to tell if it was Nil-Far or another Ghast who responded. Ultimately, it wasn't important, as long as the message got to the right person.

Duggan re-entered the *Crimson*. Once he'd passed the airlock, he removed his own helmet and returned to the bridge with it clutched in one hand. After the chill of the Oblivion, the heat of his own ship was a relief.

CHAPTER THIRTY

"WE HAVE to come up with a plan, or that Dreamer warship is going to blow us and the Ghasts to pieces," said Duggan. "I need ideas and I need them now!"

"We're fighting against the unknown, sir," said Breeze.

"No we're not, Lieutenant. We're fighting against *some* unknowns. We have information from the *Crimson's* previous encounter and we have information from the Ghast Captain. That's sufficient to make something work."

"We know we can't target the enemy with our Lambdas," said McGlashan. "We can disable the guidance systems and launch them in a straight line in the hope one of them might get a strike."

"Except the Ghasts believe the Dreamers have an energy shield," said Breeze. "We have to assume one or two lucky strikes won't disable it, else why bother having one in the first place?"

"What can we learn from the *Crimson's* first encounter?" mused Duggan.

"It fired hundreds of missiles and used the disruptors," said Chainer.

"It fired the disruptors many times," said McGlashan. "Why

would it need to keep using them? A disabled ship is a sitting duck, even for an unguided missile."

"Some of the bigger Ghast warships shrug off the disruptor effects in less than a minute," said Duggan. "And the *Crimson* itself is hardly affected, except for a spike on the core. It's certain the Dreamer ships aren't going to be disabled."

"Why fire them, in that case?" asked McGlashan. "Could the disruptors knock out an energy shield? That would allow a missile to impact with the target."

"You could be on to something," admitted Duggan. "It's still academic, since we need engine power in order to fire the disruptors."

"I was asked to submit a couple of papers on engine outputs a few months ago," said Breeze. His expression showed he was thinking hard. "I think it was in support of our own research into energy shields. Anyway, they have a preposterous amount of draw in their current form. However, in order to contribute, I did learn a few things about the field generators. One of the earliest hurdles was their susceptibility to gamma rays. The first proto-types were exceptionally vulnerable. They added shielding, of course, but it increased the complexity."

Duggan started to understand where Breeze was leading. "A crude and filthy high explosive," he said, repeating a phrase Breeze himself had once used.

"That'll do it," said Breeze. "At least to one of ours. Who knows what it'll do to this Dreamer stuff?"

"Two of our nuclear launch tubes point upwards," said Duggan.

"I see where you're going with this, sir," said Chainer. "On the off-chance we manage to land a strike on the Dreamers, won't this energy shield deflect the blast harmlessly?"

"It'll deflect the blast," said Breeze. "That's what it's designed to stop. Radiation still gets through, as if the shield doesn't exist."

"They might not even have a shield," said Chainer. "We're only guessing."

"The logs from the *Crimson* at least imply the presence of shielding," said McGlashan. "It's not beyond the scope of possibility for an advanced race to have technology that can stop lock-on targeting and can also stop explosive or plasma damage."

"I know we're working on both," said Duggan. "It's early days, though. Some of this stuff takes decades to perfect and even longer before the Space Corps is willing to modify an existing ship design to accommodate it."

"They're not going to sit there and let us chuck a couple of nukes off them, are they?" asked Chainer. "I mean, I'd love for this to work, but I think we need something more. They're going to blow us to smithereens before our missiles reach them."

"What do you suggest, Lieutenant?"

"Turn off the Lambda guidance and throw up enough missiles to keep them busy? I don't know." Chainer threw up his hands. "Hide a nuke amongst the Lambdas and programme it to explode when it detects an object nearby? Or remote-detonate a nuke by hand?"

A sketchy plan formed in Duggan's head. "How are the sensors coming along?" he asked. "If we can't see our target, we can't launch at it anyway."

"I could bring them up now if you wanted, sir. I didn't want to take any resources away from the cores, so left them off."

"What sort of range are we looking at?"

"The fars and super-fars won't be available for another day I'd guess. I can give you a good idea of anything within fifty or sixty thousand klicks. Only straight up, of course. We've got nothing that can see through the side walls of this canyon."

"Turn them on," Duggan said.

"They're running through their self-checks. We'll have vision in a couple of minutes," Chainer replied.

"Do you have an estimate of when we can fly?" said Duggan.

"The Dreamer core is astounding," said Breeze. "It's going to take us from zero to twenty percent in less than two weeks. That should be able to get us home in a month."

"A month is too long, Lieutenant."

"The longer we sit tight, the more the core can reroute," Breeze replied. "And the quicker we'll be able to go."

"How long since we landed?" asked Duggan.

"Three hours," said McGlashan. "It already feels like weeks."

"Sir, I'm getting a request from the Oblivion."

"Get me a link," said Duggan.

Crudely translated words spat from the bridge speakers. "*ESS Crimson*, this is Nil-Far - our sensors have tracked an object overhead at twenty-two thousand kilometres. It did not stop and is now out of our sight."

"Did it note your presence?"

"Our AI believes a ship equipped with equivalent technology to our own would have detected us with a probability of almost one hundred percent."

Duggan bit his tongue to stop from swearing. "We have an idea, which requires us to fire as many objects in the air as we can manage. Have you overcome your missile guidance issues?"

"Our standard missiles are not available for launch."

"Keep on this channel," said Duggan to the Ghast captain. "Lieutenant Chainer, have those sensors come online?"

"Sir, they're dressed up and ready to dance."

"Is there anything overhead?"

"Negative. The skies are clear and blue."

"Commander, I want those Lambdas programmed to fly straight. Prepare the nukes as well. They need to act as much like a Lambda as possible."

"A much slower Lambda." She gave a rueful smile.

"Sir, I'm registering a beam strike on the Ghast ship," said

Chainer. "Crap, that's a big one. It's melted about six hundred metres of her hull."

"Nil-Far," said Duggan. "You've been hit. We can't tell where from."

The Ghast responded in the synthesised tones which gave away nothing about his mood. "Our AI can detect traces of the enemy. In addition, we have tracked the beam strike to its source."

"The Ghasts have launched Shatterer missiles, sir," said Chainer. "Four on their way."

"Where are you with those missiles, Commander?" asked Duggan. "Lieutenant Chainer, I want you to find the enemy craft. The Ghasts have managed it, why haven't you?"

"They're deflecting our pings," said Chainer. "That's all it can be." He pressed furiously at his console, with his face so close to a screen his nose was almost touching it.

"I can give you four hundred Lambdas, sir," said McGlashan. "As soon as we have sensor sight."

"Get on with the nukes. Don't launch anything until I tell you."

"The Ghast missiles have detonated against an object a little over twenty thousand klicks up," said Chainer. "That helps me get an eye on them." He struck his console in excitement. "Yes, got the bastards!"

"I see them," said McGlashan.

"Fire the Lambdas," said Duggan. "Two waves of forty-eight each, ten seconds apart."

"First wave on their way," she said at once.

"The Oblivion's been hit again – twice this time," said Chainer. "They're going to be a pool of sludge with a few more of those. They're launching plasma flares and I've got traces of Vule fire in the air."

Duggan activated the bulkhead screen, which had been

turned off while the sensors were powered down. The top of the canyon was far above, and the sky was completely obscured by vivid-white flares bursting in their thousands. Thick, grey lines of Vule projectiles raked through, converging on an area far above.

"That's going to interfere with our launch," said Duggan. "Nil-Far, stop firing plasma flares. We need to launch our missiles. There's a chance we can disable the enemy vessel's shields."

"Holding our second launch," said McGlashan.

Nil-Far responded after what seemed like an age. "Very well, John Duggan. No more flares."

Outside, the whiteness faded from view. When it was clear Duggan nodded to McGlashan.

"Second wave of Lambdas gone," she said.

"When will the nuclear missiles be ready?"

"I've programmed two and we're carrying six. Want me to do the rest?"

"Yes, Commander. All of them."

"Nil-Far, how long between your Shatterer launches?"

"One minute."

"The Ghasts have launched again. Three this time."

"One of their launch tubes has been melted," said Breeze. "Their ship is a mess."

"Have we scored any hits, Lieutenant?" asked Duggan.

"There was a lot of noise from those flares. The sensors take a moment to settle." said Chainer. "I may have read a power spike somewhere. I can't be sure. The Oblivion's been hit again. The Dreamer ship is still up there."

"Our hull is heavily damaged," rasped the voice of Nil-Far. "Several of our operational systems have shut down. We will soon be destroyed."

"We're going to try and bring down the Dreamer energy

shield with nuclear warheads," said Duggan. "Hold your next Shatterer launch until after detonation."

"The channel is closed, sir. Something's knocked out one of the relays on the ground."

"Did the message get through?"

"I don't know, sir."

Duggan shouted in fury. With the communications down, there was no way for them to combine their attacks on the enemy ship above. They might only have one chance and it seemed as if it was already slipping away.

CHAPTER THIRTY-ONE

DUGGAN CALCULATED IN HIS HEAD, even while his hands flashed over his console. He sent out a cloud of shock drones. Many of them crashed into the side walls of the canyon, clattering away into the distance, or bringing down chunks of rock and stone. Some of them raced into the sky, where they transmitted wildly fluctuating signal patterns.

"Fire another eight clusters, now!" he said.

"Ninety-six missiles away," said McGlashan.

The timing was going to be crucial. The nukes travelled much slower than anything else they carried. Duggan wanted them to arrive at the same time as a wave of Lambdas. He didn't know exactly what he hoped would happen. The enemy ship's tracking systems might be confused or overloaded by the quantity of targets in the air and if the nukes didn't get through, some of the Lambdas might weaken the energy shield enough for the Shatterers to disable it completely.

"We've had a detonation, sir," said Chainer.

"A hit?"

"No sir, only fifteen thousand klicks. Must have been a Lambda impacting on a shock drone."

"That's the chance we'll have to take," said Duggan. He sent up another cloud. The drones accelerated at a similar speed to the Lambdas. The ones which made it from the canyon were lost in the endless sky. Others were visible on the main viewscreen as they ricocheted and careened off the walls.

"Lambdas almost reloaded," said McGlashan.

"Fire another hundred as soon as they're ready."

The *Crimson* rocked fractionally, an infinitesimal feeling that Duggan detected only because he'd served on spacecraft so long.

"What was that?" he asked sharply, wondering if the ground was shifting beneath them.

"Beam strike aft," said Breeze. "It's going to get hot in here soon."

"Lambdas away."

Duggan frantically checked the status of the nuclear warheads. They were still showing green. He instructed the mainframe to launch them.

"I see two nukes," said McGlashan.

"What's our damage?" asked Duggan.

"We're glowing nicely," said Breeze. "There's about thirty percent of our volume showing heat alerts. Another strike and a big chunk of the ship is going to melt."

"Three more Shatterers have launched from the Oblivion, sir," said Chainer.

"They mustn't have got the message," said Duggan. "That could see us all killed." It was worse than that – as far as he was aware, the *Crimson* and the Oblivion might well be the only surviving warships to bring news about the Dreamer arrival. On top of that, they could both attest to the fact that neither Ghasts nor humans betrayed the temporary truce between the two species. A loss of trust would make it impossible to forge peace.

"Two more nukes flying high," said McGlashan. "Four gigatons in the air."

"I can see three quick energy spikes on this chart," said Chainer. "The Shatterers got there first. I can't confirm a kill."

The *Crimson*'s nukes flew at about a thousand kilometres per second – a quarter the speed of the Ghast Shatterers. If the Ghasts had waited another two or three seconds, the first pair of nuclear missiles would have reached their target area first. As it was, Duggan remote-detonated the warheads before they flew higher than twenty-two thousand kilometres.

"Whoa, I'm getting all sorts of stuff!" said Chainer. "I'm just trying to make sense of it."

"They're not even trying to shoot our missiles down, are they?" asked Breeze.

"Doesn't look like it," said McGlashan. "Cocky bastards."

"The Oblivion's been hit again. It's like they target whatever they fancy," said Breeze. "Or have some crazy priority system."

Duggan detonated the second pair of nuclear warheads. His tactical screen showed a cluster of faint red circles, which expanded rapidly. The atmosphere was too thin for there to be much of a blast, but he'd tuned in to gamma radiation. He felt hot all of a sudden – it was warning up in the bridge. "Fifty degrees," he said under his breath. "Let's hope we don't take another beam hit."

"I'm not sure the Ghasts are going to fly that battleship any time soon," said Breeze.

Duggan kept focus on the present. "Fire the Lambdas as soon as they load," he said. "Give it everything we've got."

"The Dreamer energy readings are all over the place," said Chainer. "Up and down."

"Are their shields working?"

"I don't know, sir." He grinned suddenly. "I think we've got them! Their shields, I mean."

"Are you certain?" asked Duggan.

"Yep, the energy output from their location has dropped to a fraction of what it was. And they're changing position."

"Evasive manoeuvres," said McGlashan.

"Keep firing at them," said Duggan. "We have no idea how long their shields will remain offline." His tactical display showed the gamma radiation as it dispersed outwards. There was enough to kill anything living in a short time, yet the intensity was fading. He hoped they wouldn't need continuous, massive bursts to keep the Dreamer shields out of action. He stretched out a hand, intending to launch the final two warheads.

"They're moving again," said Chainer.

"Where?"

"I don't know, sir. They're heading east in a straight line. We'll have no launch angle in about five seconds - they're fast."

"You know what this means don't you?" asked Duggan angrily. "They're going to wait for their shields to restart and then they're going to come back and finish the job. Only this time, they won't be surprised by slow-moving nuclear missiles." He could sense impending defeat and he didn't like it. "What's our damage report?"

"Their beam weapon is much more powerful than anything we've got. Our engines have dispersed it at the cost of a huge overall increase in their temperature. I'd say a second hit will disable us permanently, with the side-effect of cooking us all to a crisp on the bridge," said Breeze.

"What about the Ghasts?" asked Duggan.

"They're a lot worse off than we are, since they took several hits in the same place. Life isn't going to be pleasant for anyone stuck in that area of their ship."

"Let's have a look," said Duggan. The bulkhead viewscreen changed to show the front and middle sections of the Oblivion, glowing and half-melted into a new shape.

"Sir?" Chainer's voice contained an infinite excitement, like a gambler rolling the dice on an all-or-nothing high-stakes game. "Two more Shatterers have just launched from the Oblivion!"

"What do you mean?" asked Duggan. "Has the Dreamer warship come back?"

"Definitely not. Look, the Ghost missiles are curving through the air. They've peaked at over four thousand klicks per second and gone to the east."

"How the hell did they manage that?" asked McGlashan.

"Maybe they get a lock on during the reload," said Duggan. "Or the Ghasts could have improved their technology already. They've had over a year to advance it." He shook his head. "For once, I'm crossing my fingers and hoping a Ghast weapon strikes its intended target."

"Nothing we can do but wait," said Breeze. "I hate waiting."

"You've got a lot of it to come, Lieutenant. Even if we win this one, it'll take a long time for the engines to come back online."

"What if the Dreamers send another ship?" asked Chainer.

It wasn't a question Duggan wanted to offer an answer to. He gave it a go. "One step at a time. Try not to think about the possibility of a second death before we've escaped the first."

"I need a hi-stim," said Chainer. "I've been trying to keep off that shit. My hands are beginning to shake from withdrawal." He laughed, the sound free of worry for a change. "One step at a time," he said, repeating Duggan's words.

They waited in the sweltering heat. Minutes passed and then hours. The Dreamer warship didn't return and Duggan convinced himself it had been destroyed. The temperature gradually diminished and the viewscreen showed the Oblivion's heat-glow had gone. The Ghost vessel was still enormously hot and it looked like a damaged parody of menace.

The next day, Chainer detected one of the Oblivion's rear boarding ramps opening. "Sir, one of the Ghasts has appeared."

"Only one?"

"I can't see any more. Looks like he's just waiting."

Ten minutes later, the boarding ramp on the *Crimson* dropped smoothly onto the hard ground. A single figure in a spacesuit walked down. This figure was John Duggan. He wore one helmet and carried a second. He placed the second helmet onto the ground and for a moment, considered returning to the bridge. Instead, he made his way steadily across the five hundred metres between the two vessels. The heat was tremendous, but his military-grade suit offered enough protection. The Ghast came forwards, clad in a bulky mech suit. Duggan looked into the alien's clear visor and wasn't surprised to see it was Nil-Far.

"Our enemies are no more," said the Ghast.

"For the time being. We don't know how many more fighters they carry on their main ship."

"We do not. A single one of their craft was a fearsome opponent. Its beam weapon had only a fraction the power of those from the mothership."

"It was an opportunity to learn. We have data to carry home to our superiors. Will your ship fly?"

"Eventually it will be able to reach home. In six months. A year perhaps."

"That is a long time."

"I would prefer it to be sooner. These Dreamers are here for war and we Ghasts do not have the ability to defeat them. We will never stop trying, as the Dreamers will soon discover."

"We need peace between our two races," said Duggan.

"Your negotiators wished us to become vassals of the Confederation. Under threat of extinction."

"I am not a negotiator, Nil-Far. Our chances of success will be greatly increased if we fight together."

"We must agree terms quickly."

With that, Duggan took his leave and returned to the *Crimson*. For the next three weeks, the ship's mainframe and the Dreamer core worked at rerouting the scrambled engines. It was frustratingly gradual progress and the crew felt trapped in slow-motion. The Dreamers didn't return and Duggan asked himself if their main ship had moved away to a different area of space and was therefore unable to send any other fighters to Prot-7.

Eventually, the engines were sufficiently repaired that Duggan felt it was the right time to depart. The *Crimson* flew directly upwards and out of the canyon, leaving the Oblivion behind. They launched into lightspeed, managing to exceed Light-K by a small margin. This was quick for most warships, but for the *Crimson* it was little more than a crawl. At Duggan's instruction, they set a course for the *Juniper*.

CHAPTER THIRTY-TWO

"THE *JUNIPER* IS DEAD AHEAD, SIR," said Chainer.

"I'll bring us in slow and steady," Duggan replied.

"I still think they're going to shoot us down," muttered Chainer.

"You told us the *Maximilian* will be able to detect our comms failure!" said McGlashan.

"Yeah, maybe they will."

"I'm going to initiate the automatic landing systems," said Duggan. "If they don't open the doors, we'll have to crash into them."

In the end, the *Juniper* did open the door to Hangar Bay One. Catastrophic failures of a warship's comms systems were exceptionally rare outside of a simulation, but it had happened before, albeit only once. The *Crimson* docked smoothly and perfectly under the direction of its mainframe. Before a contingent of the *Juniper*'s security forces could quarantine the ship, two figures disembarked, one of them being Duggan in a full spacesuit. He used the helmet to patch into the *Juniper* and reported the damage to the *Crimson*'s comms. He also obtained details of the highest-ranking officer currently in residence, as well as clearance to meet with this officer immediately.

Duggan and his companion made rapid progress to their destination, drawing a number of curious and some outright hostile stares. A group of eight security men and women followed closely; they held their gauss rifles tightly. At Admiral Teron's office, Duggan waited until the door slid aside. He entered without hesitation, finding the room exactly as it was on his last visit.

"Captain Duggan," said Teron from his seat. He kept a commendably straight face when he saw who was with Duggan. "We have much to talk about."

"Much more than you can possibly imagine, sir."

"Take a seat, please. Who is this you have brought with you?"

"Sir, this is Nil-Far, Captain of the Ghast Oblivion *Ghotesh-Q*. We've got a fight on our hands, and this time it's not the Ghasts who are our enemies."

"Captain Duggan, tell me what you've learned."

And Duggan told him.

————

The Survival Wars series continues in Book 3, Chains of Duty!

Follow Anthony James on Facebook at
facebook.com/anthonyjamesauthor

THE SURVIVAL WARS SERIES

Printed in Great Britain
by Amazon